SECRETS OF WINTER

EVA CHASE

BOUND TO THE FAE

BOOK
5

Secrets of Winter

Book 5 in the Bound to the Fae series

First Digital Edition, 2021

Cover design: Yocla Book Cover Design

Ebook ISBN: 978-1-990338-00-7

Paperback ISBN: 978-1-990338-01-4

1

Talia

 $\mathcal{I}$ adjust my position in the armchair in Sylas's study, the soft padding not so comfortable at the moment. The attention focused on me from the four figures around me is only supportive, but a prickling of pressure runs down my back regardless. Maybe because I've failed at my goal several times already.

I tune out my awareness of the Seelie arch-lord and his cadre as well as I can and stare at my cupped hands. In the back of my mind, I summon other impressions of these men I adore: smiles and wry remarks and tender caresses.

The joy of those memories blooms around my heart. I push as much of that emotion as I can into my voice. "*Sole-un-straw.*"

A glowing golden light flickers into being above my palms. I will it to expand and brighten, but just like in my earlier attempts, it wavers for a second and then fades away. I can't help letting out a huff of frustration.

August lowers himself onto the arm of my chair so he can slide his brawny arm around my shoulders, leaning in to press a kiss to my temple at the same time. "It's all right, Sweetness. Magic is hardly an exact process. Easier to bake a hundred perfect rolls than to get the same effect from a true name twice in a row."

I guess I should take comfort from his lack of concern. The pack's lead warrior is the one who's acted as my unofficial tutor when it comes to my fledgling skills in fae magic. If he thought something was wrong, he'd probably be blaming himself for messing up his teachings.

Astrid clears her throat where she's leaning against the polished wood wall near the door. "I'm plenty impressed just by that. How long have you been working true names again?"

This is the first time the wizened fae soldier who's the newest member of Sylas's cadre has witnessed my abilities, which we've kept secret from the rest of the pack, since a human isn't *supposed* to be able to draw on true names at all. My other unexpected abilities have made me enough of an object of fascination to the summer fae without adding another complication into the mix.

"I learned the true name for bronze from Aerik," I say, restraining a cringe at even a brief reference to the fae lord who imprisoned and tortured me for years. "He didn't mean for me to—I just heard him say it every time he opened my cage. I didn't know what it was then, only that it could be the key to escaping…"

Even months after Sylas and his cadre stole me away from Aerik's domain and gave me a real home, I can't completely tamp down on the flashes of memory from that time or the shudder that comes with them. August's arm tightens around me. I focus on that steady warmth, real and here in the present.

"You're quite the mystery, aren't you?" Astrid says quickly, clearly sensing that it's better not to pry farther on that specific subject. "Have you gotten the marks?"

I shake my head, and Whitt speaks up from where he's propped against Sylas's broad desk. "We're assuming it's some difference in a human using them, or else that she hasn't mastered them quite solidly enough yet, impressive though it is that she can wield them at all." The spymaster shoots me a fond but slightly crooked grin.

Seated behind his desk, Sylas leans his elbows onto its top, his hands clasped. He considers me with his mismatched eyes—both the whole dark one and the ghostly white one, which is split through with a savage scar that cuts through his brown skin from forehead to cheekbone. "You're consistently able to produce at least *some* effect at this point. Can you think of anything that might help you generate a stronger effect, Talia?"

I swallow hard. I can, but it's nothing they can give me. Mentioning it will only add to the tension that's already woven through the room despite the summery warmth of the night and the comforting scents of cedar and oak. Some of it I can't mention at all.

Tomorrow I go back to the winter realm to spend a week with the Unseelie arch-lord who's somehow my soul-twined mate, even though humans aren't supposed to have *those* either. During the first ten days I spent with Corwin and the periodic conversations we've had through our bond since I returned here, I've come to trust and even like him quite a bit… but there's still so much I'm unsure of. Not least of which is how I'm going to navigate my magical connection with him without losing the bonds of love I've already formed with the three men around me now.

My magic has always seemed to be tied to my feelings. I can only use the true name for bronze effectively when I'm scared—or remembering times when I was scared before. Air requires the sensation of swift, free movement. And light… light needs joy.

It's hard to feel nothing but joy when I'm all too aware that my heart is being pulled in two directions. As much as I could, I've spent the past week with my Seelie pack thinking only of the present, enjoying the moments I had with them as if nothing could threaten that happiness. I want to treasure this last short time with my wolfish lovers, but it's a lot harder to ignore the lingering questions about the future on the eve of my leaving.

And on top of that… Right before Corwin and I said our good-byes last week, he shared a secret I've sworn to keep for him. Just as the summer fae have been suffering from a curse for several decades now, apparently the Unseelie have faced a curse of their own, one deadly enough to have killed many of the winter fae.

My blood has worked as a temporary cure for the savagery that comes over the Seelie under the full moon, so it makes sense that Corwin is hoping something in me might help his people as well. But I still don't know the full details of their curse, let alone what I might do for it.

He said it'd be better if he can show me the rest once I'm with him rather than trying to explain with only words. And he doesn't want the Seelie knowing about the winter realm's weakness until he's sure his fellow arch-lords will negotiate with Sylas and his colleagues rather than continue their attacks along the border between the realms.

I push that knowledge aside and refocus on the room around me as well as I can. "No," I say to Sylas. "I think my concentration just isn't all there."

He nods. "That makes sense. And you'll have put quite a bit of energy into your inner wall."

He's right about that. At the start of this practice session, I summoned a barrier of imagined light inside me to seal off my connection to Corwin. I haven't told him about my use of true names yet. So many secrets I'm keeping from one side or the other.

I've held a partial wall up the whole time I've been apart from Corwin just so that I know I'm not projecting *every* thought and emotion that passes through my mind his way—and so I can quickly yank it full into place if some sensitive issue comes up. But I haven't often shut him off completely. If he's noticed, he probably assumes I'm engaging in much more intimate activities than this with my Seelie lovers.

That thought sends an uncomfortable pang through me. I refused to give up the men who won my heart before I ever knew Corwin existed, but I know it can't be easy for him to sense my affection and desire for them. The soul-twined bond stirs up plenty of guilt in *me* even though I made the decision myself. Those pangs have also gotten stronger with the knowledge that I'll be seeing him again tomorrow.

August nuzzles my hair. "Don't worry yourself. You've got a good enough handle on the true names you know that you can count on them to help a little if you should need them."

Despite his reassuring words, there's a tautness in his voice. He's been encouraging me to practice when I can so that I have every possible advantage among the winter fae. Even if I don't believe Corwin would ever hurt me purposefully, his colleagues are another story.

Maybe *all* of the Unseelie are potential threats. I haven't spent much time with any of them except my mate. They have been killing summer fae unprovoked for nearly three decades.

But I also agreed to the additional practice for other reasons of my own. Who knows whether these skills might help against the Unseelie's curse? No matter why they've been fighting the Seelie, I'm not going to stand by and watch them die if there's something I can do to fix things.

"I suppose I'll have to tell Corwin about my magic sooner or later," I say, sinking back into August's embrace. "With the bond, it's likely to slip out eventually whether I want it to or not… Better to explain things upfront."

"That may be wise," Whitt says. "But I wouldn't rush to confess if it isn't necessary."

Sylas's expression turns more serious, but he gives me another nod. "I can't help worrying about your security, but you know him best. It's your decision when you're ready to share that aspect of yourself with him, when you feel you trust him enough to be certain of his reaction."

Astrid straightens up with the alertness that made her an excellent sentry. "Are you sure you want to head back there alone? Your friend—Harper—she seemed unfazed by the last visit. Surely she'd go with you again?"

I hesitate. It was comforting having my closest summer-fae friend with me on my first visit to the winter realm when I had no idea what to expect at all. But Harper has a life here, big dreams of taking on clients from other packs with her dress-making skills and getting to visit domains all across the realm... She hasn't had much of a chance to even get settled in our new home here by the Heart, now that Sylas has been named an arch-lord.

"I can't ask anyone else to split their time between the realms like I need to," I say. "Especially when the whole pack is dealing with another move so soon after getting back to Hearthshire. Now that I know Corwin better, I think it'll be okay. I should start seeing what life would really be like over there, right? She wouldn't follow me around forever."

The shadow that passes over all of my men's faces makes my gut twist. I didn't mean those comments as if I'm thinking of moving to the winter realm permanently and leaving them behind, but we all know that's the outcome most would expect from a soul-twined bond.

None of them expresses any of their concerns, though. They've been trying so hard not to pressure me when they know how difficult the situation already is.

August strokes his thumb over my shoulder, and Sylas gives me one of his reserved smiles that still manages to convey the warmth he feels for me. "If experiencing the winter realm on your own helps you make a more informed decision, I won't object. But if you find you miss having the company, we can always arrange an escort of your choice on your next visit."

For however many trips I make back and forth before I figure out what I'm actually doing with myself and my heart. I glance down at my hands, a surge of emotion that's a weird mix of grief and hope sweeping over me.

Astrid sketches a quick bow. She's not quite in the habit of seeing herself on the same level as the rest of Sylas's cadre yet. "I'll take my leave now, if it pleases you, my lord."

Maybe she realizes we might want some alone time before I go. She's the only one other than the men in this room and Corwin who knows about my joint relationship. The rest of the pack and Sylas's fellow arch-lords believe I'm only involved with August.

Sylas aims his smile at her. "Thank you for your able service today. I continue to be glad I brought you into my cadre."

Astrid flashes a quick smile in return and retreats, shutting the door in her wake.

I curl into August's embrace, and he lets out an encouraging rumble, trailing his fingers along my jaw. But too much tension is knotted inside me for my usual desires to run free. I grasp his free hand and look at my other two lovers, who are watching me with careful but heated gazes.

"I don't—I don't want to be alone tonight," I say, "but I'd just like to have you with me while we sleep. If that's all right."

Sylas stands with a sound that dismisses any uncertainty I might have felt. "I'm sure we will all take immense delight in your presence without needing to make any greater demands."

Whitt chuckles. "Not all trysts need to be of the carnal sort. We'll be here for you however you need us, mighty one. Never doubt that."

I don't, not after everything we've been through. The only thing I doubt is whether I can make a choice that won't break more than one heart, including mine.

2

Whitt

One could say it's my job as spymaster to be constantly on the alert. Even when I'm technically at leisure, dancing or feasting or sleeping, I've trained my senses to pick up any hint of disturbance or concern around me.

So although I'm not particularly inclined to emerge from my doze in the early hours of the morning before Talia leaves us again, the stirring of her body near mine tugs me out of my dreams. After some negotiation over exact arrangements in the bed last night, I ended up sprawled at her right, my head tipped by her shoulder. The bed is wide enough for Sylas to have stretched himself out by the headboard, where he stroked her hair until she drifted off. August lies opposite me, his arm tucked against her back and his chest rising and falling with a faint snore.

Gingerly, Talia sits up in the midst of our ring of bodies and swipes her hand over her hair. I haven't opened my eyes yet, but I can sense the tension in her pose without even looking at her. Something has been bothering her since last night… perhaps for her entire week with us, only coming to a head now that she's about to return to the winter realm.

Whatever it is, I suspect it's what's roused her from slumber at this early hour. The dawn light streaming from above is still so thin it barely penetrates my eyelids.

I wait to see what she'll do, resisting the urge to wrap my arms around her and pull her into an embrace, as if I could cuddle every worry she has out of her. I can't anyway, and I want to see what she does with the space I'm giving her.

After a minute, she must decide there's no point in trying to sleep more. She eases out from under the blanket and manages to slip over August's prone form without provoking more than a slightly stuttered breath from the whelp. Her feet patter softly across the floor with their uneven rhythm, more pronounced without the help of her brace. There's a rustle of her nightgown, and then she's slipped out the door.

I lie there for a few minutes longer, debating whether to give her even more space or go after her and see what she might say when it's just the two of us. My brothers will wake up before too much longer, and neither of them is going to want to be far from her during our last few hours with our lover.

The thought of her crossing the border again, moving so far beyond our reach, makes my own chest constrict.

That soul-twined mate of hers has proven decently honorable so far, but I still can't put that much trust in him, let alone the rest of his kind. Who knows what plans they may have for our lady of the castle? If it wasn't for that uncertainty, I'd give her my true name in an instant just to know she could call out to me from anywhere in the world as long as she concentrated hard enough.

But I can't compromise the lord and brother I'm sworn to serve. Giving her that much access to my mind might compromise the safety of my entire people.

Which is the same reason that after my deliberations, I climb out of the bed with equal care and head out after her. If something's bothering her about her trip to the winter realm, I need to know for our sake as well as hers.

I pause at my bedroom to change into clothes that aren't sleep-rumpled and splash some water on my face from the basin. Running my damp fingers through the erratic tufts of my hair, I set off to locate the mite.

She isn't in her own bedroom, though from the traces of scent around it, I can tell she stopped in there briefly. I follow the woodsy sweet smell of her down the stairs to the kitchen, which isn't a surprise. Thanks to August's encouragement, she seems to feel as at home in that room as the one dedicated to her use.

I find her perched on one of the stools by the larger island, wearing the structured green dress her Unseelie arch-lord gifted her with before she came back to us and the boots Harper made for her that encompass a brace for her misshapen foot. That leg is swinging casually, but her elbows are rigid against the countertop, her hands clasped a little too tightly in front of her, her pretty face drawn.

If I could ensure she never has any cause to look that serious ever again, I'd do just about anything to accomplish it. She's had far too much weighing on her over the past few months—the past several *years*, to be honest. It's more strain than any one being should have to bear.

When I allow my steps to fall louder as I walk through the doorway, her swinging leg stills and her head jerks up. I can see how determinedly she forms the smile she gives me, as if it's a feat of strength. The clenching in my chest intensifies.

What is haunting this precious woman who's already taken so much onto her shoulders?

I grab a duskapple from a basket on the counter and toss it in my hand as I amble over to sit across from her. "Restless morning?"

She shrugs, still smiling her determined little smile that practically stabs me through the heart. I will my claws from the fingertips of my right hand and neatly cut a slice out of the apple. It occurs to me when I'm partway through the process that the gesture that came so automatically to me might disturb her, but when I glance over at her, she's watching without any hint of distress.

Well, she's ridden on my back in wolf form. If she had any qualms about the beast inside me at first, they must have been gone by then. I don't imagine her traumatic recollections involving wolfish fangs and claws had anything to do with snack time.

I pop the slice into my mouth, the tart flavor grounding me, and carve out another to offer to Talia. She takes it with a murmur of thanks but doesn't eat, only turning it in her hands, frowning at it as if I've handed her a new problem rather than a piece of fruit.

I cluck my tongue at her. "Come on now, there's obviously been something eating at you. Whatever it is, you can let it out. You may be mighty, but you should know by now that being strong doesn't mean you have to tackle the world on your own."

Talia drags in a breath, and a shiver travels through her body. My stance tenses, watching her, abruptly certain that whatever's on her mind is even worse than anything I'd have guessed.

I set down the apple. "Talia, if something went badly in the winter realm that you haven't told us—if you have some reason to be *afraid* of going back there—"

"No," she interrupts, with an almost panicked urgency that's hardly convincing. "I—I'm not afraid to go back. There's just so much going on, so many things I'm still not sure of that matter so much…"

I study her, more skepticism coursing through me. I've spent a lot of time around this woman since she came into our lives, and her response doesn't look like her typical pensiveness to me. "You might be able to lie in ways we fae can't, but I'd prefer if you didn't, even if you think it'll spare us some unrest. There's something specific on your mind beyond the general muddle things are in, isn't there?"

I thought I'd spoken calmly and evenly, but Talia pales, her fingers curling into her palms. "I'm sorry," she says, her voice even more fraught than before. "I shouldn't have—I gave him my promise—it's nothing that could hurt anyone here. Or me."

My hackles rise instinctively. The bird-brained interloper has insisted she keep something from us—

something that's troubling her. Perhaps he isn't so honorable after all. Preventing her from even talking to us properly when he can reach straight into her very thoughts…

I fight to keep the edge out of my voice. "If he'd have you go without help when you need it—"

Talia shakes her head so vehemently I stop. "It's nothing like that. Really. And I'm sure you'll find out about it soon. He just needs to get the other Unseelie arch-lords to agree to have a proper discussion with Sylas and the others." She inhales shakily with a hint of a sob. "I don't *like* keeping secrets from you. He only mentioned it at all in order to reassure me rather than leaving me totally in the dark."

My heart wrenches with guilt. I'm off my seat and by her side in an instant, tucking her close to me with a careful embrace, chiding myself for pushing her as far as I have. "Hey, now, I'm not angry. I didn't mean to upset you. If you're sure it's nothing that threatens your safety or happiness or our pack's, then it's nothing for me to pry into. I apologize. I should have trusted that you know what needs to be said or not and let it be."

She leans her head against my shoulder, but her slim frame is still rigid within my arms. "It's all right. I know it's your job to figure out everything that's going on, especially about anyone who could be an enemy."

"*You* will never be our enemy," I say firmly. "No matter how many blasted raven shifters you find yourself tied to. I can promise you that."

To my relief, my declaration manages to get a sliver of a laugh out of her. "Let's hope it's just the one. I think I've defied the laws of the faerie world enough without taking on a horde of soul-twined mates."

I give an exaggerated shudder and tip her face up so I can claim a swift but sweet kiss. "I'd like to think the Heart will be kinder to you than that."

She hums to herself, snuggling against me in a much more relaxed pose that makes me ridiculously giddy, as if *I'm* a whelp in the grips of feckless puppy love.

I suppose for all my years, in some ways I am. I haven't loved a woman like I love this one before. There's never been any being I've wanted to defend so wholeheartedly with everything I have. And that includes even my lord. Other than… other than that one misstep with Isleen I'd rather not give any more space in my head, I've never faltered in my duty to Sylas, but I can't deny there were moments I resented carrying it out.

"I wonder if the Heart would think it's actually being generous," Talia says, her warm breath grazing my neck. "I mean, I already had the three of you. I didn't *need* a soul-twined mate. So why not throw in a few more while it's already on a roll?"

Her tone is wry but not entirely joking. I chuckle. "Most things about you are only unusual because you're human, not for fae as well. And I've yet to hear of even the truest of true-blooded fae finding themselves tangled in more than one soul-twined bond. I feel reasonably confident in saying you're safe from that."

"Safe," she mutters, as if she doesn't put much stock in that word. I can't say I blame her.

"Look at it this way," I say, tugging her closer to enjoy this nearness for as long as I can before she's gone. "You've earned the devotion of not one but two arch-lords. A highly impressive feat! It's only unfortunate they're on opposite sides of the border."

She makes a dismissive sound. "It's not only Sylas and Corwin I'm taking into account."

"Ah, I wouldn't be offended if you put slightly more stock in their part in this melodrama than my own or August's," I tease, but the truth is that a twinge shoots through me as I say the words.

It may very well come down to that—to what kind of arrangement she can make between the two men with a claim who have the real authority in this world. All August and I can do is watch from the sidelines.

I shove that discomfort aside and steal another kiss, this one long and lingering. I've half a mind to see if she'll let me give her a very potent reminder of the delights we of Hearth by the Heart can offer to take with her when she goes, but my ears catch the thump of the front door as some of the servants arrive for the day. Instead, I reluctantly draw back.

I can't resist giving Talia's hair an affectionate ruffle before I pull away completely. "You've proven yourself to be awfully resourceful during your time among us, mighty one. I'm sure you'll settle on the best solution that's within the realm of possibility, whatever that may be."

And Heart willing, there'll still be a place for me in her life when she makes that final choice.

3

Talia

*L*ike the first time, Corwin crosses the stretch of glinting fog that marks the border so he can escort me to the winter realm. The last time he made the passage, one of the other Seelie arch-lords ambushed him with her men and threw him into her dungeon, so I wouldn't blame him for being hesitant. But although he glances around him with a faint air of wariness, by far the strongest emotion I sense from him is joy at seeing me again.

It feels strange, seeing *him*. Having him standing there in front of me in the flesh, tall and lean with those dark eyes watching me with their usual intentness, the blue-black curls of his hair falling around his striking face. We've spent all week in nearly constant contact during our waking hours, if often only an awareness of each other's presence rather than actual conversation, but our bond thrums so much more powerfully when he's actually near me.

In many ways, as much as we've shared, he's still a stranger. The emotions that rise in my chest are a bewildering mix of happiness, relief, and anxiety. How can I feel so close to him and yet so uncertain at the same time?

His voice travels through our bond, as cool and even as it usually is when he's speaking out loud. *It's all right. We're still finding our footing with each other. I'm just glad I'm getting more of a chance to do that. Do you need to say any further good-byes?*

He'll have noticed the good-byes I already said, hugging each of my Seelie men tightly and indulging in a few final kisses before we left the privacy of the castle. A twinge of guilt runs through me at how he might have felt about that, but he doesn't show any jealousy. I made it *very* clear during our first ten days together that if he wanted me to give him a chance, he had to accept the other sorts of bonds my heart has formed.

I guess this week will have given him a lot of practice in exercising his tolerance, even though I raised my inner walls every time things took a particularly heated turn.

I glance back at Sylas and his cadre—and Harper, who's come along to see me off too. She brought over three new dresses this morning, as if I didn't already have plenty of finery to wear around Corwin's palace. I told her more than once that I didn't mind going on my own, but I think she still feels she owes me something.

There's nothing really left to say. I raise my hand. "I'll be back in a week, right before noon."

"We'll be waiting for you," August says with a warm if bittersweet smile.

Corwin lifts the trunk with my clothes and other belongings. I step forward to join him, saying the words of the vow the Heart requires of anyone who crosses the border so close to its glowing, pulsing energy. "By the Heart, I swear to do no harm to the fae beyond this boundary. May I pass in peace and amity."

We step into the haze. It doesn't totally sit right with me, walking alongside Corwin but keeping this distance between us like awkward acquaintances. I waffle for a second and then sidle closer to slip my hand around his elbow.

The physical contact doesn't provoke the usual electric quiver and the deepening of the bond I'd feel if I were touching his bronze skin rather than only the soft fabric of his jacket, but contentment unfurls through our bond all the same. *It's a pleasure to see you wearing that dress*, Corwin says.

I brush my other hand over the light green skirt, a color I know he chose to match my eyes. He had the dress made for me shortly before I left last time, a combination of Unseelie styling and Seelie vibrance. *It seemed fitting. And I knew it already has a very good warming spell in it.*

Definitely important, he agrees with a hint of amusement, but it's also true. With each step, the temperature in the air cools until a chill tickles over my skin in brief wafts before the enchantment cast on the dress wisps the worst of it away. As we emerge onto the vast icy plain on the winter side, the breeze licks over my head.

Corwin glances down at me. "I like your hair this way."

I touch the loose waves self-consciously. Months ago, August dyed them a rich pink for me. It was a way to reclaim my identity and self-control after the years I spent in imprisonment. But over the past week, that color started to feel a little childish. It was based on my preteen tastes, after all. And I've come a long way since even those first few days in Sylas's old keep.

I'm a lady of winter as well as summer now. So when August touched up the dye this morning, I asked him to mix the pink with strands of a deeper, cooler purple.

Corwin may have picked up on some of the reasoning from my mind, but I say it out loud anyway. "That seemed fitting too. Like the dress—summer and winter together."

I can read a certain hesitation in Corwin's thoughts that he doesn't express outright. He might have made peace with Sylas and accepted the role the Seelie arch-lord and his two cadre-chosen play in my love life, but there are still immense frictions between the realms.

A lump rises in my throat. I don't want us to end up arguing so soon after I've arrived, but I can't wait much longer to understand.

We come up on the shining diamond fortress that Corwin calls home, an innate melody humming off its crystalline forms with the movement of the wind. I let it lift my spirits as I summon some of the boldness that's gradually becoming more natural to me.

I don't want to talk about the curse out loud while we're so close to the other Unseelie arch-lords' domains. I don't think they'd be happy if they found out Corwin shared their secret with me, however vaguely. So I take our conversation inward. *The curse you mentioned—have you convinced your colleagues to talk to the Seelie about it?*

I get the impression of an inner sigh. *I'm still working on them. They're essentially agreed that it would be a logical step now that we have some connection established across the border, but they're dragging their heels on deciding exactly how to best broach the subject. Caution has served us well many times before… I don't entirely blame them for being wary, as impatient as I might be to see this problem dealt with.*

I catch a flash of a memory: the iron-core collar burning around Corwin's neck when Arch-Lord Celia held him captive for that excruciating day. Maybe we're lucky Corwin himself wants to negotiate rather than go back to war.

If you're right, and my blood can act as a cure in your case as well as the Seelie's, I venture, *I suppose that might make the situation less tense?*

It may. You shouldn't feel it's your obligation, though—I may have many hopes, but I wouldn't force your assistance.

I squeezed his arm. *You don't have to. I want to help if I can. And as soon as I can. Now that I'm here, will you tell me more about the curse?*

The current of emotion that ripples through our bond contains a little regret that our reconciliation is focused on such a serious matter, but also the recognition of how deeply that matter has been weighing on me for the past week.

I'm sorry, Corwin says as he smiles at the servant who opens the palace door for us. *I thought having a partial *understanding might ease your worries more than stir up new ones. Perhaps I miscalculated. I didn't intend to leave you fretting over it.*

It's okay. I might have fretted more over not having any idea at all why the Unseelie have been attacking the summer realm and whether they might again. I just want to know what I'm dealing with, now that I can know. You said when I was back here, you could show me…?

Yes, of course. I'm only sorry that I must begin your visit with such a horrible story and such an immense request all in one.

Since my arrival, Corwin has kept his own partial wall up against our bond to stem the flow of his emotions through our bond. I'm not sure he'd want me to notice the glimpses that waver through to me now of more pleasant activities he wishes we could have shared: him playing his harp while I listen, us chatting in the dining room over one of his human chef's delicious meals. A little ache forms in my heart.

I know Corwin loves me. He admitted it to Donovan, the third of the Seelie arch-lords, in his efforts to prove he'd support a truce between the realms, and I felt the truth of the words. But he hasn't said it to me directly, maybe not wanting to pressure me when he can probably tell I'm not ready to make any declarations that intense in return. But he's been waiting a long time to find his soul-twined mate, and even though I'm not what he could have expected, he's still welcomed me.

I might not feel outright love for him yet, but I do care about him beyond the tug of our bond. I didn't just come back to see about the curse, and he shouldn't think I did.

When we've stepped into my room—the same bedroom I used during my first stay—Corwin sets my trunk against the wall. He turns as if to direct me right back out, but I stop him with my hand. At his questioning look, I ease closer to him and slide my arms around him in a tentative embrace.

With the softest hitch of breath and a jolt of delight he can't contain, Corwin hugs me back, tucking his chin over my head. I relax into his embrace, his cool woody scent like snowy forest nights washing over me, and open my end of the bond completely so he can feel just how much *I* welcome the chance to explore our connection.

Even if I'm not willing to give up my Seelie men, I'm coming to recognize how the bond the Heart forced on me may be a gift after all.

"I missed you," he says quietly. "It may sound odd when I've lived within these walls for hundreds of years without you and only spent ten days with you here, but I felt your absence every day."

The ache in my heart expands. "I missed you too," I admit. Just as I'll miss my men of summer while I'm here. For a second, the vastness of my romantic predicament threatens to overwhelm me.

As if deciding that it's best to distract me with a change of subject, even if the topic is an unpleasant one, Corwin lowers his arms and grasps my hand. "Come. I shouldn't make you wait any longer. I've just gotten word that the curse has befallen a woman in a domain about an hour's journey from here. I'll explain everything I can on the way, and then you can see the effects for yourself—and determine whether there's anything obvious you can do for her."

There's a small carriage waiting for us outside. Corwin must have assumed we'd make this journey soon if not right away.

I hold my tongue until I've settled onto the wooden bench and the vehicle has lifted off into the air on its magical propulsion. "I guess… start from the beginning? What is this curse? How did it start? When did it start?" If it struck just one woman today, then it obviously isn't tied to the full moon like the Seelie curse, and it doesn't affect all the winter fae at once.

Corwin leans against the prow of the carriage by the crystalline windshield that blocks all but wisps of the cool breeze. He rakes his slender fingers back through his hair, his mouth momentarily twisting in a rare overt display of discomfort. "We first started seeing the signs several decades ago, but it took some time before the ailment became truly serious. My father was one of the first to die from it."

That was about five decades ago, he told me before. Leaving his mother so ravaged by grief she couldn't stand to even live. "That's a similar timeline to the Seelie curse, from what I've heard. But—how do you know it isn't a regular illness?"

"No practitioner of any health-related art has been able to determine a cause," Corwin says. "Or any way of alleviating the symptoms, let alone cure them. It seems to come out of nowhere, striking down fae at random. We haven't been able to determine any pattern to who succumbs to it, and it doesn't spread in the typical fashion of a disease. Most of the time, the victims have had no contact with any other victim, and no one close to them contracts it at the same time."

As he speaks, the hairs on the back of my arms rise. How horrible to have no way of protecting themselves or predicting where this sort-of disease might appear. I swallow hard. "Does everyone who gets it die?"

He nods. "Since my father's time, yes. The last victim I'm aware of who survived was taken by the curse not long after my father was and was left with permanent weakness. And more and more of my people have been claimed by the curse as time has gone on. Back then, it might have taken only a half a dozen in one year. Now, we've already lost five across the realm in just this month."

For beings who expect to live thousands of years if all goes well, that many fatalities must be nothing short of catastrophic.

"The Seelie curse has been getting worse too," I say. "It's strange that the curses seem to be connected somehow in timing and in patterns like that, but very different in the way they affect you."

"Perhaps it is the same curse, gripping us according to our natures." Corwin's mouth flattens into a grim line. "It drives the summer fae even wilder than they already were, beyond any hope of control, bringing out their inner beasts. And for us..." He lets that sentence hang.

"What does the illness do?" I prod.

He inhales raggedly. "It's as if the victim is freezing to death, but no source of heat can warm them. Their skin turns blue and cold, their limbs become increasingly rigid until they're paralyzed, and in the end their organs shut down completely, all within the course of a few days. When our doctors have examined victims to try to understand the ailment, they've found even the food remaining in their stomachs has turned to ice."

My own stomach turns at the image. A wintry curse indeed. I could say something about it amplifying the Unseelie's rigid natures as well, but I'm not sure Corwin would appreciate the observation right now.

"You'll see when you meet this woman," Corwin says. "She should still be mobile and able to speak at this early stage, though she may appear somewhat disturbing." He pauses. "With the Seelie, the way you've brought them out of their curse is to allow them to consume your blood, I believe?"

Instinctively, I rub my forearm where Aerik's men used to drain me. "Yes. They only need a little bit—we mix it with other ingredients so it's easier to distribute as a sort of tonic. But—it only prevents the curse for that specific night. That's why I have to keep going back if I'm going to help them. I don't know... Even if my blood heals someone under your curse in the moment, the effect might not last."

"Even a stop-gap solution would be better than none at all. But of course—I wouldn't want to see you stretch yourself thin—"

I offer him a tight smile before cutting in. "I know. Let's just see if I'm any use at all before worrying about that."

Corwin stares at me for a moment before returning my smile with more warmth—and a glow of admiration that seeps through me from the inside. Just like that, our bond tugs me toward him.

Even with the images his words painted lingering in my head, the urge rises up to escape them in the giddy thrill I know his kiss can bring. Desire flares low in my belly.

The Heart won't be satisfied until we've consummated that bond in every conceivable way.

I close my eyes for a second as if that will shut out the emotions I don't want to deal with in this moment. As I open them again, Corwin gestures to the landscape beyond the carriage, speaking in a tone that tells me he's doing his best to distract me from the turmoil within. "I can take the opportunity to introduce you to a little more of our lands. You can see the frostfire forest in the distance there—the ice forms on the trees like licks of flame, cold until you break one off and then the center melts into a steaming beverage that's quite enjoyable."

He talks on for the rest of the journey, answering my questions and pointing out other features of his world. Making no mention of my brief hunger for him or how I rejected it. I might criticize the winter fae for being rigid, but I do appreciate their patience—or at least his.

The carriage slows by a keep and a sprawling village of wooden buildings—though not the same kind of wood as Sylas and his pack conjure into their homes. This is birch-pale with a weathered texture like driftwood.

The fae woman who must rule over this flock strides out of the keep with a few underlings at her heels. She bows her head in greeting. "Arch-Lord Corwin, I am honored by your visit. I didn't expect…" She trails off, her gaze landing on me with unmistakable confusion.

Corwin rests his hand on my shoulder. "I've come to see the one of your flock who's been struck by the curse. This is Talia, a guest of mine who may be of some assistance."

Those remarks don't appear to resolve the fae lady's confusion, since from what Corwin's told me, *nothing* has "assisted" against the curse so far, but she doesn't argue with her ruler. "She's at the healer's house," she says with a beckoning gesture, a thread of hopelessness wound through her voice.

The man who answers her knock at one of the nearby houses looks equally despondent. He steps back with an even deeper bow for Corwin.

The curse's latest victim draws my gaze in an instant. She's sitting hunched in a plump armchair near the healer's crackling hearth, her legs drawn up to her chest and her chin braced against her knees. Her skin, which must have been a deep tan before, has taken on a bluish shade that's turned it almost purple. Streaks of frost cling to her ruddy hair. She shivers, hugging her legs tighter.

"I would speak with her alone," Corwin says with an air of absolute authority I haven't often seen him bring out. The lady and the healer leave immediately. I guess he doesn't want to get their hopes up about my possible curative powers.

He comes to a stop in front of the woman and crouches down so their faces are level. I'd recognize the pain etched in his expression even if it wasn't coursing into me through our bond at the same time. He feels so desperately, searingly helpless in the face of this inexplicable threat.

His tone now is nothing but gentle. "I have a draught I would give you to see if it might warm you some. Would you be willing to try it?"

The woman nods with a stiffness that suggests her joints are already starting to freeze in place. Nausea churns inside me. I've never seen a corpse dead long enough to cool, but my instincts are telling me that this is what death looks like. She's nearly a zombie.

Even if I *can* cure her, how much damage has this bizarre disease already done to her?

That doesn't matter unless we can rid her of the curse to begin with. Corwin turns away from her and pulls a small flask from within his jacket. He reaches out to me, and reading his intention, I give him my hand.

With a murmured word that must be a true name, he splits open a small cut on my index finger. It barely stings. He lets a few drops of my blood fall into the flask to mix with whatever liquid it already contains and then seals my skin just as quickly as he broke it.

When he returns to the cursed woman, I struggle to keep breathing. He brings the flask to her lips, and she manages to tip her head enough to accept the drink. Then he steps back, and we wait.

A shudder runs through the woman's body. My heart leaps with the thought that she might be shaking off the effects of the curse—but then she wraps her arms tighter around her legs, and I'd swear her skin takes on an even chillier tone. After a few minutes, my gut has completely knotted, and there's no sign of any change.

It didn't work. My blood can cure the Seelie's curse, but not the winter realm's. Or if it can, it doesn't work the same way.

We tried, Corwin says silently. *It isn't your fault. It could be it'll just take more time for the effect to take hold.* But his anguish at the probable failure rings all through his inner voice.

4

Talia

inner back at Heart's Cadence is a desolate meal. The food is as delicious as always, the tender meat melting on my tongue with a delicately sweet flavor, but Corwin shows no sign of enjoying it. He says little, the connection between us mostly closed off, what I can sense from him a turmoil of uneasy emotions.

We stayed in the town with the cursed woman for a couple of hours, just in case she started to recover gradually. Corwin talked business with the lady of the flock, and I listened on the sidelines, figuring it was better to absorb all the information I can for now rather than intrude. I gathered that this isn't the first time the curse has stuck that particular flock. Over the past few decades, they've lost two others to it. As Corwin said, there's nothing tying the current woman to either of the others.

By the time we left, she'd only gotten worse. The doctor had just been moving her to a bed as her limbs had stiffened so much he was afraid she'd end up stuck in her hunched pose.

I have to think the illness *is* a curse, like Corwin and his colleagues assume, not just because of all the aspects that don't fit any regular disease but also the fact that it emerged and escalated alongside the Seelie's curse. But I don't *know* anything about undoing curses. I have no idea why my blood brings the summer fae out of their wolfish rages.

I poke at my last few slices of a turnip-like vegetable and venture a question. "Is it normal for a curse—any curse, not even necessarily one this big—to come out of nowhere? Or if there's a curse, does that mean someone must have cast it on you?" Memories of creepy Halloween stories flit through my mind, although those were human fables made up for kids.

Corwin stirs out of his melancholy reverie. "Both are possible. You've seen how much magic these lands themselves can hold of their own accord. That magic can twist into malignant shapes, though we've never faced anything anywhere near this immense. And fae can work malicious magic on each other, of course, although a spell that's afflicted our entire realm for so long… That would take an incredible effort. I don't believe one or even a few of the most powerful among us could accomplish it."

And why would anyone have wanted to anyway? I nibble at my lower lip thoughtfully. "I still don't understand why I'm tied to the Seelie curse at all, or why I would be only to that one and not yours. Unless it's because the trace of fae heritage in my background is Seelie? But that'd be the same for my brother and my mom too, and their blood didn't affect the fae who took me the same way."

"It is obviously a tangled conundrum," Corwin acknowledges. "I trust your Seelie arch-lord has taken many steps to unearth the answers."

I nod. "We haven't found out anything very specific. I wish I knew more about how fae magic and the rest work in general so I had more of a chance of figuring it out."

Corwin lowers his inner wall enough to send a tendril of affection and reassurance my way. "We can't expect you to decipher the causes of our malady when none of us who are so much better versed in magic can ourselves. But... you may yet turn out to be tied to our curse as well—if it even is a separate curse and not the same one with different expressions. Perhaps just as our curse affects us differently, the way *you* could affect it would also be different."

My spirits lift just slightly at the idea that there might be something I can do after all. "How would we figure out what that is?"

"I'm not sure. I suppose we could try as many possibilities as we can come up with—that won't make you or the cursed victim uncomfortable..." Corwin sets down his fork on his now-empty plate. "This is the sort of thing I'd prefer to consult with my coterie on rather than relying on my wits—and yours—alone. I trust that anything we discuss with them wouldn't leave that circle. But I realize not all the secrets we'd have to reveal are mine to make that decision about."

My chest clenches at the thought of admitting my role in the Seelie's curse to any other winter fae. But I've wanted to get to know the men and women Corwin works most closely with for a while. I know how careful he is. If he trusts them to be discreet, then I'd imagine I can trust them too. And they'll definitely have more insights than I can offer when I haven't spent even two weeks in Unseelie territory yet.

"How do they feel about the attacks against the Seelie?" I have to ask.

Corwin smiles grimly. "I'd say at least a couple of them are even more eager for peace than I am. None of them have argued with me about my resistance to the aggressive approach preferred by my colleagues. I wouldn't ask you to speak to them if I believed you had anything to fear."

Of course he wouldn't. His faith in them carries through our bond.

I inhale deeply. "All right, then. I'd like to meet them."

Corwin stands. "You'll only be meeting three of them —two are away seeing to more distant business—and of those here, you spoke with Olander and Zelpha briefly during your last stay. It shouldn't be too overwhelming. If you start to feel hesitant, you can always decide you've said enough."

"Okay. That's fair." The coterie members I met several days ago weren't exactly full of warmth and sunshine, but this is the winter realm, so maybe around here friendliness is simply not giving someone the cold shoulder.

"I'll call them in now and determine where we can best meet. I'll be back when everything is arranged."

As Corwin moves to go, his chef's daughter hustles into the room carrying a platter of pastries with jellied centers. "There's still dessert," she says, taking in his stance.

"I'm afraid I'll have to skip that tonight," Corwin says apologetically. "If my portion will keep, I'll have it later on."

Beth sets the platter on the table and places her hands on her hips. "Last time we made these, you regretted leaving them to get stale. I seem to remember."

I've never seen any of Corwin's fae servants talk to him that boldly, but Corwin just chuckles. "You know, I remember that as well. I suppose I can carry one with me. Thank you."

He scoops it up and takes a bite as he heads out of the room. Beth nudges the platter closer to me so I can grab as many as I'd like. I lift one that contains a yellow jelly with a citrusy scent and give the girl a closer look.

I don't think she could be more than fourteen or fifteen, still with a bit of youthful gangliness in her body as if she hasn't quite grown into all her features yet. For her kitchen work, her fawn-brown hair is pulled back in a bun, but I can tell from the curly sprigs along her forehead that it'd be pretty wild otherwise. Corwin mentioned once that she was born here in the fae realm.

"You're not worried about talking back to him," I say.

She cocks her head with a teasing smile. "Should I be?"

I find myself smiling back. "No, I don't think so. But most of the fae are pretty deferential to Corwin. I mean, he is an arch-lord and all."

Beth shrugs with a casualness that I don't think would look out of place in a mall or school cafeteria back in the human world, even if she's never set foot there. "He doesn't 'lord' it over us that much. Even if you all have all kinds of powers we don't, I don't think I could stand to go around feeling scared about it all the time. My mom always says we might as well act the way we want and ask for what we need, or what's the point in being alive at all?"

I can't argue with that philosophy—actually, I kind of admire it. But I realize I need to correct one assumption. "I'm not one of them—not fae." I touch my hair. "This is dyed. I was… taken from the human world when I was a kid."

For all her supposed nonchalance, Beth stiffens at that revelation, blinking at me. Her freckled cheeks flush. "Oh, I—I can't really tell, you know. I wouldn't have thought— Never mind." Her blush deepens, and she hurries out as if she thinks she's made some horrible faux pas. As if I don't already know how odd it is that I'm here dining with a fae arch-lord.

I wish she hadn't left. It's more enjoyable to eat with company. I still polish off the tartly sweet pastry and lick the powdered sugar from my fingers, wondering what it'd be like to have parents here, to not have the constant awareness of a whole world that used to be mine that I've lost.

Someday when everything in the fae world has settled down, I'd like to go back to the human lands just to see how the reality compares to my memories, even if I can't imagine trying to make a new life for myself there.

Just as I'm starting to get restless, Corwin returns. He stops in the doorway. "They're joining us here in the palace, where I can be most sure of our privacy. Would you come with me to my study?"

"Of course." I get up and, on an impulse, take his

elbow like I did when we were walking to the palace earlier today. As we step into the hall, a pleased warmth travels from Corwin into me.

A question that has nothing to do with the curse occurs to me. *Do your coterie know who I am to you—that I'm your soul-twined mate? And that I'm human as well?*

I explained all that they need to know about our bond while you were in the summer realm, he replies. *They wouldn't have been dismissive of any guest of mine, but I did want to ensure they treated you with the full proper respect.*

I catch a hint of pride with that statement, which I find it hard to wrap my head around. That he would be *proud* to declare me his mate, when I'm so far from being the true-blooded Unseelie fae everyone would have expected to take that role...

Corwin must pick up on that twinge of emotion. *You may not have the bloodline I expected, but in every way that matters, you're everything I could have wanted in a mate.*

I grip his arm tighter, wishing in that moment that I could say the same back just as wholeheartedly—that my heart wasn't so divided. Then he ushers me into his study, and those more personal concerns fall away as I'm faced with three members of the arch-lord's professional inner circle.

I've actually seen all three of them before, although Corwin couldn't have known that. The older man with streaks of gray in his dark hair, who's sitting in one of the study's armchairs, came to speak to Corwin right after I arrived during my first visit. I snuck over to try to listen in on their conversation but was too late.

The other two, who discussed the problem of roving beasts with Corwin while I mostly observed, have remained on their feet. The stout but agile man with the ice-pale eyes would be Olander, and the muscular woman whose chestnut hair is pulled back in a loose braid is Zelpha.

It occurs to me now as the details of our earlier conversation come back to me that they were talking around the curse the whole time. That's the reason the Unseelie have been struggling to push back the savage creatures along the fringes of the Mists—because they've lost so many people to that freezing sickness.

All three of the coterie members eye me as I limp into the room. This is the first time any of them are seeing me as not just an unusual guest of their lord's but his especially unusual soul-twined mate. My skin twitches under their scrutiny, but I keep my back straight and my head up despite my urge to retreat.

Corwin moves to the chair behind his desk, sticking to formalities even in this company—but I notice he's set up another chair next to his. He beckons me over, and I take that seat, feeling a weird mix of relief at having the buffer of the desk between me and our audience and anxiety over taking a position that marks me as almost an equal to the arch-lord.

"You know Olander and Zelpha," Corwin says. "This is Verik, the longest-serving member of coteries in Heart's Cadence—one of the first to serve my father before me. And now I can introduce you to them properly as my mate."

I rest my hands on the arms of the chair, as much as

I'd like to hug myself, and manage a hesitant smile. "Hello."

They all incline their heads in acknowledgement, but their gazes stay just as intent. "It is an honor to have you among us," Zelpha says, in a tone I don't *think* is mocking, although I can't quite believe she totally means it.

Olander turns to his lord. "You said we may have a new strategy for tackling the curse. How did that happen—and how quickly can we get started on it?"

"The how should become clear shortly. As to the other details, we're meeting in order to determine them." Corwin glances at me. "Would you like to provide the initial explanation, as much as you feel is necessary for context?"

He's letting me take the lead to make sure I'm totally okay with everything these Unseelie find out about the summer realm. I nod, appreciating the gesture as much as taking charge in any way in this setting unnerves me. His coterie members are studying me even more penetratingly now.

"You know that the Seelie have been suffering from a curse too," I begin, gathering my words. "One that forces them to shift into their wolf forms and turns them savage on the nights of the full moon? It turns out that somehow I'm connected to that curse…"

As succinctly as I can, I lay out the story of my capture by Aerik and my rescue by Sylas, and the way the Seelie have continued to benefit from my blood to stave off their curse. As I go, my nerves gradually settle.

The only real danger in telling them all this is in the possibility that one of them would see me as too valuable to allow me to return to the summer realm, but the oath I took to the Seelie arch-lords would hurt their own lord through me if they tried to hold me back. And I can see a light of hope coming into at least Zelpha's eyes as she must understand where we're going with this.

I finish by spelling our own hopes out. "Since it seems like the two curses have some connection to each other, we're thinking that I might be able to do something to help with yours too. We just aren't sure what."

Corwin picks up the thread when I pause. "I took her out to see the latest victim today. A draught with a few drops of her blood had no discernable effect, and the woman's condition continued to worsen. So whatever Talia might contribute, it clearly isn't the same as what she offers the Seelie. I'd like us to compile a list of the reasonable possibilities."

Verik gives a soft cough. "This whole situation is— well, I'd say it's preposterous if I didn't know you'd never say all this without clear verification, my lord. But for a human girl, soul-twined mate or not… I hardly think *relying* on such a person—"

"Oh, lay off with the bluster," Zelpha says dryly. "I say we rely on whatever in the lands we can, which is better than the dung-all we've got right now. Anyway, Talia showed she has a good head on her when we were hashing out the issue of the roving beasts."

Verik frowns at her but doesn't say anything further. Corwin watches their minor spat with a calm that soothes my own nerves. He doesn't see anything odd about it; to him, it's all part of the close-knit dynamic that allows them to work together so well.

He might not be best friends with his coterie, but the bonds of trust and cooperation between them hum through the air.

Olander starts to pace, apparently willing to accept the story of my powers and dive right in. "It could be *anything*, couldn't it? Not necessarily giving of her body, but some action or words or—the possibilities are nearly endless."

"Perhaps," Corwin says. "But for the start of our list, we should focus on what we can attempt without causing Talia or the victims significant distress. Or being too overt in what we're attempting at all. If word gets out that we're experimenting with possible cures, I hate to think how tensions will rise unless we're immediately successful, which seems unlikely."

Zelpha drums her fingers against her hip. "A taste of blood seems fitting to the Seelie curse, doesn't it? They go wild, looking to draw blood, and this particular blood cools the urge. What would create a similar association for our troubles?"

That's a good point. My first thought is that I could warm the victims somehow—but I don't tame the Seelie, I give them what they theoretically want. What does the Unseelie's curse drive them to do?

Nothing, really. It locks them in place, preventing them from even moving soon enough. I frown. "Maybe I could try some kind of embrace, like hugging them, if that wouldn't upset them? I guess that sounds silly, but it would be sort of holding them in place like the curse does... I don't think there's any part of me that would work like cooling them off."

"I think that would be worth a try." Corwin scrawls a note on a piece of paper he's set on his desk.

Verik speaks up in a slightly stiff but clear voice. "We should consider other bodily materials regardless of whether we can see a clear association. Skin and hair are easy enough, perhaps muscle and bone which can be derived relatively painlessly with the right magic." He considers me as if expecting me to object.

"I'll try it," I say. "If it could save so many people from dying—there isn't much I wouldn't try."

Olander draws to a halt and swivels to face the desk. "*What* we try isn't our only consideration, is it? My lord, if we go around to every fae the curse strikes with new draughts and a human girl offering embraces and whatever else, word will get around soon that *something* odd is going on. It won't escape the other arch-lords' awareness."

Corwin sighs. "Yes, I've been considering that. We'll have to come up with a suitable story, but they'll have plenty of questions regardless." He turns to me. "I can leave you out of it as much as possible. Claim it's solutions you've suggested from your experiences among the Seelie rather than anything directly *from* you."

His voice carries through our bond at the same time. *I won't let them lay one finger on you, you can be certain of that.*

My own fingers curl toward my palms, but I catch them just before my hands outright clench. Of course I can't expect to try to solve the greatest problem the Unseelie have ever faced without their other arch-lords having any clue.

"All right," I say. "Just… tell them as little as you can get away with."

Because when it comes to his warmongering colleagues, I don't trust *them* to care what happens to me or Corwin if it gets in the way of their goals.

5

Corwin

Mother is never truly calm. Even when I cast the most soothing of spells to saturate her rooms, when I enter I find her huddled in a corner or crouched by the shelter of the table. All even my extensive magical ability can accomplish is to ease the violence of her distress, and that only for perhaps an hour at a time.

Apart from a few grave missteps early on, I believe I've stepped up to the role of arch-lord rather well, especially considering how abrupt, unexpected, and chaotic the transition was. But faced with my mother, I always feel like an utter failure.

Today, she's tucked herself into the nook between the bookshelves and the wall. Her wary eyes track my movements through the strands of her stringy hair. I'm not completely sure she recognizes me at this point. Decades of desperation seem to have worn down her mind to only a few basic impulses, the greatest of which is self-destruction.

I feel like even more of a failure at the thought that passes through my head: perhaps the Heart is wrong about this one thing. Perhaps it would be kinder to let her abandon this life. She hardly seems to be taking any enjoyment from it.

But every fae life is so hard-won and long in coming, who can decide it's right to make such a sacrifice? We may yet end the curse. For all I know, it's played a part in addling her mind, and she could recover if given the chance. It would be a grave crime to steal that opportunity from her.

I tip the chair she's knocked over right side up and sit on it, keeping every motion slow and fluid so I don't startle her nerves. I will my voice to stay perfectly steady as well, holding back the anguish that's collected at the base of my throat at the sight of her. "My soul-twined mate has returned. You met her that one time. I think you'd have liked her when you were well."

Mother offers no response, only a single blink. I continue anyway. "There's a chance she might be able to stem the tide of the curse. We may soon be able to protect so many from the grief you had to experience. I only regret it's taken so long to uncover that possibility. If I could have saved Father…"

The curse moved less swiftly in those days. At first he simply complained of being mildly chilled. Once his limbs began to stiffen, he took to bed for a week before the seeping cold overcame all of his body's functions.

I remember his pose beneath the heaped covers—his

face blue and rigid, his arms and legs unnaturally straight —with uncomfortable vividness. He couldn't answer me either, the last few times I spoke to him, not so much as a croak.

Mother shows no sign of caring about my news, but it's impossible to say what might be going on inside her head. It may give her some small comfort even if she isn't fully conscious of the fact.

I take the glazed chocolate truffles I brought for her from my pocket and set them on the table. "I thought you might like a treat. Charles whipped them up this morning. I'd bring some to my meeting in the Hall, but somehow I don't think my colleagues will be swayed by sweets."

I chuckle without much humor. Mother remains still and wary. I may be causing her more distress by staying than I'm comforting her with my company.

Standing, I dip my head to her. "May the Heart shine warmly on you." Then I head out, my own heart heavier than when I came in.

Perhaps it's for the best that I approach the coming discussion carrying a somber weight within me. One wrong step here, and I could jeopardize both my mate's safety and our budding alliance with the Seelie.

As I leave the palace and set off across the plain toward the Hall, Talia must pick up on my growing apprehension from where she's joined Charles and Beth working in the kitchen. She sends a current of fondness my way alongside her soft voice. *You're meeting the other arch-lords now?*

Yes. It may take a while to hash this out. I'll find you when it's done.

Let me know if there's any way I can help. If they want to speak to me directly… I can lie.

My lips twitch with an unexpected smile. *Not a skill I ever imagined I'd appreciate, but here we are. I'll spare you their comments for the time being, unless it seems absolutely necessary.* With that, I raise my inner wall of imagined crystal against our connection.

I'm the first to arrive at the meeting room in the Hall of the Heart, but only by a small margin. I'm not often the one to call the meetings here. My colleagues' inquisitiveness over the request grows as each enters the room with the marble table, until the space thrums with unspoken questions as well as the pulse of the Heart's energy.

Neve shuffles in last, even her pale eyes alert with interest rather than clouded by their frequent haze. As the oldest of us reaches her spot at the table, Laoni clears her throat before I can begin, flicking her turquoise hair back from her brawny shoulders. "What's this about, Corwin?"

I tamp down my irritation at her insistence at always being in charge, even though in theory we're all equals. "I have no definite information yet, but there is a matter I felt I should notify you of before I put it into action. There are some new strategies I intend to attempt to defuse the curse."

I hadn't seen any point in beating around the bush. In an instant, all four of my colleagues are staring at me even more piercingly than before.

Laoni's eyebrows rise. "What new strategies are these, and how have you developed them?"

Uzziah lets out a huff, the planes of his doughy face

turning even more dour than usual. "And why is this the first we're hearing about them?"

"I only just had the opportunity to consider them myself," I say, picking my words carefully so I'm being truthful without revealing too much. *Only just* is hardly an exact length of time. "We're all aware now that the Seelie have been dealing with a curse of their own. My soul-twined mate has witnessed efforts they've undertaken that have temporarily alleviated its effects."

Terisse makes a derisive sound, folding her coppery arms over her chest. "Why would any solution those wild ones have come up with apply to us?"

"They may not," I say quickly. "But when we haven't yet found any method that works at all, it seemed to me only reasonable that we set aside our pride and try whatever we can. Our people's lives are at stake, after all."

They can hardly argue with that point—as Laoni well knows, from her frustrated grimace. "How do we know these attempts won't make the situation *worse*? Not only are they strategies borrowed from the summer fae, you're gathering them from your *human* companion, who may not have a full understanding of what she's seen."

I resist the urge to bristle on my mate's behalf, glad I blocked our connection off so she wouldn't need to hear this conversation. It's not likely to get kinder.

"Whatever her heritage, she *is* my soul-twined mate," I say evenly. "I've seen her memories; I can confirm her observations and reconsider her interpretations as need be. We certainly know that the Seelie do have an effective cure, given that they were able to shake off the curse in order to push us back during that battle three moons ago."

"There's no disputing that," Uzziah says. "It's simply a matter of caution when dealing with our enemies."

I fix a firm stare on him. "They weren't our enemies until *we* made them that by striking out at them. And my mate is eager to help us in any way she can—I can read how genuine her intentions are through our bond too."

Laoni scoffs. "The mongrels have probably addled her mind. I still don't see why you'd put up with a mate so feeble and—"

I cut her off, letting an edge creep into my voice. "Mind what you say about the partner the Heart chose for me. If you believe the source of all our power could be misguided, I'm not the one you should take that concern up with."

I motion in the direction of the Heart itself just as a fresh pulse of energy washes over us. Laoni's mouth tightens. She'd happily tell *me* that I should defy the Heart's choice, but she wouldn't take action contrary to it herself.

Neve stirs on her feet, speaking up in her reedy voice for the first time. "If this newcomer to our realm can offer a cure to our curse, then I would have to say the Heart has chosen exceedingly well."

At least I have a little support, even if it's from the most frail of my colleagues. I glance around at the others. "I'm simply informing you of my plans as a courtesy so you won't be taken by surprise if you hear reports of my visits with the next victims in the coming days. I require no further involvement unless I find a strategy that does offer concrete benefits."

Terisse cocks her head. "Do you mean to go off and

carry out your experiments without even sharing with us what you mean to do?"

"My mate prefers to share her knowledge with no one other than me and my coterie, as she has legitimate reason to worry that other parties among the Unseelie might use it to the Seelie's detriment. She may want to help us, but she still has friends among the summer fae."

Laoni's eyes flash. "Then you would take a dust-destined imbecile's word on—"

I set my hands on the table just forcefully enough to cut her off with the sound. "We're *all* dust-destined if we don't solve this curse. You all have continued to hesitate to reach out to the Seelie directly and make use of what knowledge or resources they might share with us if we explained ourselves. I've found an approach that doesn't require their involvement—you should be glad of that, not fighting it. I've been arch-lord for just past fifty years now; I have the authority to act on my own under conditions such as these."

There's a moment of tense silence. Then Uzziah speaks in a reluctant tone. "I suppose you do have a point there. If we're going to make use of Unseelie strategies, perhaps it's better if we can do so without them even knowing."

That's not the message I wanted them to take away from my proposal, but it may be the best I can get. I incline my head. "Exactly. I won't attempt anything that I can imagine doing the victims any harm. And frankly, the curse steals them away so quickly there's little we could do that would worsen their condition, is there?"

Laoni speaks up again, her voice taut but quiet. "You can't blame us for being concerned, Corwin, given the emotional feebleness that's appeared in your own family line. Perhaps this dung-body has managed to lead you astray through the power of your bond."

My jaw clenches, even though I could have predicted her taking that tactic. The memory of my mother as I left her less than an hour ago swims up through my mind. May none of the figures before me ever have to lose their own mates as horribly as she did.

I will myself calm before I answer. "Do you have any recent evidence that would suggest my capacity for reason is insufficient?"

"You have been awfully keen to make peace with the wolves, even before this mate of yours appeared," Terisse puts in.

"For reasons I've laid out with clear logic," I reply. "I could say that *your* reasons for attacking them rather than negotiating are far from logical, driven by distrust and fear rather than rationality."

Silence stretches again. Laoni rolls her shoulders with a dip of her head as she might ruffle her feathers in raven form. "Your behavior hasn't raised any significant concerns so far. But let us be clear on this: Should it appear your loyalties have been compromised, we won't hesitate to take every necessary action to diffuse that threat."

"Understood," I say, my throat tightening. "I would expect nothing less."

I know without any of them saying it that at this point, it wouldn't take much. One shred of evidence that they can spin into proving I'm no longer fit for this position, and they'll strip me of my title in the blink of an eye.

6

Talia

The next curse victim I meet is part of an Unseelie lord's household staff. The lord has set him up in a guest room in one of the turrets of his coral-like castle on the verge of a gray sea.

"Balem is our flock's best metal-worker," the lord says to Corwin in a hushed tone before we go in. "To lose him… He knows true names no one else here has gained."

"We'll do what we can for him," Corwin says. "And if you have a need of assistance later, you only need to send word, and I'll see that someone capable attends to the matter."

The lord bobs his head in gratitude and pushes open the door. As Corwin, Zelpha, and I step into the room, he gives me a curious but not hostile look. All the fae can tell I'm human once they're close enough, of course. Whatever he makes of my presence, he must assume the arch-lord knows what he's doing, because he doesn't question Corwin about it.

No one is attending to Balem at the moment. He's sitting on the bed with his skinny legs stretched out as if bending them would cause him pain, a book propped open on his lap. A glowing yellow ball of magic wafts ineffectual heat from where it hovers next to him.

His head turns jerkily to take us in. When he closes the book with one hand, I notice three of his fingers stay rigidly straight. Only a faint bluish cast colors his pale skin, but the paralysis is already setting in.

His ears show a point nearly as sharp as Corwin's—he must be close to true-blooded. Not that the fae-ness of his heritage matters to the curse. It took Corwin's father, after all.

His voice comes out a bit creaky. "I didn't—I wasn't expecting visitors." He squints as if that's necessary to properly see us, and I notice a frost-like sheen hazing his eyes. His back goes even more rigid than it already was as he recognizes Corwin. "My lord. I—it's an honor."

"I hear you're quite the metal-worker," Corwin says in a calm but warm voice. If I didn't already know how much he cares about his people's well-being, the comfort he's trying to offer in that friendly praise would say it all.

Balem brightens a little despite his chilly pallor. "I do my best. Is there—is there something I can help you with, my lord?"

"Actually, there is." Corwin walks to the side of the bed, beckoning Zelpha and me with him. "I'm sure you must be in grave discomfort, and I'd like to attempt some new methods that might ease your suffering. If you would allow us to? Some of them are rather… unusual, but I'm committed to exploring every possibility, no matter how remote. None of them should do you any further harm."

The man's eyes widen a little. "Yes—yes, of course. I put myself in your hands."

"I only need you to confirm that our attempts will stay between us until I say you may speak of them elsewhere. In such a fraught situation, I want to be sure I have a handle on how the information is spread."

Without a second's hesitation, Balem speaks up in a magic-laced tone. "I swear I will not speak of what you and your companions do in this room without your express permission, my lord."

I'm not sure whether he trusts his ruler that emphatically or he's simply that desperate for a cure. He's definitely going to be a lot more puzzled once we're finished here.

But if anything we try works, nothing else will matter.

We already agreed that I'd attempt the strategies that involve me in action first, mostly because if one of those has an effect, then Zelpha will need to whisk me off to the woman I met yesterday to see if I can help her in her precarious state as well. Verik and Olander went to see her while we came to Balem, bringing the draughts Corwin made this morning using every bodily material I could reasonably offer.

Corwin nods to me. "Talia will tend to you first. Please relax as well as you can and simply accept what she offers."

That sounds more ominous than I hope is accurate. I bring to mind the list of actions we agreed I'd take and limp forward. Balem blinks at me. "It'll just be for a moment," I say awkwardly. Then I wrap my arms around his cool torso, at first gingerly before hugging him a little tighter.

The warmth of my body seems to absorb right into him and vanish, leaving my own skin chilled. I step back, resisting the urge to rub heat back into my arms.

"Tell me about the work you're most proud of," Corwin suggests, drawing the man's attention toward a happier subject while we wait to see if there's any delayed effect. If we try more than one possibility too close together, we won't know which attempt did the trick.

The arch-lord keeps Balem talking for several minutes with no sign of any change. Bracing myself for the man's cold touch, I approach the bed again and reach for just his hand, wrapping my fingers around his. Corwin keeps talking and encouraging Balem's answers as if nothing at all odd is happening.

After a minute, I pry my fingers away. Corwin said the curse isn't contagious like a typical illness, but my joints ache from just that temporary exposure.

I still don't see any difference in the man. I swallow hard, waiting out the passing minutes until Corwin signals me again. Then I start to sing.

I'm not a major talent by any means. It's just one more idea we came up with when brainstorming—to sing a lullaby, fond and soothing. Whether the sentiment would do the trick or the idea of going to sleep would align with the gradual freezing, we have no idea.

As my voice wavers with the lilting words my mother used to sing to me when I was little, I remember a phrase she used to throw around too. *Throwing spaghetti at the wall to see what sticks.* I can't think of any better way to describe what we're doing here.

The rest of the next hour is more of the same: I offer some gesture, Corwin keeps up an amicable conversation with Balem, my heart sinks farther when we get no indication we've affected the curse in the slightest. Zelpha watches the proceedings in silence, but I can't help imagining that the hardened woman must be getting impatient. From the looks of her, she's more a warrior than anything else, like August is for Sylas. Not being able to fight the curse in any clear way must frustrate her.

Finally, I reach the end of our brainstormed list. Corwin thanks me without letting any trace of disappointment show outwardly, but I can feel his sorrow from within. He brings the first draught out from his pockets and hands it to Balem. "Now I have a few potions I'd like you to drink. They should only take one or two swallows to get down."

As the other man tips back the first, Corwin turns to me. "There's no need for you to linger here while I see through the rest of the course. Zelpha, you could take Talia to get some fresh air outside and appreciate the local scenery. You've never visited the sea before."

I open my mouth to protest and then hesitate. Part of me feels like I should stick out the entire process, that I owe it to Balem somehow. But my being here won't change whether or not the draughts work—and maybe he'll be more relaxed with just the arch-lord present and not two other strangers studying his reactions.

Plus, my spirits are so low that I doubt I'm hiding my

own disappointment as well as Corwin is. Balem shouldn't have to shoulder my burden on top of his own.

Zelpha grasps my sleeve, tugging me toward the door. "Come on then. There's nothing as bracing as the winter sea atmosphere."

Let me know the moment anything seems to work, I tell Corwin silently.

Of course. You've been wonderful—don't let our lack of progress discourage you.

I don't see how wonderful I could have been if the curse hasn't budged at all. But I follow Zelpha down the spiral staircase and along a hall to one of the palace's outer doors.

The wind rising off the frothing waters is invigorating, brisk and salty and oddly not all that damp against my cheeks. Zelpha motions for me to follow her along the rocky shoreline that stands several feet above the water.

"If you watch closely, you can sometimes spot a siren-sculler in the waves," she says.

I peer more closely at the gray water. "A siren—like a mermaid?"

"Ah, no, they're just fish, nothing more. But they have a captivating twinkling of color to their scales—it's said that they can lure sailors just like the supposed sirens could with their voices."

"So there *aren't* really sirens?"

Zelpha cocks her head as we head down a path jutting from the cliffside, closer to the water. "I suppose there might be. Not in this world. Not *all* your human fables are true, you know."

I find myself raising my eyebrows at her teasing tone.

"It's a little hard to be sure when I've found out faeries and werewolves and all kinds of other supposedly imaginary beings are real."

She laughs. "Fair. Well, even if we don't spot a siren-sculler, I'm sure I remember… Here we are! I knew there was *something* I liked about this dreary place."

We come to a stop on a wider ledge, seawater flecking my face. As I walk up beside the coterie woman, my jaw goes slack.

At the end of the path, the cliff falls away into a shallow hollow. The gray stone there has become so polished by the waves that it shines like silver. But that's not what's most striking about the spot. The silvery stone has become worn down in grooves, leaving columns jutting here and there, and as the sunlight bounces between all those shiny surfaces, it splashes images across them that must come from much deeper within the sea.

Brightly colored fish dart by. Luminescent seaweed wavers in and out of view. Glittering currents weave back and forth across the undulating wall. Staring into the hollow, it's as if I've become submerged far down in the ocean where I'd never be able to venture otherwise.

My voice comes out breathless. "Wow. I've never seen anything like that."

"Not bad for a hole in the wall," Zelpha says wryly, propping herself against the duller stone next to us.

She gives me a while to absorb all the wonders of the reflective hollow, watching it not quite as avidly as I am. Once I've taken my fill, my attention slides to her. She seems like the youngest of the coterie members I've met so far—not that any of the adult fae are "young" by human standards—but she's less formal with Corwin than the other two, as if she's more comfortable in his presence.

"How long have you been serving on Corwin's coterie?" I ask.

"Oh, not all that long, but I've been working with him one way or another since close to the beginning of his reign. My… family had become quite close to his, so we got to know each other, and I did everything I could to support him in the early years when he had, well, a lot to deal with."

Was there more beyond his father's death and his mother's grief right at the start? I guess his mother's condition deteriorated somewhat gradually. And he's indicated that the other arch-lords have never been all that keen on having him join their ranks. But Zelpha sounds like she might mean something more than that.

I don't know how to ask without sounding overly prying. And then I don't get a chance, because Zelpha rubs her hand across her mouth and gives me an evaluating look. "You're not sure of him yet. Of any of us."

My head snaps around with a jump of my nerves, but her tone wasn't accusing, at least. "I… I never said that."

She shrugs. "You don't have to. It's obvious with this arrangement you have to go back to the Seelie. You don't need to be there next week when the moon is new, but you want to be. I'm not saying I don't understand. All right, I don't understand how *all* this came to be when you're human—it'd be bizarre even for one of us to randomly contain a cure for the curse. But clearly you couldn't have been expecting the soul-twined bond, and you already have some ties to the wolfish ones. And I suppose they don't speak too kindly about us."

"You haven't given them much reason to lately," I can't help saying.

"I haven't taken part in any of the raids." She sighs. "Anyway, I only wanted to say—he's a good one. Corwin. I'm sure he comes across a bit awkward and all. He's out of practice with the whole romance thing, and after the number that's been done on him— But I can tell how much he likes you already. And I'm seeing why. You've really stepped up. I've no doubt he'll be incredibly devoted to you if you let him be. You won't find a better mate in this realm."

She can't speak to the summer realm the same way, but I hold my tongue about that. The affection in her tone stirs a twinge of curiosity in me. If she's that fond of him…

Zelpha catches my look and chuckles. "No need to speculate. I've never wanted to stake that kind of claim myself. Certainly my own mate would have a lot to say about that, Heart shine on her."

My cheeks flush at the speculation she picked up on, but in the same moment, Zelpha's laughter fades, her gaze shifting to a point behind me.

I turn to see Corwin approaching, his mouth set in a tight line. He's walled his emotions off from me, but I don't need our bond to tell how downcast his mood is. Before he even speaks, I know what he's going to say.

He inhales sharply. "Nothing worked, at least not yet. Come, we'd best be getting home."

7

Talia

When the news comes that Balem has passed away, all I want to do is burrow into my bed as if I can escape the final confirmation of our failure there. I've been moping in my room for a couple of hours when Corwin reaches out to me through our bond.

We tried everything we could think of—and we'll think of more. After all these years, it'd be surprising if we stumbled on the answer on the first or second try.

I know, I reply, flipping over on the bed and scowling at the ceiling. *It just seems so easy with the Seelie curse. I don't like that there might be something I can do that could stop people from dying, and I'm missing it.*

Perhaps more ideas will come to us if we give our minds a break from stewing over it. The unconscious can sometimes piece together problems better without our focused interference. Corwin pauses, and I sense that he's come to a stop in the hall outside my room. *We haven't had much chance to simply enjoy each other's company. Would you join me for a small outing including lunch?*

I don't feel particularly hungry, but he has a point about taking a break from brainstorming. And lying on my bed in a cloud of gloom isn't helping anyone. I shove aside the blankets and reach for my boots. *All right. I'm just not sure whether my company will be all that enjoyable right now.*

A hint of a smile travels through our connection. *I never fail to find you delightful.*

I could point out that there were at least a few times he found me less than delightful when we were first getting to know each other, like when I told him off for criticizing the Seelie or for messing with my memories of my other lovers, but he has taken those criticisms to heart with more grace than I'd have expected. Why bring up past troubles that don't matter anymore when we have plenty to deal with right here in the present?

Corwin stands just beyond my doorway, the handle of a silver basket slung over his lean forearm. "I thought you might like to get a closer look at the frostfire forest," he says. "There's a spot there I'm rather fond of. Since it isn't very far… we could fly."

I'm about to say that we were flying the last time we passed it—in the carriage—when I catch a flicker of a thought that tells me he means by his own power, using his wings. A weird shivery tingle races over my skin. He's only taken me on a short flight that way before, down into the flock village along the cliffside. It was a little scary, but also exhilarating.

And the bond immediately urges me toward him, seeking out that closeness.

I rein in the urge, but I nod at the same time. I *am* supposed to be figuring out my relationship with him as well as attempting to cure the curse while I'm here. "All right. As long as it won't tire you out too much."

He smiles, one of the rare wider ones that warms me to the core. "I'm certain I'm up to the task."

He escorts me out into the broad diamond terrace at the back of his palace, overlooking the cliff that holds his flock's village and the vast landscape beyond it. With a rustle of feathers and a warble of the wind, his wings spring into being, the black shapes fanning out on either side of him.

An even giddier tingle passes through me at the sight. Corwin never looks quite so much in his element as when he shows his raven side.

After pushing the basket all the way to his elbow, he holds out his arms to me. I step closer and let him scoop me up to his chest. My forehead comes to rest against the side of his neck, the meeting of skin against skin deepening our connection with a sudden thrum of emotion—and desire.

I do my best to ignore the more intimate sorts of heat flowing through me and brace myself for the takeoff. Corwin flaps his wings, there's a slight hitch as we leave the ground behind, and then we're soaring over the edge of the cliff.

I turn my head so I can take in the view and watch the snow-and-ice-covered terrain around us whip by. Corwin swoops in a gentle arc with a shift in the breeze, veering toward the glittering forest he pointed out to me a few days ago. I don't let myself think about the journey we were on then or how it ended.

It does occur to me that while I've been distracted by trying to tackle the curse, there are other problems I haven't really gotten answers to. Maybe having Corwin totally alone will make for a good time to ask those questions.

Corwin glides lower over the forest and falls into a loose spiral with easy flaps of his wings. We descend into a small glade amid the trees. Their dark branches, nearly the same blue-black shade as his hair, hold dozens of icicles, but rather than jutting down like I'd expect, these point upward. They waver as if they're not quite solid at all—as if they're cool blue-white flames.

"I can see how this place got its name," I say as Corwin sets me down.

He glances around us. "It can seem eerie, but I find it peaceful. And this clearing offers one of the best views with the sun streaming in and the stone providing a seat."

He motions to the large slab of mica-laced granite that fills the middle of the glade, at least ten feet long and nearly as wide. Setting the basket down at the edge, he pulls out a thin span of pale fabric. When he unfurls it, warmth wafts through the air against my face. It's got a spell on it just like our clothes.

I climb onto the rock and settle onto the blanket. As Corwin lays out the lunch he must have had Charles and Beth pack for us, I gaze around at the forest some more. The beaming sunlight really does amplify the effect, making the icicles it catches on appear to outright dance.

The breeze whispers through them with a faint melodic hum I suspect Corwin appreciates as well.

"I was digging around in our store rooms while you were gone," the arch-lord says, bringing my attention back to him. He holds up a pair of bronze spoons. "I found these—I think they must have been a gift or from a trade back when relations between the summer and winter realms were more cordial. You might have noticed we tend to favor silver here."

I hadn't really thought about it until he mentioned it just now. As I take one of the spoons from him, the true-name for bronze runs through my mind. I shove it aside with a hitch of my pulse. I haven't decided for sure when or how to tell Corwin about my other abilities.

"I don't mind the silver," I tell him.

He shrugs with a small but relaxed smile. "I thought it was fitting to bring them out while we're trying to make strides toward renewed peace."

He doles out soup from a small sealed tureen into two bowls and slides one toward me, alongside a platter heaped with dumplings I know on sight are stuffed full of spiced meats and vegetables. My mouth starts to water despite my earlier hesitation about eating. Then he breaks off two of the icicles, tipping them over into a sort of cups and offering one to me.

Like he mentioned when he pointed the forest out to me, the center of the ice is already melting with a thin wisp of steam. I bring it to my lips and take a tentative sip. The liquid that seeps across my tongue has a startling tangy, spicy flavor that reminds me of hot apple cider.

I alternate between the strange drink and the soup, the

peppery broth warming me up even more from the inside. Corwin watches me as he eats, his happiness at seeing my enjoyment radiating into me. I'm finished faster than I expected. Picking up one of the dumplings, I decide I'd better get on with the potentially awkward part of the conversation.

"Corwin… You told me the curse had something to do with why your people have been attacking the Seelie. But I haven't seen anything yet that explains the raids. Why would this strange freezing illness make anyone think barging into the summer realm was a good idea?"

Corwin grimaces. "I'm sorry. I should have thought to explain all of it right away. I keep hoping my colleagues will see reason…" He rubs the heel of his hand against his forehead. "It will probably sound somewhat ridiculous that we've carried on for so long, but I think once the idea took root and we were foiled in our attempts to test it, many of the arch-lords and lesser lords dug in their heels and became increasingly adamant about it."

"About *what*?" I ask.

He picks up a dumpling of his own but doesn't bring it to his mouth. "You have to remember that until recently, we didn't know the Seelie were suffering from a curse as well. Many Unseelie assumed the summer fae were responsible for our malady—that it was an attempt at weakening us for some later assault. So Unseelie feelings toward the wolves were… not particularly friendly in general."

"Why would the Seelie want to hurt you anyway? It's not like you have anything they need, do you?"

Corwin spreads his hands. "I don't know, but we could

have possessed something they desired without knowing it. In any case, resentment and hostility had been growing for some time, and then around three decades ago, a couple of my colleagues hit upon the idea that the summer realm might hold the cure to the curse as well as the cause. Since the condition involves extreme cold, they thought that victims brought to the summer realm might recover there—or else that living in the summer realm might prevent the curse from striking in the first place."

The pieces are starting to fall into place in my head. "But no one wanted to *ask* the Seelie if you could intrude on their territory when you suspected they might have been out to weaken you to begin with."

"Exactly. So a small party including one victim of the curse made to cross over and set up a temporary camp just beyond the border, far enough from the Heart for the vow not to be necessary. From what I understand, Seelie sentries came upon them sooner than expected, harsh words were exchanged, and the encounter ended with blood spilled on both sides."

Which the Unseelie probably took as proof of the Seelie's animosity, while the Seelie would simply have known that they'd been defending against apparently aggressive intruders. I shake my head. "Let me guess— after that they decided they had to go in fighting right off the bat."

"Essentially." Corwin dabs the dumpling in the remains of his soup. "The plan evolved into the idea that we needed to capture a decent section of summer territory to claim as our own and hold off the Seelie while we determined whether living there alleviated the curse. But we never managed to hold onto any ground for long enough to judge, and frustrations on our side—and the Seelie's, no doubt—only increased with each failure."

"You could have just asked," I said quietly. "In the beginning, before any of the fighting. I'm sure they'd have agreed to let you set up some kind of temporary settlement then."

"You may be right. But we didn't know that, and so much has happened since then…" He exhales sharply. "But now at least we seem to have reached an agreement that the fighting is only resulting in more lives lost without gaining us anything. My fellow arch-lords remain hesitant about admitting our weakness to the Seelie, though, even knowing the summer realm lies under its own curse."

His gaze has drifted away from me. Now it slides back. He considers me for a moment before saying, "I've started to wonder whether the Heart isn't responsible for inflicting this curse on all of us—as a punishment for letting our opposing sides drift so far apart in temperament and understanding and as a way of ultimately uniting us as allies once again. Perhaps that's why it brought you to us as well."

There's a rightness to that idea that grips me. "But do you really think the Heart would be that cruel to you?"

"Perhaps it wasn't totally in control once the die was cast, and our own mistakes following that are to blame for how the situation has worsened. The Heart is the power of the natural world, and nature can be harsh. Rot and raging storms serve as much of a purpose as anything of beauty."

"I guess that's true." I take a bite of my dumpling and

chew it slowly, mulling that idea over. I don't want to be a bullet point in some lesson the Heart is trying to teach the fae, but there are worse purposes to have. At least I can hope that possibility would mean the solution isn't too far beyond our reach.

"The other arch-lords *have* to talk to the Seelie about this," I say. "The sooner they can actually test out their theory about the summer realm, the closer we'll be to ending the curse."

Corwin nods. "I'm doing my best. But wariness is deeply ingrained in our natures. I think it's only a matter of time. They can't avoid seeing that it's the only reasonable approach."

"I'd like to go back to Sylas with good news about confirming the peace."

Corwin's smile comes back, bittersweet this time. "And I'd like to give you that news."

We finish the meal in contemplative silence. Then Corwin reaches tentatively across the blanket to rest his hand over mine. His touch sparks a jolt of heat. "Beyond all the concerns about the curse, how have you been feeling about this visit, my mate? Have you been lonely without your friend around?"

There's so much affection in his words and flowing through our bond that a lump fills my throat. "No, I think I'm fine without her now. We've been so busy anyway— and I'm glad that I can spend some time just with you without worrying about *her* being lonely."

"If there's anything else I can offer that you might want..."

"I know." I turn my hand to twine my fingers with his.

"I have enough." If anything, the problem is having too *much*, not too little.

But right now with our hands clasped together, I can't deny the urge to get closer to him. I scoot across the blanket and tuck myself next to him, snuggling in even more when he puts his arm around me. His air of total contentment and his foresty scent envelop me.

Our embrace doesn't quite satisfy the tug inside me. With his scent comes the awareness of how close the bare skin of his neck is to my lips. Would it taste the same way he smells?

The question and the longing it rides on stir up a twinge of guilt with the memory of my other lovers, but only for a moment. I got way closer than this with my Seelie men while Corwin waited for me on the other side of the border. Sylas, Whitt, and August all expect that I'll become closer with him.

If I indulge that longing just a little, I'm not doing anything wrong. I don't have to go any farther than I'm comfortable with.

I twist in Corwin's arms, tipping my head so my mouth grazes the base of his throat. A wave of desire sweeps through me, both my own and his through the bond.

Corwin holds perfectly still, letting me press another gentle kiss and then a more determined one against the warm column of his neck. The rush of physical connection aligning with our emotional bond leaves me giddy.

Talia, Corwin says with a hint of a groan that sends heat spiking low in my belly. Do I really want to stop at all?

I aim the next kiss higher, brushing the corner of his jaw. His arm tightens around me—and a savage shriek splits through the peaceful forest.

I jerk back just in time to see a gray, wrinkled creature that looks like some kind of panther-rhinoceros hybrid lunging through the trees toward us. It opens its maw to let out another shriek, revealing jagged teeth that glint like glass.

Corwin whips around, spitting out a spell that slams into the beast. His magic tosses it to the side just a few feet from our granite seat. The creature stumbles but whirls around as if it's barely fazed. When Corwin hurls another spell at it, it appears to leap out of the way and launches itself toward me instead.

My pulse hiccups, and my body reacts on instinct. My hand shoots out to grasp one of the bronze spoons. The syllables I've hidden for so long stick in the back of my mouth for a split-second, but I'd rather reveal the secret than risk either of us getting hurt. Which maybe is all I need to know.

"Fee-doom-ace-own!" I shout, brandishing the spoon. The true name sends a flare of power through my fingers, and the utensil jerks and lengthens into a thin bronze spear. I jab it toward the beast's chest, my other hand braced against the stone beneath me.

The flash of the metal sends the creature veering to the side again, just as Corwin snaps out another magically-charged word of his own. This time, his spell hits the mark. Rather than battering the creature, it freezes the beast in mid-lunge.

The thing wobbles and then topples over onto its side.

Corwin sucks in a breath with a muttered curse. "A searmaw, all the way out here..." He trails off, his gaze dropping to my spoon-turned-spear and then locking with my eyes. The punch of shock as he processes what I did echoes into me. "You—you used a true name."

My face flushes. "I was nervous about telling you. I don't have very much power, and I've only managed to learn a few. I don't have the marks or anything. We haven't been able to figure out why."

Our bond is open; he must be able to tell I'm being truthful. He keeps staring at me. Then he lets out a soft chuckle. "And you continue to surprise me, Talia. The Heart definitely looks kindly on you." He hesitates. "I want to hear all about it, but... I think it's best we don't let the rest of my people find out about *that* irregularity just yet. It'll be one more element for my colleagues to be suspicious about."

I nod, torn between relief that he's only startled, not upset, and a sinking sensation at his last remarks. I already knew my unusual powers might cause more controversy. Now, I can't help thinking that I could tear apart the emerging peace just as easily as strengthen it.

8

Talia

orwin's fingers dance across the harp's shimmering strings. The vibrant music reverberates through the air, seeming to seep right through my flesh into my bones. I can't help swaying with it on the bench I'm watching from, a smile touching my lips.

The instrument is enchanted, but I'm not sure any other musician could produce notes quite so sweet from it. The Unseelie arch-lord becomes totally absorbed in his playing, adjusting his stance as if he's conjuring the melody with his entire body. Music is one of the few things Corwin appears to enjoy without any bittersweet or outright tragic overtones weighing it down.

Which is why I suggested we come to the music room. After I explained and showed everything I could about my experience with true names so far, he had me demonstrate —but I struggled to will any light into being. My spirit was still too heavy from our failures over the curse.

Yesterday he asked what might bring me enough happiness that I could manage it, and we ended up in here.

It worked then, and it works again now. The delight of the moment has lit a sort of glow inside me. As Corwin lowers his arms, the last notes fading from the air, I raise my own hands and murmur to the space between them. "*Sole-un-straw.*"

A soft, golden light forms between my palms. I hold it out to him as if I could give it as a gift. From Corwin's expression and the satisfaction that trickles through our bond, it's enough of a gift just watching me do it— knowing that he can make me happy enough to create this minor magic.

"Perhaps there are more true names I'd be able to teach you, so you can continue your studies during the weeks when you're here," he says. "I appreciate you having some additional means of defense in this world that can be so dangerous even for fae, let alone a human."

Even more joy swells inside me at his offer. It was enough that he wasn't upset about me hiding my small talent from him or disturbed that I have it. For him to want to support my emerging skills in any way he can is more than I'd dared to hope.

"I'd like that," I say. "I know I'll never be on equal footing with an actual fae, but it is nice knowing I have ways of protecting myself that fit this world. Thank you."

He beams at me, and a different sort of delight flickers through me with an edge of desire. Catching it, Corwin rises and comes to sit next to me on the bench. When he traces his lithe fingers along my jaw, I tip my head instinctively to receive his kiss.

It's still overwhelming, the demanding rush of pleasure and longing that crashes through me whenever our mouths meet. After our brief intimate interlude in the frostfire forest, I've indulged the urging of the bond—and my own attraction to my soul-twined mate—a couple of times, feeling it out, deciding how much I want, and hoping my mind and body might adjust to the headiness of it so that the flood of heat doesn't carry me away quite so much. But I can't say it's become any less intense with practice.

Maybe it won't until we've joined in every possible way.

Maybe it won't *ever*. This might be one more reason why the fae treasure their soul-twined mates so much.

And it's not exactly surprising the way the heat builds, flaring hotter with each shift of my lips against his, each careful caress he offers. I'm drinking in not just my own reactions to this intimacy but his as well. I can feel him reveling in the softness of my mouth and skin, taking glee in the stutter of breath he provokes when he teases his fingertips into my hair.

I sense without him saying anything, without us even breaking the kiss, his desire to see how much more pleasure he can stroke into being. I lean into his touch without thinking, seeking what he's offering.

He hesitates for a second as if confirming my reaction and then trails his fingers down the side of my face, over my neck and shoulder, to cup my breast. At the sweep of his thumb over its peak and the giddy jolt that comes with the caress, a hungry sound escapes me. Even more heat courses through me, pooling between my legs with an urgency that still unnerves me.

Corwin feels the bond's pull just as much as I do. I can sense how much passion he's holding back so that I can set the pace. I want all of it, and yet—thinking of my Seelie lovers and all the uncertainty about my place in the realms—will it become too hard to walk away once I've given in to our connection that much?

Picking up on my conflicted emotions, Corwin eases back. He presses a gentler kiss to my temple with a sniff of my skin. "We don't have to do anything more. I will say, though—you were fertile two days ago but no longer, so there wouldn't be any lasting consequences. Consummating the desire won't bind you to me any more than we're already connected. It's the confirmation ceremony that solidifies the soul-twined bond."

I let out a shaky laugh. "Well, that's good to know." I'm still not sure my own emotional state is up to navigating that kind of closeness with him before I've decided whether I want our overall closeness to last for the rest of my life.

Corwin shows no sign of impatience. I guess for a nearly immortal fae, waiting a few weeks is like a few hours for a human. I tip my head against his shoulder, still enjoying his warmth and the feel of his lean muscles.

A different thread of tension winds through my gut. He *will* have to wait at least another week. Tomorrow my seven days here are up, and I return to the summer realm—with a few more answers but barely anything accomplished. I'm not any closer to figuring out how to handle my personal affections, and while we've discussed additional strategies for dealing with the curse, there haven't been any new victims to attempt to cure.

"When are you meeting with the other arch-lords again?" I have to ask, even though I know that subject will ruin the contented mood of the moment.

"In a couple of hours, after dinner. We need to discuss the growing incursion of hostile beasts into the domains, but I'll push the idea of opening negotiations with the Seelie again. Unfortunately, I've already put forward all the arguments I can. I suspect at this point it's simply a matter of waiting them out while I wear down their sense of caution."

Waiting them out for how long while most of my wolfish companions see the ravens as the enemy, while more winter fae die of the curse who might not have to? I itch with impatience. *I've* been doing everything I can as a frail mortal so many fae like to sneer at, and what are the other arch-lords contributing other than standing around making snarky remarks about Corwin's judgment?

I pause, my thoughts circling back. *Have* I done everything I possibly can?

Corwin runs his thumb over the peak of my shoulder. "What are you thinking, my mate? I can sense the gears turning in your head."

My mouth twitches with a smile. "I just—" I balk for a second, and then Beth's words from an earlier evening come back to me. *We might as well act the way we want and ask for what we need, or what's the point in being alive at all?*

I sit up straighter, raising my chin. "What if—what if I came with you? To the meeting? I can speak on behalf of the Seelie. I can vouch that their arch-lords would work with you all to find a solution to the curse, not exploit it."

Corwin stiffens. "I—It would be highly unusual to include you. We rarely have even our coterie members join us at the meetings."

"But you'd bring in another fae if they had something important to contribute, wouldn't you? And it's not as if the meetings are totally secret from soul-twined mates even if I'm not in the room with you."

"While that is true, I don't imagine my colleagues would see the matter as being quite so simple."

His arm tightens around me with a protective vibe, but that's not the only emotion that carries through our bond. I taste a quiver of anxiety not just about how the other arch-lords will respond to me but also how… how *he* will act in my presence.

I frown up at him. "What are you worried will happen if I'm there? I won't do anything to embarrass you. I've been around fae enough to know how to be properly polite and whatever."

Corwin's mouth opens and closes before he pulls together an answer. "It's not you. It's how I feel about you. I can keep a calm, controlled front with the other arch-lords when we're apart, but if you're right there, if I have to witness them insulting you…"

Images and bits of speech flicker to me from his memories: his colleagues criticizing his attachment to me, accusing him of being unstable, rubbing his family's history in his face. My hackles rise on his behalf. "Caring about me doesn't make you *weak*. Don't they care about their mates?"

Corwin rubs his face. "They do, but none of their mates are humans who'd face so much additional scrutiny and be less equipped to fend it off themselves."

I let out a huff, squeezing his hand. "I can fend for myself just fine. Maybe that's where your problem is. You're assuming you'd need to get upset on my behalf. I know what kinds of things a lot of the fae think about me. I've heard worse than I'm sure the arch-lords would stoop to in front of you. They're not going to throw magic at me or challenge me to a sword fight, are they?"

"No," Corwin admits, his tone going a bit dry. "As much as a couple of them might like the idea of doing so."

"Then I can handle it, and you need to give me the chance to show I can. If I can't survive four fae sneering at me, then I don't deserve to be your mate anyway."

Corwin blinks at me and then lets out a rough chuckle. I can tell he's still nervous, but he dips his head. "All right. If you can be as convincing with them as you just were with me, you might have a real chance."

When we step into the meeting room in the building Corwin calls the Hall of the Heart, I don't need any kind of soul connection to gauge his colleagues' reaction. All four of the imposing figures standing around the large marble table go rigid. The thrum of the Heart's energy, so close by, raises the hairs on my arms and the back of my neck.

"What is the meaning of this?" snaps the burly woman with the turquoise hair, glowering at us so menacingly that

Corwin stops in his tracks, halting me with him. I remember her from the night the Unseelie appeared at Sylas's coronation—the night I discovered my soul-twined bond to Corwin. She acted as if she was the leader of the group. It appears that's the case even without a larger audience.

Corwin grasps my shoulder. His voice comes out steady, but tension winds through it. "My mate has an appeal to make on behalf of both our people and the Seelie in regard to the curse. I believe it's worth hearing her out."

A depressed-looking man with bags under his eyes shakes his head. "We already granted you some leniency in attempting your treatments for the curse on her suggestion, Corwin, for all the good it's done. Our generosity can only extend so—"

I clear my throat, cutting him off. Corwin's grip tightens, but he doesn't move to stop me from speaking.

"You all have had around seventy years to find a way to reverse the curse, and so far you haven't succeeded," I say, as evenly as I can manage with my stomach twisted into one huge knot of nerves. "Isn't it a little much to call my efforts pointless after just one week?"

The woman's gaze sharpens into a glare. "This is a sacred space, no place for your kind."

I stare right back at her, refusing to cower the way she'd clearly like. "The Heart has decided to give me a soul-twined mate from among the highest of the Unseelie, so I don't think it objects to me. What exactly would hearing me speak hurt? You have thousands of years to live. All I'm asking is that you spare a few minutes to listen to what I have to say, since I'm the only person in a long time who's become familiar with fae on both sides of the border."

They think they're so high and mighty with all their talk of logic and reason—let's hear them give one logical argument to that.

The man stirs on his feet uneasily. Another woman, with tufts of dark green hair framing her copper-brown face, works her jaw but can't seem to think of how to respond.

And the fifth arch-lord, a thin, pale woman who looks like she could have been constructed out of peach fuzz and dandelion fluff, taps her wizened hand against the tabletop. Her voice is barely a wisp but still firm. "I say we let her speak."

The burly woman's jaw clenches, but apparently she can't think of any way listening to me would harm them either. "All right. Let's have it quickly, then," she says, sounding as if she's restraining a sigh.

Corwin releases my shoulder, and we walk up to the table together, slowly so my limp doesn't become too pronounced. He bobs his head. "I appreciate your open minds."

Ha. I manage not to roll my eyes and rest my hands on the cool marble. Pulling myself as tall as I can, I glance around the table, not shying from any of the gazes fixed on me, however hostile. "Tomorrow I return to the summer realm for a week. I'd like to come to the Seelie arch-lords with the news that you'll be arranging a parlay to open negotiations—so that you can determine whether spending time in the summer realm cures the curse or prevents it from taking hold."

The burly woman's expression darkens with a scowl. "Of course you'd suggest that we reveal our most fraught weakness to them. Anything to benefit your keepers."

I focus on her. "How could finding out about your curse possibly benefit the Seelie? They already know you've lost some of your population through the battles *you've* instigated. They can't predict where or who the curse will strike any better than you can. And even though it should be obvious to you by now that they weren't behind the curse since they're dealing with their own, if they *were*, then they'd already know about it. They've only become your enemies because you treated them like that instead of having a conversation in the first place."

The somber man shifts his weight again. "You can't possibly know all the means by which other fae could exploit the information."

My heart is pounding, but I fold my arms over my chest. "No, maybe I can't. But unless you can mention one of those ways, one that sounds plausible, I'm going to keep saying that you're risking more by avoiding reaching out than by finally doing it. Just in the week I've been here, two of your people have *died*. If you'd talked to the Seelie already, maybe those two people could have lived. How many of the Unseelie you're supposed to be serving are you going to let down out of this paranoia?"

Giving their caution such an irrational label makes the three main figures around the table bristle. The elderly woman is gazing off into space as if she's listening to a song only she can hear, but I'll take that over more skepticism.

"The impertinence," the man sputters.

"Did you come here to discuss the subject or to insult us?" the burly woman demands.

I gaze back at her, my muscles tensed to hold back a shiver at the power she emanates. "I didn't mean it as an insult. I'm using the word by its standard definition, based on the information I have. You're worried that the Seelie would strike out against you somehow. Why would they now when they've refused to go on the offensive after all the years you've been attacking *them*?"

The copper-skinned woman frowns. "Why *wouldn't* they want to retaliate?"

I resist the urge to grit my teeth in frustration. "They've been avoiding that specifically to hold onto the higher ground before the Heart. They don't want anything you have—they only want the violence you're committing to stop. Finding out about your curse isn't going to change that."

If only they could see how much they're like the Seelie despite all the lines they try to draw between the realms. Celia and Donovan acted on similar motivations when they took Corwin captive. But I managed to convince Donovan that peace was still possible. What will it take for these fae to recognize the same thing?

From the look the burly woman is giving me, it'll take more than I can provide. The sneer I was expecting colors her tone. "We certainly aren't going to share our suspicions and strategies with you right before you return to the rampaging wolves."

I drag in a slow breath. I'm not sure there's anything else I can say anyway, but I can't drop my case without making one more appeal to the rationality they claim to prize so highly.

"Fine. You don't have to. All I can say is that from all my observations and conversations among the Seelie, which I've had many of considering I'm in an arch-lord's pack and he respects my opinion, the summer fae have no interest in hurting you or taking anything from you. I have every reason to believe they'd let you set up a small community in the summer realm to test out your theory. Corwin can attest to my honesty on everything I've said."

Beside me, my mate nods. "I've seen it through the bond and in conversation with her arch-lord with my own eyes." The strain of staying silent during the rest of this conversation trickles through to me, but he gives me the space to go on.

I send a tendril of thanks his way and lift my voice once more. "I've told you everything you should need to know to realize you can take this opportunity to try to help your people. Either you can decide not to listen to me, because I'm a human and you judge me as unworthy simply because of that, or you can recognize how much sense I've made and act like the level-headed rulers you're supposed to be. That's up to you."

I step back from the table, my chest constricting even though I'm done. The Unseelie arch-lords are staring at me again, even the elderly one this time. She speaks first, in a slightly louder voice. "Regardless of her heritage, the girl's words ring true. The Heart did choose her for our own."

The burly woman's mouth twists, and she opens it as if

she's about to protest, but the copper-skinned woman twitches anxiously and beats her to it. "I think we should attempt the parlay. As soon as possible. We can't let our people continue dying over vague, unproven fears."

"Terisse," the burly woman hisses, but even the man is starting to nod. I don't know if they need a full consensus to make the final decision, but my heart starts to lift.

Corwin brushes his knuckles against the back of my hand. *It may take more discussion, but—I believe you have them, my mate.*

9

August

There's nothing quite like the moment when Talia emerges from the haze of the border to meet us. I always find her beautiful, but something about spending days missing her presence amplifies the joy of seeing her again to the point that my heart swells close to bursting.

She limps over to us with a brilliant smile, accepting my hug with a tight embrace of her own, but her happiness isn't as unrestrained as the first time she returned to us. A worry line has formed in the middle of her brow. As she nestles against me, she turns in my arms to look back the way she came.

Corwin followed her out, carrying her trunk. As Whitt strides over to accept it from him, the Unseelie arch-lord catches Sylas's eye. "Arch-Lord Sylas, if I could speak with you and your fellow arch-lords briefly... I'd like to see about arranging a formal parlay between all of you and the arch-lords of winter."

The Unseelie rulers are ready to have a proper meeting with ours? Sylas's eyebrows rise, but he strides over with a dip of his head. "Of course. Astrid, would you see about summoning Arch-Lords Donovan and Celia to the Bastion of the Heart? I'll meet them there." He turns back to Corwin. "Perhaps you and I should go over the gist of the situation just the two of us before bringing it to a larger audience."

Corwin smiles grimly. "I can see that might be advisable." His gaze slides past Sylas to Talia, still in my arms. I tense instinctively, bracing for hostility from her soul-twined mate at the sight of her so close to another man, but he simply shoots her a softer smile. She nods to him. I get the sense of unspoken communication passing between them before he turns to walk with Sylas.

I know how lucky I am to have this woman in my arms at all when the Heart has bound her to another, but the knowledge that I'll never have as much closeness with her as *he* does niggles at me anyway.

Whitt cocks his head toward her. "Managed to convince them to have a civilized sit-down, did you?"

Talia slips from my embrace but takes my hand as we set off toward the castle. "Corwin didn't take any convincing. He's been wanting a parlay like this for ages before I was in the picture. But... I think I might have been a major factor in swaying the others."

My brother chuckles. "I'd expect nothing less from our mighty one. Woe betide any who underestimate you."

I can't summon as much good humor as he can about

the situation, but then, Whitt can find humor in just about anything.

The Unseelie are going to speak with us—good. But what are they going to say? What if they only make demands and threats that'll make us wish they'd stuck to skirmishes along the border?

Whitt sidles up to Talia as we reach the castle's doorway and nudges her with his elbow. "I don't suppose you have more details on what this parlay will involve."

She elbows him back fondly. "I do, actually, but I thought it'd be better to discuss them somewhere more private."

"Hmm. Let us take this conversation to my office, then."

We stop at Talia's bedroom to drop off her trunk and make our way into Whitt's new office. He's moved all his belongings over from the old castle at Hearthshire now, managing to make the larger space here look full. I wonder if he's actually read all the books lining his built-in shelves and whether he really has any idea what half of the curiosities placed among them are meant to do.

His office back in Oakmeet always held a faint tang of alcohol. I find I'm relieved that his new space smells only of leather bindings and wood. I haven't seen him partaking from his flask much in recent weeks other than during his periodic revels. Talia's position here may have become more uncertain, but my brothers have found their footing with each other—and perhaps themselves—in a way I appreciate seeing.

Talia immediately drops into one of the armchairs, curling up her legs and leaning back as if she needs the support. Whitt props himself against the edge of his desk as expected, and I stay by the door I've just closed.

Talia rubs her mouth, the furrow in her brow deepening. "I guess I should jump right in. Corwin said it was okay for me to tell you this, since he'll be telling Sylas anyway, but it's better if his colleagues get to be the ones to tell the other arch-lords."

"Understood," Whitt says. "Our lips will remain sealed."

He glances at me, and I nod. Who would I tell?

"All right." Talia's hands clasp together and then release as she gathers her words. "The main thing is, the Unseelie have been facing a curse too—one that seems to have started and gotten worse on pretty much the same timeline as yours."

"What?" I burst out. Of all the news she could have shared, I'd never have expected that, even if it doesn't sound so odd once I have a moment to think about it.

The corner of Talia's mouth curves up at a wry angle. "I had no idea either until Corwin told me. They've hidden it well. And it's not as if there's been much conversation across the border anyway, right?"

Whitt has drawn himself up straighter with increased alertness. "And has it turned out you're tied to this second curse as well?"

My gut lurches as that line of reasoning catches up with me. It might not even be a different curse but the same one. If the Unseelie have that kind of claim on Talia as well as the mate bond, they might insist on having her in their realm for even more of the time.

Talia curls deeper into her chair as if under the

weight of a heavy burden. "We haven't figured that out yet, but it seems likely. Let me explain everything we know so far."

As she tells us about the freezing illness that's struck the Unseelie and her attempts with Corwin and his coterie to cure it, her shoulders tense and a hint of strain creeps into her voice. She *is* carrying a heavy burden—the thought of all the deaths she couldn't prevent, the uncertainty of whether she can stop more in the future. It's dimmed her usual hopeful light just a little.

Even though I can't blame Corwin for accepting her help when so much is at stake—even though I know Talia would have insisted on it if he'd tried to stop her, which for all I know he did—I kind of want to strangle him. Not that doing so would make *her* feel any better. I settle for flexing my hands at my sides.

Whitt asks a few questions that are clearly based on some historical or cultural understanding he probably picked up from all the books around us, and Talia answers as well as she can. She tucks a stray strand of hair behind her ear and gives us another tight smile. "I'm sure I don't know everything the Unseelie have done to investigate the curse, but you all haven't been able to figure out much about yours either, so it's not really surprising that they've struggled too."

That's true. I step forward, about to reassure her that she's clearly gone above and beyond in trying to help the blasted ravens, when the door swings open. Sylas strides in, looking even more regal than usual. "Ah ha, here you all are." His gaze fixes on Talia. "I take it you've been filling in my cadre? Astrid learned of the new developments during our brief meeting in the Bastion with Corwin."

Talia springs to her feet with a swish of her vibrant hair, her eyes wide and anxious. "Did Donovan and Celia agree to the parlay? How soon will it be happening?"

Sylas goes to her as I meant to, setting a gentle hand on her shoulder. "Everything has been arranged. We'll meet in the clearing by the Heart, where I had my coronation celebration, with the three of us taking oaths that we'll do or order no harm as the Unseelie have requested. They should be arriving tomorrow."

"All right." Talia bites her lip. "Maybe I should talk with all three of you—see if there's anything I can tell you about what to expect that Corwin might not have covered. I'm sure he's been truthful, but he won't have wanted to paint his colleagues in a bad light…"

From her tone, clearly there are bad things *she* could say about them. I bristle inwardly again.

I can tell Sylas would like to keep her out of the thick of this conflict too, but there isn't much either of us can do when she's already so entwined. He has to think of what's best for all of us.

"That might be a wise idea," he says. "Come with me, then. We were already planning on having a longer meeting after we'd consulted with our cadres."

Whitt gathers himself, since obviously as the strategist among us, his input will be useful. I waver on my feet. "What would you have me do, my lord?" The entire point of this negotiation is to *avoid* any further warfare, so it's not exactly my specialty.

"Speak to our warriors," Sylas says. "We'll want them

on guard both against violence from the Unseelie toward us and hostility from our own people toward the ravens while they're here."

"We don't want to make it too obvious that we're prepared to fight," Talia says quickly. "If the Unseelie arch-lords get any sense of a threat… They were worried enough about coming to you as it is. I don't think it'd take much to scare them off." She makes a face.

"Noted. Make sure our people take that concern into account." Sylas raises a hand in farewell, and the three of them leave together.

So I'm to prepare our guards to defend us but without being intimidating about it. That's not a job I'd have signed up for, but it's what I've got.

I gather the warriors of our pack, Astrid joining me soon after. We get a number of protests about the idea that we'd need to ensure the safety of the winter fae as well as our own, but I think I manage to emphasize how very important it is that the Unseelie feel comfortable in our domain. "We're acting as hosts," I remind them. "We'll just have to impress the socks off them with our immense hospitality."

There isn't much to discuss beyond that. Our people are well-trained, and they'll do as their lord asks regardless of their personal qualms.

After I've returned to the castle, Talia, Sylas, and Whitt send word back that they'd be eating in the Bastion during the meeting. I pace around the kitchen, wishing I could at least apply myself to making a meal as some kind of contribution. Finally, I whip up a quick dessert that Talia usually loves. But when I finally see her again, trudging in with the others, she looks so weary I can tell she isn't in the mood for sweets.

"I'm still not sure how they'll react to that arrangement," she's saying to Sylas.

"We'll approach it tentatively," he reassures her.

She stops and can't seem to think of anything else to comment on just then. I take the moment to swoop in and scoop her up.

"Hey!" she says with amused if exhausted defiance.

I nuzzle her hair. "You've been working all day. I declare it time for a rest. You're coming with me."

She sighs and lets me carry her to my bedroom, where I tuck her carefully against me on top of the covers. The tremor that runs through her body as she nestles closer brings a lump into my throat.

"They aren't your responsibility, you know," I have to say. "You didn't *have* to help us with our curse, and there's no reason you have to help the ravens either."

She tips her head against my chest. "I know. But if there's something I *can* do… I can't just let people die."

Of course she can't. I grope for an argument she'll accept. "I'm just suggesting that it'd be better if you don't run yourself ragged in the process. We've been dealing with this problem for decades. It isn't your fault if you can't solve it all in a few days—or months, or whatever."

Talia is silent for a moment. Her voice comes out thick with emotion. "The Heart chose me for a reason, right? It gave me powers no human is supposed to have; it tied me to Corwin. I might have a chance to end all the fighting and the damage the curse has done… I have to give it everything I can."

I wouldn't expect the woman I love to say anything else, but hearing it pains me anyway. I hug her closer and try to will away the ache in my heart.

What if curing everything that's wrong with this world drains her too much? It might not be the Unseelie I lose her to but the Heart itself.

And I can't think of a single way I could stop that from happening.

10

Talia

I'd imagine there's been some occasion in the history of the world when a group of people looked *more* awkward than the summer and winter arch-lords attempting their parlay, but it's hard to picture what that could have been.

The Unseelie arch-lords have staked themselves out in a shallow semi-circle just a few steps from the border with their backs to that wall of glinting fog. All of them except Corwin are poised as if ready to leap back toward the winter realm the second anyone on the summer side so much as blinks funny.

The three Seelie arch-lords face them from several feet away—because the winter fae didn't want them getting any closer. Celia stands rigidly straight, her expression sour. Donovan has his arms crossed tight over his chest. Even Sylas has an air of apprehension around him.

I tried to suggest a table and chairs, maybe some

refreshments, anything to make the meeting more comfortable and friendly. One or the other side wasn't having any of it. I'm lucky they're having *me* anywhere in the vicinity. The burly woman who likes to think she's boss of the Unseelie side—Laoni, I've learned her name is— kicked up a fuss about my presence.

Sylas pointed out that with my experience on both sides of the border, I may be able to contribute something the rest of them can't, and Corwin took his colleagues aside for a brief conference. In the end, I stayed, but not without several glowers—mostly from Laoni, but a few here and there from the gloomy man whose name is Uzziah and the copper-skinned woman whose name is Terisse. The elderly woman who's spoken up in my favor —Neve—has mostly just gazed off into the distance. I'm not sure she'll be much of an ally.

"And why exactly should we *help* you now, after you've spent so long trying to take what you wanted from us by force?" Celia asks, her voice so sharp I wince inwardly. After a couple of hours, the Unseelie have finally spit out what's going on and what they're hoping to get from the Seelie, but she clearly isn't in a generous mood. "Do you have any idea how many summer fae died during your attacks?"

Laoni draws herself straighter and stiffer, as if she's in a competition with the most senior Seelie arch-lord for who can do the best impression of a lamp post. "Many died on our side too. We have paid for our imposition."

Celia sniffs. "I don't think you have. Before we *offer* you anything, I'd like to see real reparations made to our people."

It's not an unreasonable request, I think to Corwin. Donovan is nodding along, and I'm not sure even Sylas would argue against it. *Do you think they'll ever agree?*

His inner voice travels to me with a grim edge. *We'll see how much the Seelie ask for.*

I did tell Sylas and his colleagues that the less they demanded, the more likely the Unseelie would negotiate a solid peace agreement, but I guess I can't blame Celia for not accepting peace out of hand after everything her people have been put through. I still wish she'd be a *little* less cutting in her remarks.

Uzziah's mouth twists. "That is something we can discuss. We can admit… we were at least partly at fault for going on the offensive—"

"Partly?" Donovan breaks in with a short laugh of disbelief.

Terisse raises her chin. "Our initial party into your territory disturbed no one until they were set upon by your warriors."

"We have only each side's word for how that encounter escalated," Celia says, dry but still sharp. "However, I can't think of anything our warriors could have done that was so odious it'd justify nearly thirty more years of raids."

The Unseelie stir restlessly. Laoni scowls. "We were under duress from our curse and acting in what we felt were our people's best interests. But reparations are possible—*if* you're willing to consider allowing a small settlement of Unseelie to live on your lands at least long enough to see how that affects the occurrence of the curse."

Celia exchanges a glance with the other two summer

arch-lords. "Our willingness will depend on many factors, including the exact location, the size of the settlement, how long they anticipate staying, and what restrictions we may place on their activities. However, it is 'possible.' I'd like to discuss the possibilities of our reparations before we make any guarantees on that matter."

"Fine." Laoni turns away. "We'll deliberate amongst ourselves on that subject and present you with a proposal within a few hours. You may anticipate our return at the sun's peak."

I'll do my best to ensure they're generous with their offer, Corwin says as the five of them stride back toward their realm.

As soon as they've disappeared amid the haze, Celia exhales roughly. "Wretched featherbrains."

I swallow thickly. Corwin might be going to try his best, but I suspect "generous" by the Unseelie's evaluation is barely going to be adequate by hers. If her accusatory attitude hasn't made them balk completely, that is. But *me* talking to her isn't likely to do any good when she hasn't taken much of what I said earlier to heart.

As I push to my feet, planning to stretch my legs, Sylas leaves his colleagues to join me. After a glance toward the border as if to confirm the Unseelie aren't returning already, he walks with me as I amble in my uneven way toward the nearest stretch of trees.

"What do you make of their response so far?" he asks. "Has Corwin offered any insight?"

My soul-twined mate has dulled our connection—all I can sense from him right now is a vague impression of frustration that doesn't seem promising. "He said he'd try to encourage them to be generous as far as the whole reparations thing goes. I don't know how successful he'll be."

Sylas nods. When we come to a stop in the shade of the nearest tree, he touches my arm to turn me toward him. His dark eye studies me intently. "And what of your own insights? Is there any way you feel we should adjust our approach to get through to them better?"

A flicker of warmth washes through me at the question and the attentiveness with which he's waiting for my response. I've insisted on sharing my opinions on various political matters during the time I've been in Sylas's pack, but for him to turn to me of his own accord as an arch-lord—for him to value my advice that much… It sets off a glow of happiness inside me that's close to magic without any true names necessary.

I pause, figuring out how to give my advice effectively. "I think you all need to remember how much the Unseelie are focused on logic and practicalities," I say carefully, mostly meaning Celia when I say *you all.* "Seeing that you're angry about the attacks or passionate about doing right by your people isn't going to convince them of much —if anything, they'll use any show of intense emotion as an excuse to write you off as 'savage wolves.' If you can make it sound like the reparations you'd want are totally reasonable—"

"Of course they're reasonable," Celia interrupts, halting beside Sylas with Donovan coming up behind her. "The ravens struck at us without provocation again and again, and now they think they can dodge responsibility?" She frowns at Sylas rather than me. "Why are you discussing this situation with the human rather than us? We've heard what she has to say, but these matters are far beyond her purview."

Sylas keeps his tone even. "I'd say they're well within her purview, considering she's had far more experience with the ravens in the past month than any of us has in our lifetimes."

Donovan clears his throat. He seems a bit hesitant, but he speaks up for me anyway. "I've found Talia's contributions to be sound and well-thought-out. What reason do we have to ignore them?"

Celia glares at both of them. It's almost funny seeing her act so much like Laoni, trying to exert authority over the colleagues who should be her equals, when she dislikes the Unseelie arch-lords so much. At least Celia has a fair claim on being an authority when she's held her position for centuries longer than either Donovan or Sylas. But that doesn't mean she's always right.

"What *reason*?" she says. "How about the fact that she's bound to one of those feathered fiends and owes them more loyalty than she does to us now?"

My hackles come up at her insinuation. Sylas starts to speak, but I stop him with a raise of my hand. I can fight some of my own battles. "I still consider myself part of Hearth by the Heart's pack and see that domain as my home. And I'll remind you that I've saved *you* and all the Seelie a lot of suffering by volunteering my blood, which I didn't have to do—the last time just a couple of weeks ago."

Celia stares down at me haughtily. "That proves very little."

"What about the fact that I've managed to keep my involvement in your curse a secret from all of the Unseelie except my mate? You can tell they don't know, can't you? Or they'd be trying to negotiate some control over *me*, not just your lands."

Her jaw tightens. She has no argument for that.

"I say we follow the suggestions Talia gave us earlier and that she's repeating now after witnessing the parlay," Sylas says. "We must *all* give every appearance of level-headedness and rationality, and spell out our terms from that standpoint. If we're not happy with the outcome of that approach, then we can try a different tactic."

Celia sounds as if she's restraining a growl. "If you expect me to let off the ravens for their crimes rather than taking them to task—"

"That's not what it means," Donovan breaks in, looking a little shocked at himself that he's dared to cut her off. "I agree with Sylas. We have a chance now to determine what specifically we expect and how to respond to the Unseelie when they return with their offer, not to mention the limits we'd place on their request for a settlement. We should lay it out in the most logical terms possible and stick to that approach throughout the next section of the parlay. We can still insist that they're paying heavily for the harm they've done."

Celia grimaces. "They deserve to know the pain they've caused."

"They won't care," I say quietly. "Maybe they will later on, if you can manage to form more of a truce with them as allies and your well-being starts to matter to them, but for now… It won't make them any more likely to give you what you want."

Sylas gives the other woman a firm but compassionate smile. "I understand your fury. I feel it myself. But what's more important: berating the ravens for the past or ensuring a peaceful future for our people?"

"Not only that," Donovan says. "Sylas and I are in agreement. We carry the majority. If you go against us, it'll be just as much treason as Ambrose planning his war behind our backs. I know you wouldn't stoop so low, Celia."

The oldest Seelie arch-lord closes her eyes for a second and then sighs. "All right. I hear you. As long as we're agreed that we must see progress *today* or we'll revise our strategy."

Sylas inclines his head. "We can reconvene tonight and hash out whatever we need to then."

Celia hasn't looked at me since her accusation about my loyalty, but I pipe up anyway. "Thank you. *I* want peace for the Seelie too."

She only acknowledges my words with a hint of a shrug, her attention staying focused on her colleagues. "The rest of this discussion I wish to have just the three of us."

Her brush-off stings, but the relief of knowing she's listened at least a little stops me from minding. I just hope Corwin has at least as much luck with his Unseelie companions.

11

Talia

"**W**hat about deliveries of provisions?" Terisse asks. "Our people may not be satisfied with the crops and game on your side of the border. Surely one more can join them temporarily to bring supplies from the winter realm?"

"That's easily dealt with," Celia replies with studied evenness. "Arrange a specific time frame in which regular deliveries will arrive, and members of your settlement can accept them at the border with no need for those bringing them to linger."

They eye each other across the wooden table the arch-lords finally agreed to sit down at—after Sylas and his colleagues conjured it—yesterday morning. From my seat at the edge of the gathering, I watch the Unseelie side carefully, braced for another argument. But those have been coming fewer and fewer across the two days these negotiations have stretched over. After a moment, Terisse and Laoni incline their heads.

"That is reasonable," Laoni says, managing to keep a pompous tone even when she's giving in.

Corwin speaks through our bond with a hint of amusement. *Wonders never cease.*

The corners of my mouth twitch upward. *Hey, I'm just happy you all have managed to make some kind of agreement instead of stomping back to the winter realm.*

It does look promising, but I'm not holding my breath for a quick finish. I'm sure my colleagues have approximately a thousand more details they'll want to nitpick apart before they're satisfied.

The final negotiations haven't been the most exciting spectacle ever. I lean back on the stump-like stool, soaking in the early afternoon sun, and footsteps rustle across the grass behind me.

"There's our mite." Whitt comes up beside me and gives my hair an affectionate ruffle. "Still enjoying the show? Sylas said there wasn't much left to discuss."

I suppress a yawn. "It seems like there's a lot, but it's minor details now." Everything we hoped for is actually going to happen: the settlement, the experiment to see if the winter curse can be cured by the two realms sharing resources. A little thrill races through me at that thought.

Then my stomach gurgles. Whitt chuckles. "And that's why I've come to get you. Celia's people are preparing a meal for the arch-lords, but August wanted me to convey you back to the palace so you can have a break from all the politicking. Your reward will be whatever elaborate feast he's whipping up right now for the three of us."

I'd protest that I intended to see the negotiations through to the end, but my mouth immediately starts watering at the thought of August's cooking—and it isn't as if I've had anything to contribute so far today anyway.

We've kept our voices low, but of course Corwin doesn't need to use his ears to pick up on our conversation. He gives me a mental nudge. *Go on. I'll let you know if any disaster looms that requires your attention.*

It seems like the most likely disaster you'll have to deal with is a plague of boredom, I reply, and he swipes his hand across his mouth, hiding a flash of a grin.

I push myself off the stump and shake out my legs before limping after Whitt back to Sylas's castle. Sweet floral scents lace the warm summer breeze, a few birds are twittering in the trees—the atmosphere couldn't feel more peaceful. I'll take that as a good sign.

We step into the palace to even more appealing scents: fresh-baked bread and some kind of spiced meat that involves cloves. When we walk into the kitchen, August is just finishing slicing up a melon as a fruit accompaniment. He's already laid out three plates on thin wooden trays.

He beams at the sight of me. "Good, Whitt managed to tear you away."

"I don't think I'm missing much. They've finished the major deliberations." I bob up on my toes to give him a quick hug and am struck by the sense of how normal this moment feels—like how my life was in the brief periods of peace before I became entangled with the Unseelie. There are plenty of issues that are still up in the air right now, but there's nothing wrong with pretending for a little while that it's just an ordinary, cozy day with two of the men I love, is there?

Whitt cocks his head toward the counter. "What's with the trays? Are we going somewhere?"

August's grin widens. "I thought since this one has been running herself ragged"—he bends to kiss my temple—"we should get in as much relaxation time as possible while we've got her. We can bring the food down to the entertainment room. Sylas's whole collection has been moved over now. You can pick whichever movie you want, Sweetness."

Suddenly, nothing could sound better than vegging out with delicious food in front of the TV. A smile springs to my own lips. "Perfect."

It takes me a few minutes of pawing through the human-world movies Sylas has accumulated before I settle on one. He's mostly collected comedies for his own relaxation, but I suspect Whitt, at least, won't be too impressed by anything full of slapstick antics or bathroom humor. I do want them to enjoy our time together too. In the end, I settle on a British film that appears to be more clever than silly.

We all hunker down on the sofa while we eat. Seeing my two men laughing along at the early jokes warms me as much as my own laughter does.

When we're all finished with our lunches, August stacks the trays off to the side and scoots closer to me. I end up tucked between him and Whitt, my legs over August's lap and my head tipped against Whitt's shoulder. Whitt strokes his thumb over the back of my hand while August massages my bare calf with gentle pressure.

We haven't gotten to enjoy each other in more intimate ways much since I've returned, I've been so wrapped up in either thinking about or monitoring the negotiations. A deeper warmth blooms inside me, pooling between my legs. By the time the movie's over, every inch of my skin is tingling in anticipation.

"Imagine getting into that much trouble over a serving dish," August says with a laugh, and nuzzles my hair. "It did make me think, though—you've gotten pretty solid with bronze. Maybe I should teach you the true name for silver next. You mentioned that's in more common usage on the winter side, didn't you?"

"It is." I pause, considering. "Corwin said he'd start teaching me true names as well as he can while I'm there. Maybe it'd be better if he handled anything that's more of a winter fae specialty."

"Ah." August sounds a bit startled, and his muscles tense for just a second where I'm resting against him. "That would make sense. And an arch-lord would have a better grasp of the magic anyway."

"You've taught me just fine," I say, nudging him with my heel, but his smile in return doesn't look quite as bright as before. I find myself remembering that comment Whitt made before my last trip to the winter realm— something about how he wouldn't be offended if I cared more about Sylas and Corwin than him and August, just because the other two are arch-lords. Whitt and August don't really think the other two men matter more to me than they do, do they?

For the first time, I wish I had *more* soul-twined bonds instead of fewer. It's so much simpler to let Corwin know how I feel about him when all I need to do is offer my affection through our bond. I can say and do all kinds of things to try to show my devotion to my Seelie men, but I'll never be able to express it quite as plainly and undeniably as I can to the Unseelie arch-lord.

And maybe it's not surprising that they might both feel a bit pushed aside when I've spent most of my first few days back in the summer realm focusing on the arch-lords' parlay.

An ache forms around my heart, and more desire flickers low in my belly. I do love them—and want them—just as much as I always have. And maybe I can't offer up a direct line inside my mind, but there are other ways we can connect that should make my interest *very* clear.

A discomforted twinge travels to me from the bond I do have, but before more than a brief prickle of guilt can hit me, Corwin's voice follows. *It's all right. They've earned their place in your heart—I'm not going to dispute it. I'll just keep my own walls up until you need me again so I'm not distracted from the parlay.*

I send him a rush of appreciation before summoning my own inner barrier of light. Then I focus on August, curling my fingers into the fabric of his shirt. "Thank you for all of this. I definitely needed the break. But there's something else I need." I glance over my shoulder at Whitt. "From both of you."

Whitt hums and leans closer. "And what would that be, mighty one?" he asks in a suggestive tone that floods me with heat.

I reach up to graze my fingers along his jaw and look at August again. "I need you to let me show you how much you matter to me. How much I enjoy being with you in every possible way."

August's eyes light up with an eager flare. His voice comes out husky. "I think we can manage that. Do you want to go upstairs to the tryst room?"

I shake my head. "I don't want to wait even that long. It's been too long already."

I tug him to me, and he captures my mouth without a moment's hesitation. Whitt teases my hair to the side and kisses the back of my neck. Just like that, we come together in a mass of shared adoration.

How could the Heart ask me to give this up when I feel so much like I belong here?

But maybe that isn't what the Heart wants at all. Maybe I'm meant to unite summer and winter in my heart as well as in political negotiation. To accept love from both sides and create a different sort of truce.

If only I could figure out how exactly to make that more personal truce work in practice.

I don't want to think about that right now, though. I want to celebrate what I have and these amazing men who've cherished me every bit as much as I cherish them. We've come so far, and I've overcome so much. I have to believe I can find a way through this dilemma too.

Kissing August hard, I swivel to straddle his lap. Whitt eases closer, marking a trail down my neck and across my shoulder with his skillful mouth and a hot wash of his breath.

As August's tongue coaxes my lips apart, he cups my breast, provoking an eager whimper from me. Whitt reaches to the other side of my chest, drawing my nipple to a stiffened peak with a flick of his fingernail across it. A jolt of pleasure ripples through me and stirs up an unexpected impulse.

I pull back from August just a bit, touching his face and then Whitt's as I gaze into their eyes. "I love every part of you, the wolfish parts as well. I want… I want to enjoy those parts of you too. What happened in the past shouldn't stop me from appreciating your fierceness. I'm stronger than that."

Whitt's expression turns so tender it makes my throat constrict. He brushes his thumb over my cheek. "Being affected by the horrible events of your past doesn't make you weak, mighty one. Not in the slightest. We all have our scars."

I froze up once before with him when he nipped me with just his regular teeth. But I know how exhilarating it is to be swept up in the full power of a fae man. That one day when Sylas took me with the wild passion of a lover refusing to accept it might be our last time… I want to experience that intensity again and again, as many times as I can.

"You wouldn't hold back your fangs and claws with a Seelie woman, would you?" I say. "I'm not afraid of them; I'm not afraid of anything about you."

August ducks his head to press his lips to my neck. He electrifies the skin there with a swipe of his tongue and a heated murmur. "I'll give you everything you ask for, Sweetness. You just say the word if it's too much."

His teeth graze the sensitive skin with the sharpened points I know are his wolfish fangs. He traces them across my skin so gently the panic I was worried I'd have to conquer never rises up, only a quiver of giddiness.

I know these men would never hurt me. What made my former tormentors monsters wasn't the wolf in their nature.

The tips of claws glide across my upper back. Whitt gives my shoulder the lightest nip and then drags his claws downward. They neatly sever the fabric of my simple dress. The rasp of the splitting cloth and the feel of it falling away across my skin sends a thrill straight to my sex.

With increasing urgency, I seek out August's mouth with mine. He kisses me back with equal furor, his fangs just barely nicking my lips. Moving around behind me, Whitt teases both of my nipples between the cool edges of his claws. A moan tumbles out of me.

The spymaster works me over until I can't help grinding against the bulge forming in August's slacks. Then, testing his teeth against my shoulder, Whitt slits the fabric of my panties as well.

I arch up to let the cloth fall away, and Whitt retracts his claws to delve his fingers between my legs. As they slide across my clit, I gasp.

August takes the opportunity to capture the tip of my breast between his lips. He suckles me with alternating flicks of his tongue and grazes of his fangs. Whitt tips my head so he can claim my mouth for himself, still fingering me. A possessive growl reverberates from his throat, but I know it's not aimed at August, only the thought of any intruders on our shared love.

I rock between them, bliss building in my sex and lighting up my skin. Just when I think I might die of frustration, August wrenches down his trousers and frees his erection. He pulls me down over him, filling me with the ecstatic burn I've come to appreciate so much.

He grips my thighs, his claws forming little pinpoints of pain. When I whimper, he jerks his hands back, but I grab his wrists and bring them back.

"No," I mumble between kisses. "It was good." Like a hint of sour bringing out a deeper sweetness in a candy.

Whitt trails his own claws down my spine, sparking a path of giddy shivers in their wake. When he reaches my bottom, his touch stops, the claws vanishing again. His lips move against my shoulder, his voice low and sultry. "If you're in an experimenting mood, dearest, there is a way you could have both of us at once."

My breath hitches at both the new, adoring nickname and the implication in his words. "What's that?" I ask, already suspecting it before he skims his fingertips across my behind to the opening there.

I've never given that part of my body much thought in terms of sex, but the delicate stroke he gives it brings a flicker of pleasure and another whimper to my lips. "I'd be careful with you," he says, repeating the gesture. "I'd like to see what heights we could take you to working in tandem."

August lets out a rough encouraging noise. I can't see any reason to deny any of us that experience. I nod. "Yes, please."

Whitt chuckles. As I sway over August, taking him deeper, the spymaster continues to massage my other opening, gradually adding pressure and a slickness formed with a whispered word of magic.

It feels strange but so good I can't help shifting my posture to open up to him. Then he slips a finger right inside me there, and my breath shudders out of me with the pulse of pleasure.

"Good?" he asks, pumping in and out with a little more pressure to warm up the muscles. "Would you like more of me there, mighty one?"

I manage an inarticulate sound of agreement. So much ecstasy is swelling through me now that I can barely think, let alone speak.

He adds a second finger, and then a third, with a surge of bliss so strong I cry out. "Oh, I think you're ready now," Whitt purrs, more cat than wolf now.

There's a rustle of his slacks as he drops them and kneels, and then the hard length of his cock brushes against me. I go still over August as the other man carefully eases into me.

It's a different sort of burning, tighter but headier because it's so new. I find myself panting, overwhelmed with the sensation of being doubly filled.

I'm Talia McCarty, a human who survived the fae and now stands beside some of the most powerful in the realm, and I will take every delight my men can offer me.

I start to move again, slowly and then gaining speed as the three of us find our joint rhythm. August brings my mouth back to his, our kisses shaky with broken breath. Whitt groans, embracing me from behind. Their rigid shafts plunge into me in unison, and the incredible sensation expands all through my body. I grip August's shoulder, Whitt's arm where it's tucked around my torso, my breath breaking into giddy pants.

With so much stimulation, it doesn't take long before the wave cresting inside me crashes over its peak. I shudder and clench, coming with a cracking of bliss so intense it blanks my mind.

August's grip on my thighs tightens as he bucks up and follows me over the edge. Whitt thrusts inside me a little longer, tossing me straight into another orgasm with a renewed blaze of pleasure, before he stiffens against me with a choked sound he muffles against my back.

For a few minutes, we linger in our combined embrace, our bodies coming down from the high of the encounter. Then we untangle ourselves slowly, Whitt moving back to the couch in time for me to collapse half cuddled by both of my lovers. I wrap an arm around one of each of theirs.

"You're mine," I say with a little wolfish fierceness of my own. "And you're staying mine."

August kisses my sweat-damp forehead, his smile back at its usual brightness. "No argument at all from either of us, Sweetness."

Too bad solving all the fae's problems isn't this simple.

Talia

"So which place is your favorite?" Harper asks me a little breathlessly, swinging her legs where she's perched on her crafting table. I've been hanging out with her in her new house here by the Heart—where she's living on her own now rather than with her parents— telling her about the sights I saw on my second visit to the winter realm.

I tip my head to the side, considering. It's a little hard to focus with the awareness that just a short distance away, the negotiations between the arch-lords are finally wrapping up. Corwin told me he expects they'll be finished within the hour. After three days of hashing things out, the Unseelie arch-lords have finally become at ease enough to be willing to let the Seelie host them in the Bastion, where both sides will swear oaths when the agreement is totally worked out.

"I think the painted forest is still the most impressive out of everything," I say. "So I'm glad you got to see that."

"The frostfire trees sound pretty amazing too. And that cave by the ocean!" Harper gives a gleeful shiver. "It has been good getting some time to settle in here, but eventually you'll have to give me more of a tour."

The corners of my lips twitch upward. "I guess once I've seen all the best sights, I can make sure I take you to the highlights." Assuming I still have a place in the winter realm by that point—assuming a summer fae would be welcome as a visitor...

I can't fully sink into the conversation with all the uncertainties and secrets hanging over me. I'm not sure I've been a great friend this morning. The things happening in Harper's life right now are so distant from what I'm going through, and she doesn't know the half of it to even try to understand.

I get up from the armchair I was sitting in. "I think I'm going to see if they've finished with the negotiations." That's not totally true—I know they're not, because Corwin would have told me otherwise—but it's a reasonable excuse to leave that won't hurt Harper's feelings.

She bobs her head with a smile that shows she isn't offended. "You're here for another couple of days, right? I'm going to make you another dress for your next trip across the border."

A twinge of guilt hits me. "You really don't have to. Your work is absolutely gorgeous, but the winter fae seem to care mostly about practicality... No matter how friendly the realms end up getting, I'm not sure you'll pick up many new clients over there."

Harper shrugs. "It's not for me. I like knowing you're over there looking like a real lady. Put anyone who'd think less of you in their place."

I won't argue with that motivation. "Well, thank you," I say, wishing I could give her more than travel stories in return. I should ask Corwin if there are any special kinds of fabric or embellishments used in the winter realm that I could bring back for her to experiment with.

Outside, the air is crisper against my skin than it was yesterday, with a hint of coolness in the summer warmth that suggests a light rain might fall tonight. It doesn't seem to ever rain during the day near the Heart.

I set off through the scattered trees around the pack village, drawn by the rhythmic pulsing of that glowing spot that determines so much of what goes on in the entire faerie world. The Heart's energy tickles over my body more noticeably as I emerge from the trees and cross the vast field toward it. The table from the earlier negotiations has been removed. There's no sign it ever existed amid the pale pink and blue flowers bobbing with the breeze.

I limp right up to the vast glowing area in the border, its power rising to a thrum. When I'm standing just a few feet away, the mass of the Heart stands at least twice as tall as me and far wider than I could ever reach, its light pulsing in time with its energy. Staring into its golden depths, I have to catch my breath.

What do you want from me? I think at it. *What am I supposed to do here?* Questions I don't dare ask out loud, in case some passing fae overhears. And also, *Why me?*

If it chose me for some special purpose, shouldn't it give me more of an explanation? I have no idea what role it expects me to fulfill—whether I should be focusing completely on uniting the summer and winter fae, whether I'm meant to be paying more attention to the curse itself. Whether it even has a purpose for me at all or its effect on me is actually simple random chance.

As many good things as I've discovered in the faerie world, I'd hesitate to call that chance "luck."

The Heart doesn't give any indication it's heard me. It just pulses steadily on, the thrum starting to make my bones ache while I'm standing so close. It overwhelms my senses to the point that I don't hear footsteps approaching until Astrid comes to a stop beside me.

"You look like a woman thinking deep thoughts," the old warrior says in a gently wry tone.

I let out a huff of breath. "I just… I don't understand why I've ended up so connected to this place. It seems like the Heart must have something to do with it." But I got straighter answers from the tree-bound sage we visited, in all his vague rambling.

Astrid's mouth twists into a slanted smile. "The Heart's ways are difficult to discern even for those of us who've drawn on its magic for over a thousand years. I tend to think of it as something like the sun rather than some sort of conscious entity. Its power fuels our lives and strength, but it simply *is*. Any patterns that arise are merely the natural order of things."

I can't hold back a snort. "I don't think there's anything natural about a human with curse-healing blood and a soul-twined mate."

Astrid raises an eyebrow. "Maybe it's just a natural order too complex for us lesser beings to fully comprehend." She turns to the Heart, tipping her head back to soak in its glow, which seems to smooth the wrinkled planes of her aged face. "I find it's easiest not to worry about what those patterns might be. I trust that my intentions were shaped by the same power, so therefore what I decide to do with myself should fit in with any grand plans one way or another."

I wish I had the same faith. But then, there isn't much I *can* do other than keep going the way that seems best to me, is there?

"Thank you," I say, because it is a little comfort to know that even a fae woman with centuries upon centuries of life behind her finds the Heart as mysterious as I do.

Corwin lets down his inner wall a little more, giving me a clearer glimpse of the circular meeting room in the center of the Bastion and the voices carrying around him —filled with relief and satisfaction. The oath-taking must be over. The truce and the agreement for the Unseelie settlement are confirmed. At least that one thing has wrapped up smoothly.

Smiling, I set off toward the Bastion, Astrid ambling alongside me. I'm halfway across the field when Corwin and his colleagues emerge.

I feel the second that Laoni lays eyes on me. Her gaze sends a chilly prickle down my spine, but she pitches her voice low enough that I only hear it through Corwin's ears. "I still say your mate is too close for comfort with that one Seelie pack."

"She does seem to spend a great deal of time with them and to look to them for guidance," Terisse agrees.

Laoni's gaze travels past me toward Sylas's castle, even though she won't be able to make it out from that angle. "Especially those *men*. Are you so sure of her loyalties?"

I bristle and shudder inwardly at the same time. Have I given away more about my relationship with Sylas and his two cadre-chosen than I'd have wanted to?

All I sense from Corwin is irritation and defiance, though. "Her association with Arch-Lord Sylas played a large role in ensuring the success of this parlay. I'd prefer that to her being the sort of woman who'd drop her loyalty to those who've earned it the second the wind changes course."

Without waiting to hear his colleagues' response, he breaks away from the others to stride to meet me. *Don't mind them. The Seelie arch-lords could have offered us half the summer realm, and they'd still find something to grouse about.*

Astrid makes a gesture of farewell and leaves me to my mate. The other Unseelie arch-lords hustle on past us toward the border, apparently eager to return home and stay there this time. I can't say I'll miss them.

Corwin on the other hand… "I guess you need to get back to Heart's Cadence," I say as he reaches me.

"I have been somewhat neglecting all my duties there over the past few days." He takes my hands in his. "I didn't want to leave without a proper good-bye, though, even if you'll be rejoining me in a short while."

There's no more judgment in those words than in his

retort to Laoni, but I can taste the bittersweet undertone. He can't help wishing I was coming back with him now.

The wind whips across the field, sending a burst of bright petals spiraling. Suddenly it seems absurd that he's spent all this time in the realm that was my first home among the fae while barely seeing any of it.

I squeeze his fingers. "Can you hold off on those duties for another hour or two? You've shown me some of your favorite spots in the winter realm—I could show you some of the summer realm's magic."

I brace instinctively for him to dismiss the idea, but instead one of his rare brilliant smiles crosses his lips. "I'd like that very much."

I glance down at my boots. "It'll go faster if you fly us. It's a little bit of a hike from here. If you don't mind bringing your wings out around the Seelie, that is."

"I should be asking you whether you wouldn't be shunned if you're seen with one of us ravens," he replies with a hint of dry humor.

"It'll be fine. Just don't go waving any swords around."

He unfurls his wings, stretching them to their full span before folding them closer to his body again. In the summer sunlight, the black feathers shine with a faint iridescent gleam I never noticed before. I let him scoop me up and give him directions that take us over Donovan's domain.

Like on the winter side, the area around the Heart here is a broad plateau. Most of the way around that hill, the climb to its broad peak is a relatively easy slope—not that I'd enjoy trekking up it very far with my warped foot. But in one spot in Donovan's territory, one Whitt told me about back when we still lived in Oakmeet and showed off to me a couple of weeks ago, the land falls away in a narrow, sheer cliff with an equally narrow waterfall.

I have Corwin set us down on the grassy bank near the bottom of the falls where the thin river winds away into forestland. He gazes up at the waterfall. It isn't as expansive or fierce as the falls in his domain, but the cascading water glitters with an effervescence that puts even his diamond palace to shame. I swear you can see every color in existence, including some I've never known existed, twinkling off the torrent.

"They call it the Shimmering Falls," I tell Corwin, sitting down and running my fingers through the silky grass. It gleams a green as vibrant as an emerald. All of the plant life around the falls has absorbed some of its vividness, the flowers and ferns beaming in a blazing mass of color that would be overwhelming if it didn't feel so harmonious at the same time.

Well, it feels that way to me. Corwin blinks hard, the scenery so intense and so different from what he's used to that I sense his eyes outright stinging for a moment. But as he adjusts, awe sweeps away any discomfort. "It's spectacular."

"I wouldn't want you to think the winter realm had all the best sights," I tease, and lie down on my back. The grass caresses my arms, and the sun grazes my skin, and I feel wrapped in a cocoon of contentment. It's even better getting to share this beautiful spot with someone who's never been here before.

I guess this must be how my fae men have felt showing

me so many remarkable sites for the first time. Now I understand why they enjoy playing tour guide so much.

Corwin sinks to the ground next to me and strokes gentle fingers over my hair. The affection traveling from him into me has a tang of sadness to it. I look up at him, about to ask what's wrong, but he beats me to it.

"You love this place very much," he says.

I shrug as well as I can in my current position. "Like you said, it's spectacular. It makes me feel like... like I'm floating on some kind of song made out of color."

I'm not sure that description makes much sense, but Corwin smiles. "Yes." He pauses. "But that's not what I meant. I meant this *entire* place—the summer realm itself."

"Oh." A lump rises in my throat. "Yeah. I mean, I haven't pretended I don't."

"I know. It's simply different experiencing it myself and through you at the same time, seeing you as well as sensing your impressions..." He exhales slowly, and the sadness expands. "I can't take you away from this. I could never—to ever expect you to dedicate yourself completely to the winter realm..."

I sit up abruptly, reaching for his hand. "We found a way around that, for now at least. I don't mind going back and forth."

"It can't continue that way forever. I know you're aware of that as much as I am." The same pensive uncertainty that's dogged me for the past few weeks echoes from him through our bond. "When I go back, I'll have some time before you're with me again. And a lot to think about in that time."

I grasp his hand tightly with a wrench of my heart. "Don't go making any decisions *for* me. I don't want to lose you either—and the rest of the winter realm is growing on me."

Corwin tugs me closer to him and slips his arms around me. "I promise I won't take any action without consulting you first. Let's not worry about that. For now, I'd like to just enjoy this piece of happiness you're sharing with me."

I nestle into his embrace, but my own happiness has taken on a bittersweet tinge. For all the beauty and magic the fae world has to offer, this one thing I want so badly feels as far out of reach as ever.

Sylas

It wasn't hard to determine where Arch-Lord Corwin had gone. The Unseelie are a rare enough sight in the summer realm, and especially this close to the Heart, that I had multiple reports back from my sentries of a raven-winged man carrying Talia toward the Shimmering Falls before I even set out to look for him.

I don't have to go very far to find them. As I expected, he brings Talia back close to my castle, tightening his embrace for just a moment before he sets her down on her feet. I pause where I've been waiting in the shadows of the trees along the edge of the field. When he bends to give her a quick kiss, my wolf roars within me, longing to charge at him and tear him away from her.

But he has a much more legitimate claim on her affections than I do. I haven't even been able to admit my interest in her to anyone outside my cadre.

That thought—and the memory of how close I'd been

to claiming her as my mate before her soul-twined bond came into being—makes me bristle in a different way. I clench my jaw to hold back a snarl that's not really directed at anyone in particular, only the situation at large.

This Unseelie arch-lord *is* her Heart-given mate, and I have to respect that if I want to maintain any kind of relationship with her. I only wish it was easier to be glad that he's proven himself worthy enough that she hasn't turned her back on him. If he'd been a villain, we'd have so much more turmoil on our hands.

Talia leaves Corwin to head back toward the castle, her gait typically uneven but her windblown hair and flushed cheeks giving her a wild beauty that sends a twang of desire through me. I tamp down on those urges and focus on the winter arch-lord now turning toward the border.

Striding forward across the grass, I catch his attention before I've spoken. He glances at me and stops just a few steps shy of the wall of haze. He's withdrawn his wings, but I can see the raven-ish apprehension in the tilt of his dark head.

"Arch-Lord Corwin," I say evenly. "Before you head home, I was hoping I could speak to you just the two of us."

"Of course." He glances around, perhaps wondering whether the subject I wish to bring up is safe around potential eavesdroppers.

I intone a quick spell to give me a sense of the nearest fae in the area and motion for him to follow me back toward the trees, where our conversation should proceed uninterrupted. As he falls into step beside me, there's a certain reluctance to his movements that I can't help noticing.

He's consulted with me before, but only when it helped his cause. I'm not sure whether he's more unhappy about my presence or uneasy about how I'll respond to his.

In the shelter of the trees, I face him. "I simply wanted to confirm, before she's due to cross the border again, that as far as you've observed Talia is adapting to her time in the winter realm and to the transitions back and forth reasonably well."

Corwin's eyebrows rise slightly. "Isn't that a question you should be asking her?"

I have to respect his response even though it rankles me that he'd think I don't value her own assessment. "I'd imagine you've gotten to know her well enough by now to realize that she's hesitant to admit any worries or weakness if she thinks she can overcome them on her own. She doesn't like coming across as a burden, even though I've never considered her one regardless. It seemed wise to get an impartial perspective. Or at least a perspective less skewed toward keeping up that resilient front of hers."

Corwin's expression stays implacably calm with the coolly detached air all of the Unseelie seem to have. "And if I said she was experiencing any difficulties with the present arrangement, would you use that as justification to suggest she shouldn't continue her visits after all?"

My fangs itch in my gums at the insinuation, but I will them back. "I'd hope that by now you're aware that I wouldn't stoop to such underhanded tactics. I've been fair in my dealings with you, haven't I?"

Corwin offers me a smile—small and tight, but unexpected enough that it diffuses my irritation. "I apologize. You have. Perhaps I've spent too much time in my colleagues' company these past few days, and it's put me too far on the defensive."

Interesting that he'd blame *his* colleagues for that rather than my own, although I have gathered from both him and Talia that he doesn't see eye-to-eye with the other Unseelie arch-lords on a variety of subjects.

"I'm concerned about her well-being, nothing more or less," I say. "If there *is* anything she's been struggling with, I'd want to do what I can to help her while she's with us. And since she wants to continue exploring the soul-twined bond, that would include helping her be at ease in your realm."

Corwin inclines his head. "I think she's been taking to the new environment well. She's clearly very adaptable to have found a place for herself so quickly among your pack in the first place. The greater difficulty may be encouraging everyone *else* to adapt to having a human woman standing by an arch-lord's side, but if they see that she's been instrumental in tackling our curse... those hesitations should be smoothed over without too much trouble."

I consider him. "She's said her blood didn't have any effect on the victims of your curse, nor any of your other attempts. I assume that's why you switched your focus to creating the settlement here. Do you believe there's much chance that the atmosphere of the summer realm will really be all the cure you need?"

The Unseelie arch-lord glances away for a second, his

expression darkening. "I don't know. I'd like to have faith in the idea, especially after all the pain we've put your people through striving toward that goal, but… it feels too simple to me. Even Talia's blood hasn't been a full cure for your curse, only a temporary one. I can't shake the sense that there's something more to this, a missing piece we require to get to the heart of the problem."

His sentiments echo my own so well that I find myself unexpectedly reassured even though we're no closer to the answer. "Indeed. At least we're proceeding with the trial, so we'll know more than we did before. And I expect that being able to collaborate to whatever extent between our realms should speed our progress toward a real cure even more."

Corwin's smile comes back, perhaps a little brighter than the first one. "I'm glad we were able to reach that point. And Talia can certainly take a great deal of the credit for it." He lets out a soft chuckle. "She's skilled at seeing the best in any person and situation she encounters —and finding ways to bring it out into full view."

The warm fondness in his tone, so different from his usual cool demeanor, puts me even more at ease than before. Perhaps I was still somewhat concerned about how her theoretical mate valued her. It couldn't be more clear that he appreciates her for much the same reasons I do.

Now it's even more difficult to resent his presence in her life.

"She does," I agree. "One of her many impressive qualities. I'd challenge anyone who claims she can't hold her own among the fae to point to more than a handful of our own kind who've shown as much fortitude and compassion."

Corwin hesitates, and then says, with an awkward twitch of his hands, "I'm also glad she has you. The three of you. It was hard, at first—sometimes it's still hard—but with every day I spend with her, it's easier to understand how she could have won so many hearts and found room in her own to offer so much love in return. I know how much you mean to her. It's not my wish to wrench her from you completely. I simply haven't determined a better arrangement than what we currently have."

A constricting sensation winds through my chest. Both because of the generosity in his words—and the unstated fact that we're nonetheless both aware of, that our current arrangement *can't* be the final one. It's suitable for the short term, but we can hardly jerk Talia back and forth between the realms week by week for the rest of her life.

And I haven't come up with a better proposition yet either. Corwin and I both have our duties to our peoples as arch-lords. We're bound to our sides of the border as much as she's bound to him.

"I appreciate that," I say, hoping he can tell how genuinely I mean the words. "I'll do whatever I can to find a solution that allows us all our happiness." Drawing in a breath, I step back. "Thank you for speaking with me. I won't delay you from your journey home any longer."

I'm not sure whether I feel better or worse for the conversation as we part ways. I definitely feel worse seeing Celia stalking across the field toward me when I emerge from the stand of trees. From her expression, she's gathered that I've been talking with the Unseelie—or one of them, anyway—alone.

She may have toned down her animosity for our negotiations, but she still isn't remotely friendly toward them.

She glances toward Corwin's figure vanishing into the border's haze and comes to a halt abruptly in front of me. "Making some additional negotiations?" she demands with her typical imperious air.

I swallow a sigh. Celia approved of my appointment to arch-lord, but she wasn't as enthusiastic about the prospect as Donovan—and since he and I joined together to overturn her decision to take Corwin prisoner, she's aimed more of her temper at me than usual.

"We didn't discuss the Unseelie settlement or the peace accord at all," I say. "I was merely inquiring about the more personal matter of Talia's visits to their realm, which seemed better dealt with between just the two of us."

My colleague's stance relaxes a little, but her expression stays stern. She eyes me with a penetrating gaze I don't particularly care for. "You're very invested in what goes on with this woman."

"She's the closest thing to a cure we have for our own curse. Why wouldn't I be?"

"It isn't just that, though. The oaths protect us from losing the benefit she provides." She pauses. "Your cadre-chosen who was enamored with her—I still see them showing affection to each other. Does her Unseelie mate know about that?"

I catch myself just shy of gritting my teeth. "Of course he does. It would be difficult for her to hide something like that while they're bonded. Talia has insisted that she not have to give up the other sorts of bonds she's formed, and so far her mate has respected her wishes on the subject. We're waiting to see how that plays out. At the moment, there have been larger issues to focus on."

Celia hums to herself. "And perhaps it also matters to you on a personal level more than it should. You can *like* the creature, but don't forget that the security of your people must come before your concerns for any one individual—especially when that individual is a mortal we've already outlived at least twice over."

Without waiting for my response, she turns on her heel and marches off. I watch her go with a sinking sensation in my gut.

Corwin spoke of his people's acceptance of Talia as his mate. I've been contemplating how to keep her in my life while she's tied to him as well. But I have the problem of my own peers too, don't I? Even if the Unseelie arch-lord and I can reach a happy compromise, how will I explain it to my fellow rulers in a way *they'll* understand?

And what obstacles will they throw in our way if I can't?

Talia

After a week in the summer realm, the first day back in the chill of the winter side is always jarring despite the warming spell on my clothes. It doesn't help that within an hour of my arrival, my lunch with Corwin was interrupted by a message that the curse has struck a woman in another domain. Corwin, Zelpha, and I have been riding in one of the Unseelie carriages for what feels like ages.

At the speed my soul-twined mate has pushed the vehicle too, some of the icy wind whips past the crystalline shield meant to protect us from it. A thin haze of cloud has turned the sky gray and dimmed the sun. I've tucked myself as close to the windshield as possible, my knees drawn up and my arms wrapped around myself, trying not to let my nerves overwhelm me.

There are strategies for tackling the curse that we discussed after the last time but haven't had the chance to try yet—mostly attempting more than one of our past ideas in combination. And this is the first time I'll attempt to heal a victim so soon after the curse has hit them. But I can't get rid of the uncomfortable knot in my stomach at the thought of failing yet again. Of knowing that our failure will mean this woman's death.

Corwin has been putting together his "draughts" while we travel, taking the particles of my blood and skin and even my bones so carefully I feel only a faint, split-second stinging with each one. Zelpha studies the landscape beyond the carriage, even her usually nonchalant expression turned serious.

"If this doesn't work," I say, "she could still join the settlement in the summer realm, right? You wanted to see if a stay there could cure the curse as well as whether it can prevent it."

Corwin frowns. "I'm not sure the preparations will be ready in time. They haven't finished constructing all the buildings or ensuring the initial supplies are in place. As you could probably tell from the parlay, neither side was eager to rush into anything."

"I was due to head over and see how things are progressing tomorrow anyway," Zelpha says. "It was meant to be ready within the week. I might be able to hurry things along."

But it'll be easier if something we try today works and the summer settlement doesn't need to factor in at all. I drag in a breath and gird myself for the coming attempt as well as I can.

Corwin sinks onto the bench next to me, slipping his arm tentatively around me. When I lean into his embrace, he hugs me closer to him. Sharing his warmth eases my worries just a little.

Just the fact that you're trying so hard is incredibly admirable, he tells me. *And we might not have the settlement being created at all if it wasn't for you.*

I know. And I want *to help. It seems so much easier, the way I can wake the Seelie out of their curse. I don't know why there isn't something more simple for you.*

His hand glides up my arm to rest on my scarred shoulder. *I wouldn't call what happened to you to make that discovery "easy."*

Fair point. The memory of the attack ripples through me with a shudder I can't quite suppress. Corwin's arm tenses around me, a wordless apology traveling through our bond.

I really hope I don't have to lose as much as I did that night to unravel this side of the fae's curse.

"Here we are," Zelpha says, straightening up.

I twist on my seat to peer through the crystalline windshield. We've dipped into a valley between two sheer cliffs. Like in Corwin's domain, the flock village has been formed along the rocky face—on both sides. The houses here are formed out of the same stone as the valley walls, though, as is the craggy castle that juts up toward the sky near the edge of the cliff on the right.

A man waves to us from a terrace partway down. There isn't anywhere for the carriage to come to rest there, so Corwin draws it up alongside the railing and lets it hover while we clamber out.

"I'm glad you could come so quickly," the man says, his face both flushed and drawn. He looks sick himself, though not in the way of the curse. "I hope—if there's anything you can do for her—"

"We'll try our best," Corwin says. "Will you give us the space to make our attempts in private? We can't be entirely sure how any external factors will affect the situation."

We have no reason to think having another person around would change anything—it's never been a factor when it comes to helping the Seelie curse—but we're still trying to keep it quiet just how involved I am in our "attempts."

Unlike past supporters, this man hesitates, wavering on his feet for a few seconds. His mouth twists as if he wants to argue. Then he ducks his head. "Whatever you think is best, my lord. I just want them to be okay."

Them? I puzzle over that remark as we step through the doorway into the man's home. Either with his fae senses or simple instinct, Corwin passes through what looks like a living room to another doorway beyond.

As soon as we come into the bedroom there, understanding hits me with a lurch of my gut.

The woman sitting in an armchair by a small hearth has her arms cradled around her rounded belly. She strokes it and shivers, her voice lilting in a faint crooning.

She's pregnant. Fairly far along, by the size of her, but maybe not enough that the baby could survive being born just yet.

But if the curse takes her, if it freezes her straight through… the baby will die too.

The knot in my stomach multiplies into a dozen. I

swallow hard as Corwin walks to the woman's side. "How are you doing?" he asks, calmly but gently.

Another shiver ripples through her. She looks up at him, barely seeming to register who he is. Grief is already etched throughout her expression.

What agony must she be in, knowing not only is her life on the line but her child's—a child she might have waited hundreds of years to have a chance to bring into the world?

"Cold," she murmurs. "I'm cold, but it's not too sharp yet. I can still move all right. Well, as much as I could before in this state." Her arm tightens around her belly protectively. Then she blinks, some of the distance drawing back from her eyes. "My lord, you think there's something you can do?"

She gazes past him to Zelpha and me, and the hope that darts across her face nearly kills me.

"We're going to try everything we can think of," Corwin reassures her, his own distress radiating through our bond into me. He knows more deeply than I do how treasured children are among the fae, who bear so few. "I've brought a couple of my people with me to assist. Are you comfortable here, or would you like to lie down?"

The woman glances toward the bed where the cover lies neatly across the mattress and shakes her head. "I'll stay here by the fire unless you need me elsewhere."

"Right there should be just fine." He inhales slowly, and I can feel him steadying himself for the task ahead as much as I did on the carriage.

I have no idea how to rein in my nerves now. As Corwin draws out his first draught, one that combines two aspects of my body, I wrack my brain for any tactic we might have missed that I could add to our plans for today. But we've already gone over so many possibilities together. The heavy thumping of my heart only makes it harder to concentrate now.

Zelpha touches my back in a tentative gesture. "If there's a way, we'll find it," she murmurs, and I realize she's attempting to reassure me. My anxiety must be showing. I shove it down as well as I can, not wanting to add to the immense distress the cursed woman must already be experiencing.

Because it would take an awfully long time to go through every possible combination of bodily contributions and actions, we agreed the last time we had a discussion about tackling the curse that we wouldn't worry as much about separating out the effects. If something works, then we can look at all the factors that were in play around the moment the victim seemed to turn the corner and separate those out more later.

What really matters is giving the victim every possible chance of surviving.

So, as soon as the woman has swallowed the first draught, I step up to her and hold out my hand. After a second's hesitation, she takes it. Wrapping her hand in both of mine, I sing the same lullaby I offered up to the victim before her.

A burn starts to creep up behind my eyes. I learned this song from my mother. Maybe she sang it to me before I was even born, like this woman was singing to her child.

Her skin is chilly to the touch. Nothing I'm doing, not even the press of my fingers against hers, seems to warm her. Her other hand shifts over her belly as if she's felt her child moving inside her.

Corwin offers up another draught, and then another and another. My throat gets hoarse from singing that tune and then a few others I throw in, because why not? I give the woman quick but emphatic hugs, hold her hand, and massage her shoulders and then her feet. She gives me a small smile of thanks even though I can tell that whatever comfort I'm offering her isn't fixing the larger problem.

Zelpha brings out some snacks I helped bake back in Corwin's kitchen, quick little sugary treats that didn't require much preparation before we left. The woman straightens up to eat them and flinches with the movement.

I can tell in an instant that her back is stiffening up. She holds her posture awkwardly as she chews, a little more of the color draining from her already grayed face.

Nothing's working. She's only getting worse.

I offer every gesture I can again and finally step back, my heart aching. The woman slumps back in her chair with a wince. The angle of her jaw looks tight now too.

How much longer does she have before she'll barely be able to move at all?

Another mother and another child dead because I couldn't do enough. Because I couldn't act the right way when it mattered.

The burning fills my eyes, and I turn around before she can see the tears that overflow. A sob clogs my throat. I force it down, swiping at my face, but I can't hold back the tears completely. They streak down my cheeks and over my hasty fingers. I manage to stay quiet, but my breath comes out shaky.

Talia? Corwin says, his inner voice taut with concern.

Just focus on her. I'll get myself together as quickly as I can.

I've never cried in front of him before, I realize. He's seen me upset but not like this, not in reality rather than my memories. I can tell from the emotions whirling through him that it's an unusual sight in the winter realm. That's not surprising when the Unseelie value emotional control so highly.

All the more reason I need to get a grip before I freak out the woman I'm supposed to be helping.

Zelpha comes up beside me, her brow knit. "Is there anything I can do?" she asks quietly.

I shake my head and focus on breathing slow and steady. After a minute or two, the burning eases off enough that I can blink the last tears away. I wipe at my cheeks, knowing they must be splotchy and my eyes red-rimmed, but there's not much I can do about that. Maybe I should just go outside until Corwin's finished with the last few steps.

Before I can move to go, the woman's soft voice reaches me. "You're weeping—for me and my baby?"

I turn toward her, not wanting to speak with my back to her but hesitant to let her see how affected I am. "I'm sorry—I just wanted so badly to make things better for you."

She stares at me, but she doesn't look offended, more amazed. "I'm honored that a companion of the arch-lord cares so much."

The tension inside me twists with a bittersweet pang. On an impulse, I step toward her instead, touching her cheek as if I can pass on how much I do care through that contact the same way my emotions can travel to Corwin more easily skin-to-skin.

But of course, I don't have any kind of bond with this woman. I get no sense of inner connection. I'm about to pull back when she grasps my wrist, a gasp spilling from her lips.

And then I feel it. The faint warmth blooming beneath my fingers across her cheek. Her hand is warm where it grips my arm as well. Her eyes widen, the awkwardness of her posture easing.

She takes a big gulp of air. "It's—it's going away. The cold. I can feel—I can feel the fire again. And the warming spell on my clothes."

I clasp her hand, rocked by the surge of joy that rushes from Corwin into me. But my own burst of happiness is tempered by the knowledge that the cures I offer have never been enough to chase away a curse completely.

Maybe we've figured it out. Something I just did tipped the balance. But how long will she have until the cold creeps over this poor woman again?

15

Whitt

I can't say I'd been looking forward to spending the day hanging around a bunch of mangy ravens, but it's certainly interesting seeing how similar and yet how different the Unseelie folk are. They've grouped together to work on the buildings of their new settlement with similar focus, summoning the same sorts of materials our kind can. The voices raised in approval or suggestion around me could have belonged to Seelie just as well.

On the other hand, their gestures have a subtle but noticeable bird-like quality I'd never had much chance to observe before. After ambling along the fringes of the settlement for a couple of hours watching the progress of the construction, I suspect I could have picked out a winter fae in a crowd of Seelie without even being close enough to scent them.

Although it's no trouble scenting them here with so

many together. The spot we offered them in between two Seelie domains near the border now stinks of raven.

Stepping back to take in the entire area at once, I have to reflect that it's an odd-looking town for either realm. With mate-pairs from various Unseelie domains coming together and no lord overseeing them, they've all constructed their homes out of the materials they feel most comfortable with. The result is a jumble of wood, stone, metal, and any other material that can be raised or woven into walls.

I don't know how large a typical Unseelie flock is, but this village makes a decent-sized pack. Sylas and his colleagues agreed to allow a hundred of the ravens to make their home here. They've all had to take an oath that they'll do us no harm as long as we don't attack them unprovoked, although there's no telling whether one or another will try to find a loophole.

Of course, as Sylas pointed out, there shouldn't be any reason for them to undermine our rules if the ravens are telling the truth that the only reason for the attacks was to take control over some of our territory in the first place. I suppose we'll just have to see whether it turns out our lands help offset their curse. If living here shields them from that icy death, we may have an invasion on our hands. It's not as if we'll want to trade and take their frozen terrain in return.

For now, the newcomers are eyeing the few of us wolves prowling around the edges of their new home with wariness that I'll admit is understandable. We're here both to make sure they're settling in without issue and to ensure all the requirements we insisted on are being met.

So far, no one I've seen has put a toe—or a talon—out of line. But I can't shake a creeping uneasiness that something about this situation isn't quite right.

It's merely a vague impression. It could be simply the discomfort of having so many of our recent enemies on our soil right in front of me. But my instincts are well-honed, and if something's telling me I'm missing a factor of concern, I'm inclined to trust that sense.

I continue circling, watching several fae performing the magic to allow working pipes into their homes for drinking and washing, and another group getting a garden started with vegetables that may or may not take to our climate. No doubt August will have all sorts of questions and tips for them when it's his turn to check in on the settlement.

When my gaze passes over a woman I recognize as one of the Unseelie arch-lords—not the loud, arrogant one, but not the friendliest of their number either—I pause. She's swiveling on her heel in the midst of several of the half-formed houses, her head cocked in contemplation. When her eyes catch mine, they narrow. Only for a moment, but enough to know she doesn't like us keeping an eye on them.

Can I blame her for that? Maybe not. That doesn't mean I should completely ignore the understated hostility, though. They're our guests, here by our grace only.

A wry voice pipes up from just behind me. "Don't mind Arch-Lord Terisse. She's mostly annoyed that she got stuck with overseer duty today."

I turn to find a woman almost as beefy as August standing nearby, her deep brown hair tied back in a loose braid. She's a raven—no whiff of wolf breaks through the overall birdish odor that permeates this place—but she's being awfully familiar with me for one. I wouldn't expect even one of my fellow Seelie to speak that casually about one of our arch-lords to me, let alone to a potential opponent.

Possibly she's hoping to catch me out in some sort of insult. If so, she picked the wrong wolf. I smile back as mildly as I'm capable of, keeping my tone equally inoffensive. "I suppose it's understandable that the transition would cause some stress."

The woman rocks on her heels, watching the other Unseelie in their preparations for a moment. Why isn't *she* helping them? How many overseers do they need? From the muted point of her ears, she doesn't have the authority of a true-blooded lady.

"Well, different folk among us have different levels of enthusiasm for our duties," she says, and shoots a much broader smile than mine at me. "I'm Zelpha, by the way. I'm part of Arch-Lord Corwin's coterie. He wanted an update on the progress that's been made here."

That explains why she's here but not why she's talking to me. I continue to study her reactions carefully. "Was there something in particular you needed from me?"

She lets out a bark of a laugh that makes me like her despite myself. "I was talking to one of your wolfish brethren, and he mentioned you're a cadre-chosen of Arch-Lord Sylas's. I figured I might as well come over and introduce myself, seeing as we have a significant mutual friend now."

"Talia," I say, still uncertain of her true intentions.

"That would be the one." The Unseelie woman's smile softens in a way that eases some of my suspicions. "I think she's as anxious to know how things are coming along here as my lord is. I'll be sure to tell her I spoke to you and that we haven't pecked you to death so far."

A snort of amusement escapes me before I can catch it. All right, I'll admit it, I do like her. And if this is the sort of fae Corwin picks for his coterie, perhaps I'll have to like him a little better too.

The thought of Talia sends a bittersweet twinge through my gut. It's only been two days since I last saw her, and she seems to integrate herself into Unseelie society better with every visit—but that isn't exactly a comfort.

"How is she, beyond that anxiety?" I have to ask, still careful with my tone. Corwin might know exactly how much the mite means to me, but Talia's indicated that they've kept it quiet from everyone else in the winter realm as we have here.

"Oh, running around trying to save the whole world with her own two hands like usual," Zelpha says breezily, in what does sound like an accurate summation of Talia's typical approach to any problem. The Unseelie woman tips her head in the opposite direction from the village, lowering her voice. "There's been a development as far as the curse goes as well, but one I'd prefer to discuss with less of a potential audience."

Her tone stays light, but the words themselves are ominous. I don't imagine I have anything to fear immediately from one of Corwin's chosen. If I can take her word on her being one. She does sound pretty familiar with Talia. I'll stay on my guard nonetheless.

I nod, and we meander farther from the village until we're a safe distance from eavesdroppers. It's a particularly hot day, and the breeze that sweeps over us has the feel of a furnace. I soak it in with an appreciative stretch of my neck, but Zelpha shudders. "I don't know how they're all going to get through the next year with it being this blasted *warm* around here all the time."

I chuckle. "I suppose they'll all have to hope you get answers about your curse before a whole year is up, then, won't they?"

Practically speaking, it could take much longer to judge the effectiveness of this tactic. Moving winter fae who are already cursed to the settlement to see if they recover will provide some information, but it could take some time before they can be sure that the curse won't strike anyone already on this side of the border.

If that's the case, would they start going wild under the full moon instead? Part of me wouldn't mind witnessing that chaos just once. Maybe they'd quit their snarking about our savagery if they were brought to it themselves.

"It may be sooner than that," Zelpha says, still quiet. She looks toward the border, her expression tensing a little. "Corwin, Talia, and I went to call on a victim of the curse yesterday, and it seems Talia was able to at least temporarily ward off the curse's effect."

My eyebrows jump up. "Then why is the settlement still being built?"

The Unseelie woman gives me a baleful look. "Because we don't know how temporary the warding off will be. As you've found, it may return—it's possible the summer realm will offer a more permanent solution. And we also haven't had a chance to try to repeat the process. We're not entirely sure how she did it. There were a few different things going on at once, and many we'd tried not long before the obvious turn-around."

"Not very scientific of you," I say.

"Well, we had a lot to get through, and there's no way of knowing how long we'd need to wait to be sure one or another thing *wasn't* going to work. And it's hard on Talia, the longer we're there trying." She lets out a breath, the corner of her mouth curling upward at a wry angle. "She grows on you, doesn't she? I've never talked much with any human before. Maybe that was a failing of mine, not theirs."

I hum to myself while mentally giving her another several points of favor. "Based on my experience, I'd say that Talia is an extraordinary figure in general, all considerations of heritage aside."

"I guess that's why the Heart chose her for… whatever it is her role is supposed to be. Well, hopefully we can figure out the exact element that made the difference quickly so it'll go much faster in the future. Anyway, I thought you'd like to know she's had some success. It's definitely put her somewhat more at ease, though I get the impression she won't rest easy until she's cured the lot of us."

"She does like to take on a lot." I pause, contemplating the woman in front of me. She's given every indication of knowing Talia as well as she says and of being honestly fond of her. I doubt she'd be aware of many of the things she's mentioned to me if she wasn't working closely with Corwin. A touch of hopeful warmth lights in my chest.

If this is the sort of fae we're dealing with on the winter side, at least in some respects, then I might be able to believe that we could reach a more permanent compromise between our realms, even if I can't imagine what that would look like just yet.

I'm not about to let my tongue fly loose without absolute confirmation of this woman's station, but I can extend a little trust of my own. I motion toward the village. "You'll know your people better than I do. While you've been here, have you seen any signs of outright unrest—more than a general discomfort at adjusting to the change in environment?"

Zelpha frowns thoughtfully. "No, I would have noted that. The last thing we need is more fighting. Why, do you have reason to suspect there's a larger conflict brewing?"

"No. Nothing concrete." I study the town again. "It may simply be that it feels too much like an ideal setting for something to go wrong, more so than that something already is. If you do notice anything, you'll pass on word to Arch-Lord Sylas?"

"I can do that." She dips her head with total confidence, but the niggling sensation inside me isn't satisfied by that either.

Whatever may be coming, we'll just have to face it once it's here. At least Talia has one more fae on her side to shelter her from the worst of any impending storms.

16

Talia

"It has to have been the tears, I'd say." Verik rubs his mouth where he's standing near one of the bookcases in Corwin's study. The light filtering through the diamond walls brings out the streaks of gray in his dark hair. "We didn't even consider attempting to use them originally—I can't think of the last time I saw one of our own weeping—"

He pauses with a sidelong glance at me and an awkward tensing of his mouth as if he's concerned I'll take offense. I can't help noticing he's become a little more deferential to me since finding out I've managed to heal one of his people.

I give him a tight smile in return. "I know the Unseelie aren't much for emotions. And *I* didn't think of it either. It's not like tears are a typical bodily material or whatever that're always there."

"But you could encourage yourself to produce them,"

Corwin says from where he's seated next to me behind his desk. "If you're willing. I realize it'd require bringing up memories of past pain."

You really don't need to put yourself through any more anguish, he adds through our bond.

I shift on the chair he set up for me as before, almost but not quite as if I'm ruling side by side with him. It won't be fun dredging up the thoughts of my family and the torment Aerik put me through to force those emotions to the surface, but... "If the alternative is fae dying, I think I can handle a few minutes of discomfort."

Olander paces the study in his typical restless way. "We can't discount the other factors. The woman *noticed* you crying and was affected by that. And you touched her cheek right when the effect was taking hold. Had you made that exact kind of contact before?"

It's hard to remember every individual gesture I tried during our previous attempt. "I don't think so. It wasn't something we'd specifically discussed. It could definitely have been that."

There's a light knock on the door. "Come in," Corwin calls.

Beth nudges the door open with her shoulder, carrying a tray with glasses of a steaming beverage the winter fae are fond of that tastes like warmed, creamy root beer and fried dumplings. "You said I should bring refreshments," she says with a smile.

Corwin gestures for her to set the bounty on his desk. "Yes, perfect, we may be here a while yet, and it's getting on toward lunch."

Verik turns to me, apparently not fazed by the other

human now in our midst. "I'd say we try every possibility at once, all the factors that were present when that woman recovered, just to ensure you *can* cure the curse again. Once we have that certainty, we can worry more about narrowing it down."

I open my mouth to agree, but I'm startled silent by the widening of Beth's eyes as she spins to gape at me. "*You're* curing the curse? That's—I know it's been a problem since before I was born. How did you manage it?"

The fact that I'm directly involved in providing the cure isn't a secret anymore. It would have been pretty much impossible to keep it one after what happened with the pregnant woman two days ago. But this is the first time I've had to say anything about it to the residents of the winter realm, since Corwin has done the other sharing of the news.

My cheeks flush. "I've only done it once. It's hard to explain—I don't even understand it. I seem to be connected to the curse somehow, magically or through the Heart. We're not sure."

She stares at me a few moments longer, maybe re-evaluating me all over again like she did when she found out I was human. Does this weird magical aspect make me even more unsettling than if I were fae?

My stomach twists at the thought, but I don't know what to say to her. I had kind of hoped I might have another friend in the palace once I got to know her better—someone who understood the human aspects of my life. Before I can come up with anything to ease the tension, she's bobbing her head to Corwin and hustling out of the room with an apology for the intrusion.

My mate doesn't show any concern about her reaction. As he picks up his glass, he nods to Verik. "I agree. We'll attempt to recreate the last few minutes before the woman recovered as accurately as possible. I'd also like to attempt a draught with a few tears in it to see if that might have an effect on its own. Then Talia wouldn't need to be present every time someone falls ill."

Which will get awfully inconvenient when the curse strikes while I'm on the summer side. I bite my lip, and another unnerving thought hits me. What if the woman it seems I saved gets sick again while I'm gone, and we lose her and the baby after all?

"She's seemed okay so far, right?" I ask. "The woman I already cured? The curse hasn't come back at all?"

Olander pauses long enough to give me a mildly reassuring look. "All reports seem promising. I realize that the Seelie re-experience their curse every month regardless… I suppose there's no way to know what kind of timeline ours might run on."

"All we can do is wait," Verik says. "And hope we're able to meet whatever new challenges present themselves."

He's partway through that sentence when Zelpha bursts into the room. "I'm not sure what you're talking about, but we've got some kind of challenge right now. A nearby one, at least. A fellow in Uzziah's domain has just caught the chill."

Corwin springs up, his expression darkening, and I don't think just at knowing another of his people is facing the curse. We haven't needed to deal with the arch-lords directly so far.

I push myself out of my chair, my chest constricting. Uzziah will have some idea that I'm providing the cure now, but he's never actually seen me try to work it.

"We'll go right away," Corwin says, and glances at the refreshments we hadn't gotten to yet. "Do you want something, Talia—to shore up your strength…?"

The thought of trying to eat anything before I attempt to repeat my previous success only makes me queasy. "No," I say quickly. "I'm fine. Let's see what we can do right away." What would the other arch-lord think if I turn up nibbling on snacks like I think I'm at a tea party?

"We'll fly." Corwin releases his wings as he steps into the hall. "Zelpha, you join us in case you can think of some factor we forget from last time, and Verik, why don't you come as well to observe. Where exactly is the afflicted man?"

The other two fae unfurl their own wings, Zelpha's a deep brownish black and Verik's speckled with gray like his hair. "Uzziah has already brought him into his castle. I told the messenger to let him know to expect us shortly."

Getting into position for Corwin to lift me up for flying has become a practiced motion. I settle against his chest, taking a little comfort from his solid warmth. The three fae sweep out onto the terrace and spring into the air without hesitation.

Zelpha and Verik contract into full raven form, since they don't have anyone to carry. They swoop ahead of us, dark graceful shapes against the stark blue of the sky. Corwin soars after them, tucking his head close to mine.

We know what we're doing now. We know we can fix this. There's nothing to worry about.

He can say that, but I know his emotions aren't totally settled either. I lean into him. *I'll do my best. I know the arch-lords were already skeptical. Maybe if they see it with one of the folk of their own flock, they won't mind having me around so much.*

They shouldn't have minded in the first place, Corwin says, but a matching hope flows from him into me.

Uzziah's domain lies on the other side of the Heart. His castle is a broad, gloomy fortress of dark metal that reminds me a lot of the solemn man whose family must have created it. The sight doesn't inspire much in the way of uplifting thoughts.

We land just outside the imposing doorway, Zelpha and Verik shifting into human form in mid-flight. A servant opens the door immediately to usher us in.

We find Uzziah with his typically stern expression down a narrow hall deep within the castle. The metallic scent trickling off the walls gives me the unnerving impression of raw meat. As Corwin inclines his head to his colleague and gives his condolences, I have to swallow another surge of queasiness.

"The curse-struck one is in here?" my mate asks, motioning to the door Uzziah was waiting outside of.

The other arch-lord folds his arms over his chest. "Yes. Do you need to make any preparations before you see him?"

"No, we have all we need. We'll work through the process on the spot. Since we've only managed the effect once before, it'll most likely still take a little trial and error." Corwin draws in a breath. "If you'll give us an hour or so, I feel reasonably certain we'll come to you with good news within that timeframe."

Uzziah's eyebrows arch. "Come to me? I'll be with you. I'm not having you work this strange Seelie magic on my people without bearing witness." At the rapping of footsteps from farther away, he glances down the hallway. "When Laoni got word, she said she'd come to observe as well."

Oh, great, the only winter fae who makes me *more* nervous than Uzziah.

Corwin draws himself up straighter as the imposing Unseelie woman comes into view at the end of the hall. *I'm sorry,* he says only to me. *If I try to prevent them from observing, they'll only be more suspicious of what we're doing. I don't have any grounds to outright bar them from the room.*

I gather my nerve. *It's all right. It had to happen sometime, I guess.* At least now I have a halfway decent idea of what I'm doing.

When Laoni reaches us, with a narrow glance and a nod at Corwin and no acknowledgment of me at all, Uzziah leads the way into the room. "We have visitors who may be able to sort you out," he announces.

The man who's sitting cross-legged on the floor near the hearth looks up at us. The curse must be gripping him quickly—a hint of blue already stains his cheeks. He's the youngest of the fae I've tried to help so far, maybe not yet out of the fae equivalent of his teens.

But that's okay. I'm going to stop the curse from leaching any more of life's warmth from his body.

"Let's start with the gestures we can attempt right

away, and then move to the more involved possibilities," Corwin says a little stiffly. I can tell from my impressions through our bond that he means we'll hold off on the crying part until it's absolutely necessary.

Uzziah and Laoni take positions beside the hearth where they have a clear view of the proceedings. Ignoring their penetrating stares, I crouch down beside the young man and raise my hand. "I'm going to touch you, only for a moment."

He peers back at me and shivers. "All right."

I brush my fingers tentatively against his cheek and then hold them there more firmly. The chill in his face seeps into my skin. No warmth expands from where I'm touching. Well, it was probably too much to ask that the solution be quite that simple.

I ease back and straighten up. "Now...?" I say, checking Corwin's expression.

He glances at Zelpha. "Was there anything else that happened right before?"

She shakes her head. "We'd tried giving the woman the confections we brought, but that was at least ten minutes before any effect showed. After that, Talia stepped aside. You talked with the woman a bit. I'm not sure how much of a difference that made."

"It can't hurt to include it." Corwin turns back to me. "Prepare yourself, and when you're ready, let him see."

"Okay." I inhale deeply and swivel so my back is to the young man, like I did in the room with the pregnant woman. Maybe it makes a difference for him not to be sure what's happening right away too.

I can't compare this young fae to my mother, but what

about—he's about the age, in fae terms, that my brother would have been now if he'd survived, isn't he?

What would Jamie's life have been like if Aerik and his cadre hadn't killed him? What things might he have done? There's so much he missed out on—so much he should have had… And if I can't come through, this fae man will lose so much time he should have had too. He's barely had time to come into his own.

It takes longer than last time for the burn to well up behind my eyes, maybe because of the pressure of multiple gazes watching the proceedings. I tune out my awareness of my spectators' presence as well as I can, focusing on the memory of Jamie's shrieks and the glimpses I caught of his savaged body, on every milestone that was stolen from him, on all the joy he'd been able to express at just eight years old and how much more he could have experienced…

And it was my fault. Maybe not completely, maybe not even mostly, but in some ways, it can't be denied. I led him on that chase into the woods. I teased him into following me.

If I hadn't been playing games, he'd still be alive.

If I can't pull myself together to help the young man right here, *his* death will be on my shoulders too.

A lump creeps up my throat. Moisture forms in the corners of my eyes. The first tears trickle out slowly, but once they've started, more stream out, faster than I can blink them back.

But I don't want to blink or wipe them away. The fae man needs to see them—to see that I'm crying for him.

I turn back around. Corwin is ready, having sensed my

emotions. "See how she weeps for you," he says to the young man, gesturing to me. "It pains her to know you're suffering. She cries to think your life might be cut short."

"What is this about?" Laoni breaks in, her voice stiff with what sounds like horror. "How is your human having a meltdown going to cure anything?"

I wince, but I force myself to step closer to the young man anyway.

"Give her a chance," Corwin insists. "This is how it worked the last time."

Uzziah lets out a discontented mumble. The other arch-lords are both scowling now as well as staring. Apprehension prickles down my back. I can't see any change in the young man yet.

With tears still trickling down over my skin, I touch his cheek again, trying to replicate the exact angle and motion as I did with the woman two days ago.

Then, it felt so natural in the moment. Right now I only feel awkward. I will the warmth to chase away the chill in his skin, but nothing happens.

"I'm not seeing any grand effect," Uzziah mutters.

Laoni steps toward us. "This is a ridiculous spectacle. Whatever you're trying to prove, it's clearly misguided."

Panic flickers from Corwin through our bond. "Let me at least try—" He swipes his forefinger across my jaw to collect a few tears and brings them to the young man's lips.

Laoni lets out an indignant sputter and leaps in to yank his arm away. It's too late. I can tell Corwin managed to give the young man a taste of them. I hold my breath, pleading with everything I have in me for the blue to vanish beneath a healthy flush of life, for there to be *some* sign that what we're doing here made a difference.

But nothing comes. Laoni marches Corwin out of the room, motioning for Uzziah to usher me after them. Zelpha and Verik follow, their expressions stormy. They won't speak out of place among the other arch-lords unless Corwin prompts them to, though.

"What in the lands was *that* meant to be?" Laoni snaps once we're out in the hall. "You're likely to sicken him more seeing this dust-destined mortal so overwrought."

"I swear to you, we're only repeating what worked in the previous case," Corwin says emphatically. "Please, if you'd let us continue—there may be some pattern to it we haven't identified—"

"Maybe it was the confections beforehand?" Zelpha ventures.

Laoni ignores her. "What else would you do, exactly?"

Corwin's uncertainty travels into me. We went through all the basics of what worked with the other woman. "Perhaps… Perhaps he needs to have spent more time with Talia first, to feel more comfortable with her…"

"So you want to badger this one of my flock with even more hysterics while he's already suffering?" Uzziah says.

"He's going to suffer anyway," I break in, unable to stay quiet. "We *know* something worked before. Is there really anything that wouldn't be worth trying if it ends the curse?"

The fae around me fall silent. Then Laoni turns to Corwin, her gaze icy. "You will prepare everything you offered to the woman you cured and have it on hand. Then you may return with your 'mate' and make another attempt. But if that one fails too, then I think we must assume the previous recovery was simply a milder case, not a curing. Our people don't deserve to be put through even more torment in their final moments. We'll send him to the summer realm and hope for better luck there."

Corwin dips his head in a jerk of acceptance. "It shouldn't take long. We'll return as soon as we're ready. Come."

He holds out his hand to me, beckoning to his coterie with the other. I grasp his fingers, but a sense of hopelessness too big for me to shake sweeps over me.

They're giving us another chance, sure. But what if we still can't get it right? What if that one moment before *was* some weird fluke, or some specific synergy that formed between me and the pregnant woman for reasons that no longer apply?

If we can't cure this man, the other arch-lords will have even more reason to dismiss everything Corwin suggests for the rest of his reign.

Talia

It's late evening by our second return to the palace from Uzziah's castle. Stars are glinting into sight all across the darkening sky. It should be a beautiful sight, but I can't appreciate it. My eyes are stinging, my heart thumping heavily in my chest.

That's it, isn't it? I say to Corwin, not wanting to discuss our failure—*my* failure—out loud with his coterie members too. *They said they'd give us one more chance. They won't let us see him again.*

If we think of something we missed, they'd have to give us the opportunity to offer it, Corwin says, but his inner voice is as downcast as I feel.

Laoni said they're going to send him to the summer realm settlement right away.

I'll take you there if I think we have a chance.

I don't know why the chances we had today didn't get us anywhere. Maybe my tears were too forced, or I didn't manage to produce enough of them? It isn't like bleeding, where all it takes is a nick of my skin and the fluid springs out. Or was it some aspect of my interactions with the pregnant woman that none of us noticed that drove back the curse?

My blood can snap *all* of the Seelie out of their wildness. Surely whatever I can do for the Unseelie curse wouldn't be restricted to just pregnant women—or women —or people who make me think of my mother—or any other random criteria?

But then, none of the magic that's tying me to the fae makes sense to begin with, so who can say?

Just inside the palace, Corwin turns to Zelpha and Verik, who stayed with us and offered whatever suggestions they could through our second visit with Uzziah's afflicted flock member. The arch-lord dips his head to Zelpha. "If you remember anything else from the other day that might serve us…"

"I'll let you know right away, my lord," she says, her usually energetic voice somber. She manages a stiff little smile, and the two of them head off.

"Are you hungry?" Corwin asks me.

I've had nibbles of things here and there throughout the afternoon—we thought maybe sharing a meal with the cursed young man might help somehow—and my stomach is too tight for the thought of eating more to appeal to me. I shake my head. "Just tired." And frustrated with myself. And horrified for that fae man I haven't been able to save. A stew of unpleasant emotion churns inside me.

If I were back in the place I still think of as my main

home, with Sylas, Whitt, and August, right now I'd go to one of them and let them wrap me up in their arms. It wouldn't make all the wrong things about today right, but it'd ease the pain inside me a little. None of them are here, though.

But my mate is. I look at Corwin, taking in the distress etched on his own face and the worries for his people overshadowing every other emotion I sense from him, and nothing in me balks. He *is* my mate. I care about him, and I trust him. Maybe I don't feel exactly the same way about him as I do my Seelie lovers, but his embrace would be a comfort too.

I just feel guilty asking for it when I'm the one who let us both down.

I can't bring myself to put the request into words, but the longing rises up strongly enough that Corwin must catch it anyway. He meets my eyes as if checking to confirm and then holds out his hand to me.

Whether I'm being selfish or not, I can't help myself. I twine my fingers with his, letting the affection he's sending through our bond wash over me, and walk with him back to my bedroom.

On the threshold, he hesitates again, even though the comfort I'm desperate for isn't anything especially intimate. I just want to be held. I squeeze his hand and lead him in, and he follows with a flare of happiness he can't suppress—or maybe he doesn't want to.

At the edge of the bed, he scoops me up much like when he's flying me somewhere and settles us on top of the covers together, my head tucked under his chin, his arms encircling me, our legs folded against each other.

He strokes his hand over my hair. I press my head against his chest, his wintry forest smell filling my nose. Even after all the tears I forced out over the past several hours, new ones prick at my eyes.

I thought his embrace would give me some comfort, but instead I only feel more guilty. He probably has other, more important things he needs to be doing to repair whatever damage I've done to his reputation.

"I'm sorry," I mumble, not totally sure which of the vast array of failings I can think of I'm apologizing for.

Corwin's arms tighten around me. A flood of compassion and tenderness courses through our bond, so intense and undeniable it brings a different sort of tears to my eyes.

"You have nothing to apologize for," he says. "You're giving so much of yourself already. No one could ask for more than that."

"But it hasn't been enough. There must be something I'm missing that made things work with the woman before but not today. And now the other arch-lords are blaming *you* for everything."

Corwin lets out a faint huff. "I'm sure they'd have found something else to blame me for if it wasn't this. You know they were never that fond of me, from well before you ever set foot in our realm."

"They've threatened to remove you from your position if they think your judgment is off," I have to point out. "If you lose Heart's Cadence because of me—"

"No," Corwin cuts in firmly. He pulls back far enough to tip my chin so he can meet my eyes. In the dim twilight of the room, his glint like black diamonds. "They can try, but they won't succeed. And nothing they do is *because* of you. Talia—" A roughness creeps into his voice. "I couldn't be more impressed by your strength and generosity when it comes to my people. You can feel that, can't you? You barely know us, and you've set aside every other thought to contribute whatever you can, no matter how much strain it puts on you."

The truth of his words resonates into me. I swallow hard. "I just don't want to give them excuses to attack you."

"You don't need to worry about that. It's *my* job to defend you from my colleagues. They're for me to deal with."

He brushes a gentle kiss to my forehead before meeting my gaze again. "They think love makes a person weaker, that you have to keep it reined in or it'll break you like it did my mother. I started to believe that too. But you've shown me that it's the opposite. Having you in my life, loving you—it makes me *stronger*. Every challenge is easier to meet. Every setback easier to face. Never doubt that you have made my life better in every possible way."

I stare at him, hardly daring to believe him—but there's no denying the conviction that rings through his words and sings through our bond. It strengthens my own resolve.

This problem is complicated and difficult, and I hate that we haven't solved it yet, but we're not done fighting. And I'm not fighting it alone. I found my footing among the Seelie, but Corwin is helping me uncover new determination and confidence within myself too. While I might not know yet why the Heart tied us together, I'm glad that it did.

Another longing swells inside me, one that might also be unfair since I can't offer the same in return just yet, but I'm not sure I could hide it from my mate when we're this closely entwined anyway. My voice comes out in little more than a whisper. "You've never said it to me."

Corwin blinks. "Said what?"

"That—" My cheeks heat as I fumble with the words. "How you feel about me. I've felt it, and you told Donovan, and you talked about it just now, but you've never…"

"Oh." He caresses my hair again, studying me. "I didn't want to make you feel pressured to return the sentiment. You *shouldn't* feel pressured. And I suppose I'm still not the most adept at expressing my emotions." He drags in a breath. "I love you, Talia, and I will wait however long it takes to earn your love in return. I couldn't have asked for a better mate among the truest of true-blooded fae."

His love shines into me like the glow of the summer sun, so bright and warm it's hard to believe it could have come from a man who normally has a lot in common with the cold, impenetrable lands he grew up in. I want to soak it all up, in every possible way.

I want to offer everything I can back. I might not be ready to say the same thing just yet, but I can't deny that I'm falling for him.

Why should I deny myself any of this?

I run my fingers into his thick curls and bring his mouth to mine. Like always, the kiss sparks a sharper heat right down the center of me. But this time, I don't try to dampen my reaction. I let the flames keep kindling inside me as I meld my lips even more perfectly against his.

A soft groan escapes Corwin. He kisses me back hard, his own desire roaring to life. The sense of how much he wants me fuels my own hunger and sets off a fresh wave of his, on and on in a blazing cycle between us.

It's scared me before—the intensity of our connection. But I know I'm strong enough to revel in it without losing myself. I've got to have at least as much faith in myself as he does.

I roll onto my back, pulling him with me. Corwin follows, his nerves lighting up as his body comes to rest on top of mine with a tingling eagerness that races into me. I want—I *need*—this man so much it's hard to imagine I ever pulled away from him before. His yearning smolders just as hot.

He kisses me on the mouth again before charting a searing path along my jaw and down the side of my neck. When he finds a sensitive spot at the crook of my shoulder, I gasp. My hands fumble with the collar of his shirt, searching for the snaps to loosen it.

His fingers skim up the side of my torso, burning with eagerness. *Talia?* he says without lifting his mouth from my skin. It's both a question and a plea, so much longing in it my skin quivers.

Yes. I want… I want to feel all of you.

He lets out another groan, his lips moving down over my collarbone as he finds the fastenings on my dress. *When this happened, I meant to take it slow. To treasure every moment. To ensure you experienced every pleasure. But I don't know—I've wanted you so much. I'm not sure how well I can hold back.*

Don't. His fingers delve beneath the dress's bodice, and I arch into his touch. *You don't have to hold back or pretend with me. I like seeing you as you are.*

With a strained noise in his throat, his mouth crashes down on mine. I manage to peel back his shirt to trace the lean muscles underneath. His thumb swivels over the peak of my breast, sparking a jolt of pleasure.

Everywhere we touch, the flames of desire flare hotter. The rush of pleasure spikes higher with his thrill at my reactions, with the shivers of delight that course through his flesh beneath my hands. We're alight with not just our own pleasure but each other's, or maybe it's all the same, one immense wave of bliss sweeping through both of us in tandem.

With a series of hasty tugs, Corwin unwraps me from my dress and tosses it aside. His mouth roves over my body with gentle nips and avid swipes of his tongue, as if I'm the greatest delicacy he's ever consumed.

When he sucks one nipple between his hot lips, my head tips back with a whimper. As I dig my fingers into his hair, he teases the nub to a stiffer peak with a swirl of his tongue, the graze of his teeth. Giddiness shimmers between us. I can't tell who's enjoying the moment more, only that with every fresh spark of pleasure, it grows on both sides.

I wrench him back up over me, claiming his mouth, exploring his tautly muscled body now that I've managed to strip off his shirt completely. The responses that ripple from him into me tell me exactly which caresses provoke the greatest effect. For a few minutes, I'm content to summon as much heated bliss in him as I can just by running my hands over his chest.

Finally, I dip my fingers right down to the waist of his trousers. The bolt of lust that shoots through our connection has me drenching my panties even though he hasn't touched me that far down yet.

An oversight that can be quickly remedied, Corwin says with fervent amusement. As I grapple with his belt buckle, he slides his hand down between us to cup it between my thighs.

The electric tingling at his touch, at how pleased *he* is to feel my arousal, reverberates through my veins. I can't help pressing into his fingers, chasing the heights they promise. A growl slips from my mouth that pleases him too.

Then I yank his belt away and ease my hand into his trousers, and all conscious thought evaporates from his mind with my grasp around his already hardened erection. The heady sensation searing through him radiates into me. I buck into his hand, melting and soaring at the same time.

Between scorching kisses, he kicks off his trousers and boxers. As I stroke his rigid length up and down, my brain short-circuits at just how much pleasure I never knew this gesture could summon. Corwin keeps his head enough to make short work of my panties.

I raise my knees on either side of his hips, welcoming him. Pure joy races through his body. He lines himself up and plunges into me in one swift stroke.

Oh! It's even more overwhelming than the flood of

impressions before—feeling his hardness stretching me, filling me; feeling my slickness clenching eagerly around him. I've never experienced anything like this before, and somehow I'm still spiraling higher and higher.

I pant for air, pressing back into the pillow. Corwin ducks his head next to mine, hot breath and shaky kisses marking my neck.

My love, he says with his inner voice, punctuating each thrust with words radiant with happiness. *My heart. My soul.*

My mate, I answer automatically, my hands gripping his shoulders.

The words somehow set off an even headier surge of need than before. We rock together wildly, spurred on by each other's blaze of passion as we hurtle toward our release, and I can no longer tell where his body begins and mine ends. It's just *us*, twined together, merged into one being of bliss.

The giddy pressure builds and builds—and finally crashes over us in a breathtaking maelstrom. I quake beneath Corwin, and he clutches me to him with a groan —and oh, God, if it could have been like this from the start, why have I been resisting this for so long?

We come to rest still linked together. Corwin kisses my temple and then my cheek, and I taste the salt of my sweat on my skin through his lips. The joyful satisfaction resonating through him echoes my own so well it brings a smile to my face.

More than worth the wait, he tells me, as if he picked up my earlier thought.

My muscles have gone so slack I can barely move.

Corwin eases down next to me and nestles me against him like before. I sink into his embrace with a happy sigh. But as I relax there in his warmth, three truths settle over me with a weight I can't shake off.

I'm falling for this man. It may not be long at all before I can say I love him. And I still have no idea how to reconcile that growing devotion with all the love I have in me for my lovers back in the summer realm.

18

Talia

The atmosphere during breakfast is a strange mix of contentment and somberness. After sleeping next to Corwin all night—and rediscovering just how good our bodies can feel together this morning—a happy glow infuses our bond. Every time I look at him, a flutter passes through my chest, giddier when he happens to be looking back.

But at the same time the knowledge hangs over us that the young man from Uzziah's flock will have been taken to the summer settlement last night. Maybe the warmth and the vibrant surroundings will melt away the curse's grip on him. If they don't, then it'll only be a couple of days before he's dead.

And we have no idea why I couldn't help him.

We don't communicate much other than wordless wisps of fondness through our connection. I suspect neither of us wants to break the spell of our recently shared passion by bringing up any of the many subjects we'll need to get back to discussing. But we don't get to linger in that peace very long anyway.

Just as we're finishing up the last of our meal, a headier warmth filling me as Corwin tracks my tongue licking traces of honey from my thumb, a fae man I recognize as one of Corwin's servants hustles into the room. "My lord," he says with a deep bow. "Apologies for the intrusion. Domhnall sent a messenger who wishes to speak to you as soon as possible."

My mate lets out a noise of concern and gets to his feet, a serious cast coming over his face. "I'll be there at once." He turns to me. "Domhnall is another of my coterie members—he's been traveling the realm on my behalf. If he's reached out without feeling he could return to speak to me himself, it must be a grave matter."

I push back my chair. "Do you think it's to do with the curse?"

"It may."

As I stand, Corwin pauses, and I sense that he didn't expect me to come with him. But he recovers within seconds and gestures for me to follow him. *As my mate, you should be aware of anything critical going on in the realm. I'm simply not used to having the company yet.*

It's all right, I reply. *I know it's still an adjustment.* For me as well as him. But after what we've shared, both between each other and in facing the curse, I can't stand to hang back while he takes this new problem on by himself.

He shoots me a smile. As we walk toward the terrace, he keeps a measured pace to account for my limp.

The messenger stands just inside the door to the

terrace, the thin sunlight filtering through the broad windows making her look like some kind of snow nymph with her pale skin and equally pale clothes.

"My lord," she says, with a bow just as deep as the servant's. "Domhnall wishes to have your presence as soon as you're able to reach him. He didn't convey all the details to me, but it's in regard to the incursions of beasts farther in from the borders. He's waiting for you in Lakeshine."

A flicker of discomfort passes through Corwin, there and then stamped out so quickly I'm not sure I didn't imagine it. I glance at him, but his expression has taken on its impervious lordly mask. I feel as if the walls around our bond have risen just slightly.

He shows no outward distress. "Thank you for your haste. I'll set off immediately. Do you require passage back?"

The messenger shakes her head. "I have business in a domain nearby, and I can make my own way easily enough. It was a pleasure to serve my arch-lords."

She slips out onto the terrace, unfurling her wings as she goes. When she fully transforms, her raven is a muted gray that blends into the snowy landscape the moment she soars off over it.

Corwin murmurs a scrap of bark into being with a few words marked on it and sends it off like I've seen my Seelie men do with leaves to send a message. "I'll bring Olander," he tells me. "Better to have too much support than too little."

"And me," I put in. "I should know what's going on, right?"

My mate hesitates again, this time with a deeper

twinge of uneasiness that reminds me of his earlier discomfort. "I wouldn't want—if it's a matter to do with the beasts, you'd have trouble defending yourself."

The memory of the searmaw that attacked us in the frostfire forest comes back to me with a shiver, but I hold my ground. "I'll have you and two of your coterie members right there. I promise I won't go wandering off or anything stupid like that. If it's *that* bad, I can just stay in the carriage and you can make it hover ten feet off the ground. Unless some of these beasts fly?"

Corwin's lips twitch with a hint of amusement. "No, the creatures we've been dealing with have been land-based."

"I do want to be a full participant here," I go on. "I need to understand every part of your work as an arch-lord. And maybe there's some other way I can help."

Since I'm struggling so much to help with the curse, I don't need to say. A waft of compassion wraps around me, and Corwin's expression softens. "All right. I know I can't be treating you as if you're so terribly fragile. But do stay close to us while we're there."

"Of course. I don't want to end up as a searmaw's breakfast."

I'm not sure if Corwin and Olander would have flown by their own wings to Lakeshine if I wasn't coming along, but it's too far for him to carry me. We go out onto the icy plain beside the palace, and by the time Olander meets us there, the arch-lord has summoned a small carriage into being.

Olander gives me a slight nod but doesn't say anything to me, which I'm okay with. Hopefully my participating in situations like this will show him that I do have a legitimate place alongside his lord. I tuck myself into my favorite spot near the bow, and Corwin and his coterie member lean against opposite walls of the carriage.

"Domhnall didn't say what specifically he's so concerned about right now?" Olander asks. "We've been having these issues with the beasts for months now."

Corwin shakes his head. "Perhaps it was too sensitive for him to want to pass the information on through a messenger. Lakeshine is pretty far inward from the fringes… Years ago, it'd have been unusual to see any beasts of the most hostile sort in that area. If there's been a particularly large influx, that might have been enough to worry him all on its own."

"But not really worth keeping secret." Olander frowns. "He has a good head on his shoulders—not the type to panic. It must be bad. I don't like this at all."

"Neither do I." Corwin sighs. "Have you continued to work on the true name for chimeras? I know you can handle a searmaw already, and just about anything else we could run into."

"I've been meditating on it, but it's always difficult without direct interaction. And I think chimeras will be a tricky one to master in general. If you can spare me to spend some time on the fringes where I could 'commune' with them more, I'd get there faster."

Corwin hums to himself. "I think our current situation is too precarious for me to want to send you off that far. But if we can get matters relating to the curse more settled, then it might be feasible."

One more thing being delayed by my difficulty with

the curse. I suck my lower lip under my teeth but manage to hold myself back from worrying at it.

Are there any simpler true names that could help against the beasts? Maybe we could work on one of those to start on my magic training here, and I could actually get involved in fending them off—

No, Corwin interrupts, gently but firmly. *Your Seelie men have kept your additional powers secret from the rest of their kind for a good reason. If you show them publicly, I have no idea how my colleagues or the rest of my people will react, but I suspect it'll cause more chaos than joy.*

When my spirits sink, he adds in an even softer tone, *But that doesn't mean we can't see where we can get with those true names one on one. I just hesitate to have you use them in a meaningful way in public until your position here is more secure.*

Of course. I understand. Even if I don't like it.

I'm getting tired of having to hide so much of who I am. As if it's my fault the Heart's magic has ended up twined through me in so many unexpected ways. As if it's a problem when you'd think it should be a gift.

But then, how can I be frustrated that the Unseelie may not totally accept me when I haven't even totally accepted my soul-twined mate yet? I haven't let myself really become a part of this world in every way it wants me to.

I chew on that thought for some time, not liking any of the conclusions it leads me to. When the carriage finally starts to slow, I shake off my reverie and stand up to take a good look at the domain we're arriving in.

Unsurprisingly, Lakeshine's castle and village stand by

a large, glassy lake. The water lies so still, only the faintest ripple caused by the breeze reveals that its surface isn't frozen solid. The castle and its buildings have been formed out of dark gray stone that sparkles with patches of mica.

As inert as the lake looks, there must be life in it, because the air that meets my nose when I climb out of the carriage has a faint but distinct fishy odor. The breeze is almost warm by winter realm standards, though.

I stick close to Corwin as he strides toward the village. Before we reach the nearest houses, a man hurries over to join us: short and spindly-limbed, with hair so short it's merely a dark sheen on his brown scalp. He bobs his head to Corwin and raises a hand in greeting to Olander, his gaze stopping on me only for a moment with a fleeting trace of curiosity.

"My lord, if you'll come with me. I think you'll understand why I've called you in once you have the whole story."

He sets off around the edges of the village at a swifter pace than I'd expect from someone so delicate-looking. I keep up as well as I can, ignoring the prickling of pain in my warped foot when I push myself faster.

Around the far side of the village where the lake is no longer in view, three large beasts sprawl in pools of blood. A mix of fur and scales covers their massive forms. I step even closer to Corwin, just in case they're not quite as dead as they appear.

The man who must be Domhnall lowers his voice. "It's odd enough to have them coming in this far. But the thing with these three is—scouts spotted them two domains away. They headed straight here, ignoring the other villages closer by that they passed."

Corwin's forehead furrows. "Did no one try to stop them?"

"Of course. But there wasn't anyone with solid enough true names to hold them back, and they were quite determined not to be diverted. Word went out, and I arrived here just as they did. It took a considerable amount of power to tackle them here when they'd rather have ignored me and continued on into town."

"As if they were being driven—or summoned—by magic," Olander says, and I remember the tuskcat some of Ambrose's pack-kin sent after me months ago.

"Who would they have been after?" I ask without thinking.

Domhnall gives me another quizzical glance, but at Corwin's nod, he answers. "I don't know. I've asked around the village—surreptitiously so as not to provoke too much anxiety—and it doesn't sound as if there've been any major conflicts between anyone of this flock and another in recent times. I'm not even entirely sure these three *were* magically compelled. I've checked them over and found no trace of any but their innate magic. I thought possibly with your keener awareness, you might decipher the spell, my lord."

Corwin moves forward and kneels by the first of the creatures. He intones a few words under his breath and stretches his hands out over the monstrous body. They hover over each part of the beast before he draws them back and rubs his mouth. "I don't sense anything in that one. Let me try the others."

As he works, a small crowd of villagers gathers a short distance away. Olander and Domhnall stop them from getting any closer, but the coterie members seem to feel it'd be worse to try to shoo them away completely. The villagers stir restlessly on their feet, looking plenty anxious already.

When he's examined all three, Corwin straightens up with a clouded expression. "If there was magic on them, it's already faded. That could be the case if it was tied to their life's energy. But it's quite an odd tactic regardless. To settle a dispute this way—and so far from the fringes, where the beasts' presence would immediately draw notice—is highly unlikely to have a controlled outcome."

Olander hums. "Beyond the savagery of it, it's not particularly smart, is it?"

"It doesn't appear so. But perhaps I can unravel the mystery more." He turns to our small audience. "Since you're already here, I hope you won't mind if I ask you a few questions."

There's a snort from the back of the bunch. My gaze lands on a stout, middle-aged woman who's crossed her arms over her chest. Several other gazes zero in on her, including Corwin's. A tremor of uneasiness passes from him into me.

"Did you have something to say, Pippa?" he asks in the most carefully even voice I've ever heard from him.

She wets her lips. Something hostile sparks in her eyes and then fades. "I'd only say if it turns out these things *were* sent our way on purpose, I hope you'll make sure the punishment for the crime is just."

She turns and walks off. The others from her flock

focus on Corwin again. He smiles tightly, but his emotions are roiling behind his impassive front.

What was that about? I have to ask.

Nothing to worry yourself about. She won't say more than that.

But why would she want to? It's obviously upset you. It bothered you as soon as you heard we needed to come here. What's—

Corwin's inner voice breaks through mine with unusual sharpness. *Let it* be, *Talia.*

I'm so startled I take a step back, as if he's physically pushed me away. Corwin's gaze jerks to me, his eyes widening. *I'm sorry,* he says quickly. *I—there are things I try not to think about, let alone discuss. But I suppose you deserve to know.* He draws in a breath and faces the flock again. *We can't talk about it while there are others around. When we get back to the palace, I'll explain, I swear.*

His apology and his promise ring true, but all the same, a lump fills my throat as he steps closer to the folk of the flock to ask his questions.

What can my mate have managed to hide from me that he's even more hesitant to share than his family's tragedy?

19

Corwin

Talia's impatience trickles through our bond for the entire journey back to Heart's Cadence. I hate that after we've come so far, I'm shutting her out more than I have in days—after she welcomed me into her bed, after we shared the greatest physical intimacy we can. But I don't want her glimpsing too much of the tumultuous emotions inside me either.

I'm annoyed at myself for letting Pippa affect me, for showing any distress at all about going out to Lakeshine. Frustrated that I couldn't come up with any answers to explain why those beasts homed in on that village. Dreading the conversation to come and how Talia might react to me afterward. What if hearing this account chills all the trust I've won from her?

I wouldn't have avoided the subject forever. At some point, this part of my history would have to come up. I'd just hoped it'd be after we were more formally united and solid in our bond.

But perhaps I deserve to have it out in the open now. I'd like to think it doesn't define who I am in the present in any way, that it was a lapse driven by a culmination of circumstances that could never repeat themselves, but that doesn't ease the pang of old guilt that's risen up through my turmoil.

We can't hash it out just yet. Even in the relative privacy of the carriage, I don't want to start the conversation with Olander present. The words exchanged through our bond might be imperceptible to outside eyes, but our reactions to the subjects we touch on aren't. I can't focus completely on Talia when I have to consider how one of my coterie will be noting my behavior as well.

To give her credit, Talia doesn't badger me about it. For all her internal restlessness, she holds her tongue, not saying anything even through our bond until the carriage lands outside the palace. Olander sets off for his home in the village, and my mate glances at me with a question she doesn't need to put into words in her eyes.

"Let's go to my study," I say, wishing my voice hadn't come out hoarse.

She nods, and then after a second's hesitation, reaches to grasp my hand. The simple gesture makes my throat constrict even more. I haven't lost her trust *yet*, in any case.

Whatever it is, you need to let me decide what to make of it, she says, lacing her fingers through mine. *I don't believe it can be anything all that terrible. Maybe I don't know everything about you yet, but I do know you.*

Heart help me, let her be right about that.

We reach my study, and I shut the door firmly behind us. Then I find I have no idea where to start, even though I've had hours to consider it.

Talia settles herself into what appears to have become her favorite armchair in the room, slipping off her boots and pulling her legs up next to her. I stay on my feet. I manage not to pace, but I can't will myself to relax enough to sit down either.

"Something happened with that woman in the past," Talia prompts.

"In a way." I inhale deeply and turn to face her. "I want you to know from the start that I'm ashamed of the decisions I made—they were born out of anger and pain rather than reason and good sense, and while those emotions weren't unjustified, I believe I owed better to those involved."

Talia studies me, her calm expression unwavering. "Okay, I'll keep that in mind."

It's too awkward after all just standing here motionless. I cast about for something to hold onto and finally sink into one of the other chairs, though not the one behind my desk. I don't want any reminders of my authority between us while I explain.

"There's a custom among the Unseelie that the few fae who are blessed with multiple children may send a child to one of the arch-lords' courts to be fostered there," I begin. "When a family already has one or two to carry on their own legacy, it gives the additional child a special opportunity. They generally integrate into the arch-lord's flock and remain there as adults, and frequently they become close enough with the arch-lord to enter the coterie."

"That makes sense," Talia says. "Was someone like that sent to Heart's Cadence?"

"Yes. When I was still a child, my parents took a boy a couple of decades younger than me as a foster. Lazlo."

Even though the moment is more than two centuries distant now, the memory of our tentative first meeting sticks vividly in my mind: that young version of Lazlo ducking his head shyly even as his bright eyes glinted with curiosity. "He lived here in the palace," I go on. "We essentially grew up together. It didn't take long before we were close friends."

Talia's gaze weighs on me. I can feel her putting together the pieces before she speaks. "I haven't met him. He isn't here anymore?"

"No. He— I—" I pause, rubbing my forehead. The words catch at the back of my tongue.

I want to lay it out as dispassionately as I'd need to before my fellow arch-lords, as if it were something that happened millennia ago to someone I never met. But that will only make Talia see me as being as cold and cruel as Pippa no doubt does.

I'm just not sure—I've never really *let* myself grieve. I'm still not certain I even deserve to.

"The world didn't end when you told me about what happened to your parents," Talia says softly. "I don't think it will over this either."

"I know. But this is different. That was something that happened around me—this was something that happened *because* of me. When I was at my worst." I've only just realized how badly I must have let Lazlo down, with Talia showing me that I don't have to stay quite so bottled up to fulfill my role as arch-lord after all. If I'd met her back then—if she'd existed back then—

Of course, if I'd had my soul-twined mate by my side, *everything* would have been very different.

I force myself to continue. "Lazlo did everything he could to support me when my father died. I took on Verik, Domhnall, and Meriol, who you haven't met yet, from my father's coterie, but Lazlo was the first who was solely my choice. But as my mother deteriorated, as I struggled to find my footing among my colleagues and they began to judge me based on her behavior—you know that I've closed myself off."

"You tried to make yourself like ice," Talia says, with a hint of affection. "Or maybe like diamond. Hard and unshakeable."

"And cold. Even with Lazlo. I didn't want to appear partial or to risk our friendship affecting my judgment… so I started holding him at a distance. Speaking to him about little other than the business of the realm. Showing no interest in the rest of his life. He tried to maintain the rapport we once had, but he couldn't do it on his own. Looking back, I can tell I hurt him badly."

I let those memories wash through me, knowing Talia is catching glimpses of them too. The smiles that cooled and faded over time, the laughter dwindling into silence, the overtures he simply stopped making, aware of what my response would be.

I told myself it was for the best. That the loss I felt was

a necessary sacrifice. I can't imagine my sense of purpose did anything to ease *his* loss, though.

Talia extends a tendril of sympathy that I'm not sure I'd receive if I'd finished the story. "He ended up leaving?"

"Yes, but not quite as you're thinking." I clasp my hands together in my lap. "There was also—after I'd settled into my responsibilities and found ways to at least… stabilize my mother, I took notice of a fae woman in the flock who was unmated." Just the thought of her sends a sharper jab of guilt through me, as if I've betrayed Talia somehow before she was even born.

"It's okay," Talia says, though I catch a tremor of discomfort through our bond that presumably she can't control either. "I know it's normal for the true-blooded fae to take other lovers when they haven't found their soul-twined mate yet—and even when they have."

I bristle instinctively at her final remark. "You won't need to worry about *that*." Reining in my emotions, I gather myself. "But yes. I wanted that sort of companionship, and I liked Ensley a great deal—and she liked me as well, as far as I could tell—but I always kept her at a careful distance for the same reason I held myself back from Lazlo. I didn't want to become too emotionally entangled, especially after seeing my mother so affected by a broken heart."

"I think that's understandable."

"Perhaps. But it did mean two people very close to me who spent a lot of time in each other's company because of that didn't feel they could count on me or that I cared very much about either of them." I grimace, more at myself than anyone else. "Lazlo and Ensley fell in love and began a relationship in secret. I'm not sure exactly how long it was going on, but—she became pregnant. With his child, she knew because of the timing, but she implied that she'd discovered it sooner than she had to give the impression that it was mine."

Talia stiffens in her chair. "She lied to you about *that?* Or—as close to lying as I guess she could, being fae? That's awful."

I spread my hands, unable to summon any of my anger from back then. It all burned out decades ago, leaving nothing but ash. "They decided together to lead me to false conclusions. Even if the child wouldn't be true-blooded, it would have been better off believed to be an arch-lord's. And they were also afraid of how I'd react if they revealed their relationship at that point. I hadn't given either of them any reason to expect compassion."

Talia's voice goes quiet. "But you obviously found out somehow."

"Yes." I can't sit still any longer. Pushing myself out of the chair, I allow myself to stalk through the room as if the movement will make the rest come out easier. "I was very excited by the thought of a child, as much as I tried to rein my emotions in. I started attending to Ensley more closely and stumbled on the truth. And then..."

I stop at my desk, bowing my head for a moment before swiveling again. "The deception and the realization that the child wasn't my own hurt me—so much more than I'd been prepared for. I think the fact that I'd become so invested without knowing it fueled my anger more than the betrayal itself. Which wasn't fair to them. I should have simply sent them away to seek a home in some other domain. It might not have made much difference, but at least I'd have spared them a little suffering."

"What did you do?" Talia asks, tracking my path across the room.

I force myself to meet her gaze. "There's an area on the fringes where criminals are sometimes sent. The work they're tasked to do there is grueling. I banished them both there. And that might even be why—it seems to strike a little more frequently in the outer domains—a few years later, the curse took them both."

The image that has featured in so many of my nightmares wavers up from the depths of my unconscious: the rigid blue-white faces of my former best friend and my former lover. I hadn't heard until they were already gone, not that I could have saved them at that point anyway.

"It's the only case I know of where two people in close contact fell victim to the curse at the same time," I say roughly. "So I can't help thinking my actions had something to do with it. I never found out what happened to their child—likely they sent him or her off to another domain to have a better life than the fringes would offer. I stole parenthood from them too, for the short time they'd have experienced it."

Talia's tone stays even, but I can taste the trickle of horror that ripples through her. "And how does that woman in Lakeshine fit in?"

"She's Lazlo's mother. She feels, understandably, that I punished him far too harshly. Not that she'd dare spell it out so clearly to my face."

Talia is silent for a long moment. The clash of her

emotions carries through our bond and shows in her tensed posture.

I swallow hard. "It's a lot to hear all at once, and it isn't —it isn't how I'd want you to think of me, but I realize you can't simply dismiss it out of hand."

Her hands twist together in front of her. "Have you really forgiven *me* for being with other lovers?"

I'm so startled by that question that I hope she can recognize the truth of my answer. "It wasn't something for me to forgive in the first place. You've been honest with me the entire time. You've never tried to trick me or mislead me. Even if you *did*, I wouldn't let my temper and my fears get the better of me like that again."

"Okay," she says, but there's something different in her expression when she looks at me, a wariness I haven't seen since her first few days here. It sends a lance straight through my heart.

She gets to her feet. "It is a lot. I just—I just need some time to let it sink in, all right? I'm still glad you told me."

I'm not. There wasn't anything else I could have done, but as I watch her leave the room, I can't shake the looming sensation that I've just soured everything good we had together.

20

Talia

I haven't generally ventured outside Corwin's palace on my own, although he's assured me that his domain is totally safe. But after an uneasy night's sleep and an awkward breakfast, I find myself slipping out the door to walk along the river's bank all the way to the cliff edge where the water tumbles over in the broad torrent of the falls.

There's no wall or any other kind of barrier along the cliff. I guess when most of the beings around here can shift into a bird in an instant, no one has much fear of heights. The roar of the waterfall and the knowledge of the sheer drop just a few steps away jangle my nerves, but after I've stood there for several minutes, gazing out over the spectacular if chilly view, they settle down. There's something reassuring about the fact that despite the chaotic natural phenomenon going on right next to me, I can remain steady on my feet, like I've made it through so much else.

If only I had a better idea what might be waiting for me on the other side of all this confusion.

I don't hear the approaching footsteps over the rush of the water until Zelpha is nearly at my shoulder. She stops next to me, folding her arms over her chest. For a moment, we both stay silent, just taking in the sprawling landscape beyond the cliff: snowy plains, dark forests, icy rivers, and distant mountains.

"So, he told you," she says without preamble.

My gaze jerks to her. Did Corwin say something? Does she even definitely know *what* he told me?

I'm not sure how much I want to say, although presumably she already knows the whole story. She was probably here when it all happened. "I… What do you mean?" I ask.

She looks sideways at me. "It wasn't hard to figure out. I heard you went out to Lakeshine yesterday, and there's been a virtual cloud hanging over the entire palace since you got back. Corwin obviously thinks you're unhappy with him. Are you?"

I open my mouth and then close it again, grappling with my answer. "I don't think unhappy is the right word." It's just that the thought of him being so vengeful—and not really that long ago in fae terms—has shaken me.

For now, he's accepting the Seelie men in my life. For now, he isn't blaming me for being unwilling to completely devote myself to him. But what if he gets impatient? What happens if I fully accept the bond and he starts thinking of me as entirely his?

I've seen so much of him, gotten to know him from the inside out, but he hid that part of his past from me. There could be more I haven't seen. And it isn't as if I've had a shortage of experience with how cruel the fae can be.

"It doesn't fit with how I thought of him before," I continue finally. "I'm having a little trouble wrapping my head around it." That sounds like a polite enough way of putting it when talking to a coterie member who's obviously on his side.

Zelpha nods. "That's fair. I just thought you should know, whatever account he gave you is totally colored by the fact that he's been beating himself up over his decision for more than thirty years. I'd imagine he came across *worse* in his version than he was in reality. And this is coming from someone who was not only there but had plenty of reason to be pissed off at him over it if his actions hadn't been understandable."

I blink at her. "Why would you have been upset?"

She gives me a crooked little smile. "Ensley was my little sister."

"Oh." My eyes widen. She did say her family had been close to Corwin's. "And you—you thought she deserved to be banished to that awful part of the fringes?"

"I think everyone could have made better decisions, but that Corwin's were the most reasonable of the bunch given his situation. You probably haven't been living here long enough to understand how precious children are to us, especially to the true-bloods like him. To allow him to believe he had a child on the way only to tear that joy away from him, when he'd lost all the other family he had less than two decades before..."

I might not totally understand, but I've heard enough of the fae refer to their feelings about children to know it's an incredibly big deal. "Why would she do it, then?"

Zelpha shakes her head. "She might have been my sister, but I didn't always understand what went through her head. She had to know the truth would come out eventually and hurt him horribly when it did, but she decided to mislead him about it anyway. If they'd told him what was going on as soon as they realized she was pregnant—by the Heart, if she'd broken things off with Corwin to begin with when Lazlo caught her eye—a whole lot of pain could have been spared all around."

"I guess she must have been scared."

"Not of Corwin, I wouldn't think," Zelpha says. "He's never been anything like a tyrant. Ensley did care about him, but she also liked the prestige that came with being attached to an arch-lord. I think she was hesitant to lose her position in case things didn't work out with Lazlo, and she justified it by telling herself Corwin wasn't that invested in their relationship anyway, that she hadn't made any official commitments. Of course, all that went out the window once there was a baby in the mix."

She turns more fully toward me. "I wouldn't have sent them out to the workcamp, no. Simply banishing them in general would have been enough. But they still had opportunities. The camp has a debt system, and if you work hard, you can earn your release. They were together—he didn't insist on separating them. They could have arranged to recover their child once they earned their way out. No one could have predicted that the curse would take them. Corwin certainly had no control over that."

Okay, that doesn't sound quite as dire as Corwin put it. But… "Lazlo's mother seems to blame him."

"Yes, well." Zelpha shrugs. "A lot of people had a lot of thoughts about Corwin in those days. He was young to take over the arch-lord position, and the situation with his mother had noticeably affected him, as well as it being rather unnerving all on its own. Some folk in the flock muttered about his judgment after the fact. But I wouldn't be surprised if they'd have accused him of being too lenient if he'd picked a gentler punishment. When they saw me speaking up in support of him, as Ensley's sister, that calmed things down pretty quickly. That's actually how I took my first steps toward joining the coterie."

My eyebrows rise. "You haven't been in it for very long, then?"

"No, only about fifteen years. It took a while for him to realize I'd keep having his back, but it's hard to fault him for being skittish after all that went down. It's a hell of a lot of work sometimes, but it's work I enjoy. And… maybe I feel I kind of owe it to him to help keep him on track after my sister's deception threw him so off course."

She turns to me with a crooked grin. "Do you want to come down into the village and get to know more of the flock? Maybe spending some time with them, hearing how they talk about him, will help you get your bearings."

I hesitate, but what else am I going to do? Mope around here or in my bedroom? I'm not going to clear my head that way. And before too long, this flock might be mine nearly as much as it is Corwin's. "All right. Do—do we need to fly?"

"Ah, no, there's a path for walking too if you'd rather go by that route. Just takes a little longer."

"That's okay. I'd like to know how to get there on my own anyway." It still feels a bit odd letting Corwin carry me around. I'm not sure I want to get into the habit of letting his coterie do it too.

Zelpha leads me a short distance along the cliff edge and shows me what looks like just a notch in the rock that turns out to be a flight of stairs when viewed at the right angle. The path *does* have a railing, probably because any raven shifter using it mustn't be confident in their flying. I grip it firmly, following Zelpha down the cool passage toward the village. The roar of the waterfall dulls to a muted rumble.

I can just see the closest terraces up ahead when the path flattens out and veers inward. Glowing crystals on the ceiling light our way into the cliff itself. I'm about to ask Zelpha where we're going now when we emerge into a huge cavern so large it could hold the entire castle at Hearth by the Heart.

As I look around, my breath catches in my throat. Even though we're deep within the cliff, radiant light beams down over us, seemingly reflected by diamond fixtures across the ceiling near small openings that must reach to the surface. An invigorating mineral scent fills my lungs.

Fae from the village move all around the space. At one end, a few are tending to some sort of underground garden. Another group appears to be assembling a large piece of furniture together. A couple of younger-looking fae simply stroll through the place, chatting with each other. What appears to be a small band start a song and then stop to discuss how to best shape the melody from there.

"The village common," Zelpha says. "We like having access to the open air from our homes, but it's hard to gather together to get much done right on the cliff-face, as you can imagine."

"Of course." I bite my lip. "Who should we talk to? Everyone looks pretty busy."

"Oh, I don't think that'll be a problem." Zelpha chuckles. "Here we go."

A couple of the garden workers have noticed us and left the plants to meander over. At first I think they assume Corwin's coterie member must have something important to say, but then I realize their gazes are fixed on me with restrained curiosity.

"You're the arch-lord's human companion," the woman says when they reach us, her hands squeezing shut at her sides. "The one who's been working on a cure for the curse?"

Word has spread quite a bit. I shove down my twinge of discomfort. "Yes. I've been trying."

"That's fantastic. I never would have thought—" She cuts herself off, maybe about to say something not entirely complimentary about humans, and lets out an awkward laugh. "Is there something *we* could help you with? I haven't heard that you've come down here before."

"I just… haven't spent much time in the winter realm in general yet," I say weakly. Maybe I should have insisted on visiting sooner.

I glance around. What can I say that would get me the

kind of answers I need? "It must be frustrating waiting so long without knowing how to stop the curse."

"We can endure. We've always known our lord is taking every step he can to ensure our safety."

There's an opening I can use. "I understand it's been a little... difficult for him since he had to take on the arch-lord position so suddenly."

The man stiffens as if I've tossed out a grave insult. "Arch-Lord Corwin may have needed a little time to grow into his role, but he's never neglected us. I doubt any of the other arch-lords come down to speak with their folk directly so often."

"He comes down here a lot, then?"

"Nearly every day," the woman says with a prideful air. "There's rarely any need to trek up to the palace and call on him, because you can always count on him coming by soon enough to see if there are any matters of concern."

I smile in a way that I hope will soothe any ruffled feathers. "I didn't know—he hasn't mentioned it, and like I said, I haven't been here very long."

The man hums to himself. "He keeps his own council, as well one should. But if there's anything required of him, he'll see it through. You never need doubt about that. Better action than empty words any day."

When I ask about their garden, they happily show it off to me, prompting more inquisitive comments from their colleagues. By the time Zelpha and I have made the rounds, I've ended up talking to at least a dozen folk of the flock, and I'm at least convinced that everyone here has faith in Corwin's ability to lead reasonably and conscientiously.

"Thank you," I say to Zelpha as we head back up to the top of the cliff. "Talking to them does help put some things into perspective."

"Hey," she says lightly. "You're going to feel what you feel. I can see why hearing that story all of a sudden would put you out of sorts. I just…" She hesitates, and her tone goes more serious. "I'd already found the mate I wanted to be with before Corwin ever became arch-lord. I wouldn't want to see him lose out on the same sort of happiness because he painted himself in too poor a light, that's all. It's been obvious how much you mean to him already."

As if to punctuate that point, Corwin's voice carries through our bond that moment with a whiff of panic. *Talia, where are you?*

Despite my tangled emotions, my automatic response is guilt and concern. *I just went down to the village common with Zelpha. We're coming up now. I'm fine—I'm sorry if I made you worry.*

His tone smooths out immediately. *No, that's all right. It's good for you to see more of the village. I only— Would it be all right if I came out to meet you?*

He's asking me permission to move around his own domain? *Of course. Maybe… maybe we should talk some more.*

A flicker of hope touches me. *Yes, I'd like that.*

When we come out onto the open plain at the top of the cliff, Corwin is already there waiting for us. Zelpha gives him a bit of a bow. "I didn't lead her too far astray, my lord."

Corwin gives her a baleful glance at her teasing and

turns to me as she heads off. "What did you think of the village common?"

That wasn't what I expected we'd be talking about. "It was… it was lovely," I say. "It's silly, but it didn't occur to me there had to be somewhere the flock could get together. Everyone was, well, pretty welcoming. I think they all still find my being here a little strange."

"They'll adjust. I'd see that they view you with all due respect." He studies me carefully. "Is there anything else I can tell you? Anything you'd want to know?"

He doesn't mean about the village now, clearly. I waver, but maybe there is.

Can you be totally open with me? I ask silently. *No walls up at all? I don't want to pry; I just want to be sure I'm seeing everything.*

Corwin's stance tenses and then relaxes. He closes his eyes. *Yes. I can do that. I'd want for there to be a time when we're often completely open with each other.*

He holds out his hand, and I grasp it. As the last fragments of his inner barrier fall away, the rush of impressions from him sweeps over me even more forcefully than before.

There's so much emotion inside him that doesn't show on the outside, whirling and rippling this way and that. His worries about the curse, his frustrations and anxieties about his colleagues, his devotion to his flock… and his love for me. It washes over me, pure and unhampered by any resentments or jealousies. I even catch a twinge of *affection* for Sylas and how well he's protected me.

It isn't all exactly positive. I can sense his regret that my Seelie lovers have had more time with me and got to know me before he ever could. He's afraid that I might still choose them over him and shut him out completely. But the emotions tied to that regret have the flavor of loss, not anger.

My fingers tighten around his. Suddenly there's one more thing I want to see. He's shown he'll let *me* see the vulnerabilities he tries so hard to hide, but will he be able to let go of a little of his rigid exterior if I need him to? I don't want him disgracing himself in front of the other arch-lords, but I don't want a mate who can never reveal his fondness for me in public.

I tug him closer and rise up on my toes. There's no one nearby, but we're in view of at least one other castle and anyone who might be flying near the Heart, if they happened to look.

The awareness of those facts and a momentary balking pass through Corwin, and then he dips his head to meet my kiss.

It's short but sweet. When I draw back, my heart feels both lighter and heavier.

If I don't really need to worry about Corwin, if he's learned from his mistakes in the past and grown beyond them… then the only person holding us back from the bond we're meant to have is me with my divided loyalties.

Corwin bows his head to kiss my temple with a wash of tenderness that suggests he caught my uneasy thought. "Come with me," he says. "There's something I should show you."

Talia

I walk with Corwin past his palace and on toward the border. Curiosity prickles at me, but I stay quiet, knowing he can feel my eagerness and that he'll answer it when he's ready.

We stop several feet from the hazy barrier that separates the winter and summer realms. Corwin glances around, confirming there's no one nearby to overhear. His nervousness seeps through our bond, but it's tinged with hope. He thinks I'll be happy with what he's going to say but doesn't want to assume.

He takes one of my hands and runs his thumb over my knuckles, looking down at it. Then he raises his eyes to meet mine. "I've been thinking about this— well, I've been thinking about possibilities since I first understood your ties to the Seelie. But after spending that time in the summer realm last week, speaking with Sylas, seeing how our peoples can find a compromise if we work at it hard enough, a clearer idea started to form."

"A clearer idea of what?"

"How our future could look—one where you aren't constantly traveling between the realms, constantly going without people you care about no matter where you are. It seemed overly ambitious at first, but I've pored over all the records I can find and tested my magic and meditated with the Heart, and I've come to believe there's a good chance of it working."

"*What?*" I say again, a glimmer of excitement rousing my impatience. Has he really figured out a solution?

"It'll depend on Sylas agreeing and working with me on it," Corwin cautions. "The one thing I'm certain of is that for the magic to come together, it'll require cooperation from both sides. But—I know how much you mean to him and his cadre—it seems there'd be a good chance—" He cuts himself off with a small noise of frustration. "Let me just show you what I'm picturing. That'll be easier than trying to explain with only words."

He releases my hand to step away from me, opening the space between us. In a low, steady voice, he speaks the syllables of a true name—or perhaps more than one.

The sounds form a slow sort of melody, like an echo of the song the wind makes as it winds around his palace, and something glitters in the air. After a moment, I realize it's frost. He's conjuring a shape out of delicate ice—and particles of what looks like stone, fine as sand.

I peer at it as the elements expand and multiply. It's starting to look like… like a building, with an arched doorway and impressions of windows. No, like a castle, drawing higher and broader with each murmur he makes. Turrets rise up, spires glint in the morning sunlight.

But it isn't like any fae palace I've seen before. He's mixing the ice and the bits of stone together in an odd sort of merging. At first I think they're combined fairly evenly, but as the building continues to solidify, it becomes clear that one end is made primarily of ice and the other side of the rock, which as the bits gather is showing a brownish-gray color and a texture almost like bark. It's only in the center of the building that the two materials twine together, forming a swirling pattern on the wall.

When Corwin's voice falls silent, the delicate model he's created stands nearly as tall as me and as wide as my outstretched arms could reach. I step a little closer, taking in every detail but afraid to so much as breathe too near it in case I shatter the thin walls.

"I doubt what we'd come up with would look *exactly* like this," Corwin says. "It's only an approximation to illustrate the basic idea. But I don't see any reason why our strengths shouldn't work in harmony. The trickiest part will be adapting the border magic."

I glance up at him, still not totally following his line of thinking. "The border magic?"

"Yes." He turns toward the wall of shimmering fog. "Sylas's domain is just across from Heart's Cadence. I believe with our combined efforts, we should be able to construct a castle that straddles the border. We'd simply have to bend the spell that requires the vow of nonviolence to encompass a slightly wider section of land, where either end protrudes beyond the typical borderlands. Which would simply mean that anyone setting foot inside the building would have to swear to do no harm at the entrance. You couldn't ask for better protection than that."

It takes me a few seconds to wrap my head around everything he's saying. "You want to build a new castle that's right on top of the border? You and Sylas together? *Oh.*"

My gaze jerks back to his model. The rocky part has a bark-like texture and color for a reason. Corwin was trying to give the impression of the wood Sylas and his pack use to construct their castle and homes. And the icy area is a stand-in for Corwin's diamond. It's a castle born from their strengths working in harmony to produce a single structure.

A giddy tingle shoots through me that I'm afraid to focus on too much in case I've misunderstood. "It'd be a *shared* castle?" I clarify. "One for both you and Sylas to use?"

"Yes!" Enthusiasm lights in Corwin's eyes as he must sense my own growing excitement. "As a symbol of commitment to the continuing cooperation between the Seelie and the Unseelie… A space where we can regularly touch base and stay in tune with what's going on in both the realms. We could frame it to the rest of the arch-lords as Sylas and I being ambassadors to each other's people."

I can't help looking back toward the diamond palace that's been in his family for generations. "But—you wouldn't want to completely give up your original home."

"Oh, no, I don't imagine we'd live in the border castle permanently. We could move between it and our usual palaces as need be. But—" He pauses and comes around the model of the castle to touch my face. "*You* could live there. You could see any of us as often as you liked without having to go back and forth. And any time you wanted to go right into either realm, it'd be as simple as stepping through a doorway. I was already picturing—we could make fine quarters for you right in the center of the castle where the two sides most closely merge…"

He skims his fingers up the side of the model. I can almost picture it myself: a bedroom with diamond and wood woven together across the walls, warm light streaming in through the crystalline panes, and at least some of the time, *all* of my men within reach just down a hallway or two.

A smile stretches across my face. "That would—that would be amazing. It'd be *perfect*."

Corwin beams back at me. "I'm so glad you agree. Of course, we can't know whether the Heart will actually accept a structure across the border until we try it… but I'd very much like to try it."

A wave of affection sweeps through me, so immense I can't contain it, can't compress it into words. I throw my arms around Corwin and hug him tightly. He returns the embrace with a sense of such utter joy that I can't doubt anything he's said.

But I still have to ask one thing. I nestle my head against his chest and speak through our bond. *Are you sure you'd want to live like that—with your soul-twined mate always having other men around? Won't people ask questions about why I'm living there rather than just with you in Heart's Cadence?*

Corwin presses a kiss to the top of my head. *How much we tell them is up to you. You're my mate, and that will be true no matter how many other men you love. It will be my honor as your mate to give you all the happiness I can. If you want to be open about your affections, I'll tell anyone who asks just that. If you'd rather keep that part of your life private, we can simply say you're living there out of respect to your ties to both realms—as far as the curse and the rest goes.*

He sounds totally calm, totally certain. And suddenly I am too. I didn't know before what I needed to hear—I couldn't have predicted this is what would do it—but any doubts that might have been lingering in the back of my mind dissolve.

How can I worry that this man might lash out at me or my Seelie lovers when he's spent the past several days devising exactly how I can still be with them as well as him?

But it's more than just that. A strange, heady burning sensation spreads through my chest, as if something inside me has cracked open to emit a flood of warmth.

I squeeze Corwin tighter, tears that are all joy prickling in the back of my eyes. *I love you. I—Whenever we can arrange it—I'm ready to confirm the bond.*

Corwin exhales sharply with a flicker of surprise. He'd hoped to reassure me about the future, but he obviously hadn't anticipated it'd affect me quite so much.

"Are you sure?" he murmurs, leaning his head close to mine. "It isn't a requirement of putting this plan into motion. If you wanted to wait and make sure Sylas will agree and we can manage to pull it off—"

"No. There'll be less argument from the other arch-lords and whoever else anyway if I'm officially bound to you, right? And..." I breathe in his woodsy scent, still afloat on the swell of emotion filling me. "I know I want to stay in your life, no matter what happens. I can see that even if this plan doesn't work out, we'll figure out something that does. You've offered this to me, and I want to offer you the clearest demonstration of *my* love that I can."

Corwin leans in to kiss me, his adoration rushing in to join mine for him. It's a longer kiss than the one we shared by the cliff, potent and passionate. By the time he draws back, I've practically melted into him.

"It doesn't take long to prepare the ceremony," he says. "A day or two—we could arrange it before your next return to the summer realm. If you don't think that's too quickly."

After the weeks of agonizing uncertainty, part of me wants it settled right now. "I think that would be fine."

"Then I'll set things in motion at once, my soul." He kisses me once more, quickly but tenderly. Then he gives his model of the border castle a regretful look. "As much as I admire my own conjuring, I think I'd better deconstruct it. It'll raise too many questions if it's noticed."

"It was just a practice run for the real thing anyway," I say.

His smile comes back. "Yes. The real one will be much more spectacular than this, besides."

With a wave of his hand, the frost and bits of stone disperse. He wraps his fingers around mine, and we head back toward the palace.

We've only taken a few steps when a carriage hurtles into view from farther down the border. It races across the snowy terrain and slams to a halt just ahead of us. An Unseelie man leans over the hull, his face strained.

"Arch-Lord Corwin," he says in a ragged voice. "I came as quickly as I could—the summer settlement has been attacked!"

Talia

"All right," Corwin says. "Tell me exactly what happened and why you believe the Seelie are responsible."

The young fae man who raised the alarm stiffens where he's sitting on the bench at the opposite side of the carriage. He must have constructed it hastily, because the pale walls and floor vibrate with the speed the vehicle is moving at. Corwin only paused long enough to get the gist of his story and then call his nearest coterie members and a few of the flock's warriors before setting the carriage back toward the Unseelie's summer settlement.

"We were just finishing setting up the last few houses," the young man says. "Almost everyone's already moved in now—we even managed to get some of the plants we wanted growing there—I don't know about those summer crops…" He halts and shakes himself as if to get back on track. "Then there was this shrieking sound like a horrible ice storm descending on us."

Zelpha raises her eyebrows where she's leaning against the side of the carriage a few feet away from me. "An ice storm struck in the summer realm?"

The young man grimaces at her. "No, it just sounded like that. I don't know *what* it was. But the next thing we knew, one house and then another were collapsing like they were being blasted over by some kind of gale, all in a row right along the edge of the new village. A lot of them had people inside—they couldn't get out in time—the man Arch-Lord Uzziah sent who's bad with the curse can barely move as it is, and he was in one of those hit."

Corwin's expression is rigid. "You said before that our people were hurt. Do you know how many—how serious the injuries are? Did we lose anyone?"

"I'm sorry, my lord—I'm not sure." The other man looks down at his hands, which have clenched where they're resting on his knees. "I don't have much magic that'll help for healing. The people who do were rushing in to help—I thought the best thing I could do was hurry back to the Heart for help. You said if I saw anything concerning, I should let you know. You can't get much more concerning than *that*."

"No." Corwin rubs his face. "I can't see why the Seelie would attack the settlement after we came to such a firm agreement, though."

"It was their arch-lords you made the agreement with, wasn't it, my lord?" one of the warriors ventures. "I doubt many of the wolves are eager to have us on their territory, and they're not exactly known for keeping their animosities to themselves."

I tense instinctively at the insult, and Corwin fixes the woman with a measured look. "Neither have we for quite some time, and most of *our* animosity was born out of a misunderstanding. I don't think we should start laying blame until we've had a chance to properly investigate."

His reaction brings down my hackles, but my mind spins back toward something else the man from the settlement mentioned. "The man from Uzziah's flock—the one who was cursed. He hasn't gotten any better since arriving in the summer realm?"

A shadow crosses the young man's eyes. "No," he says. "He was still a little mobile when he was brought in, and the chill has gripped him even more since then. From what I last heard, he was past the point of talking or motion. Unless it turns around very soon, I don't imagine he'll make it through the day." He pauses, and his expression darkens even more. "If he even made it through the attack."

"Are we sure it even was an attack?" Verik asks in his coolly thoughtful way. "We're unfamiliar with the weather patterns and such on the summer side. For all we know, this blast was a natural phenomenon like one of our storms."

"That just happened to strike our settlement in the right spot to destroy a dozen of the homes?" the young man says.

Several pairs of eyes turn to me, presumably recognizing me as the only one in the carriage who has much experience with the Seelie realm.

I spread my hands helplessly. "I've never seen a storm like that, but I haven't been out in the summer realm weather for all that long either. I don't think it's impossible it's just a coincidence."

I don't think it's very likely either, but it seems wiser not to say that in this company.

We'll sort it out, Corwin says through our bond. *The Seelie have had their representatives watching over the settlement too—I'm sure they're already aware and are making their own investigations.* A thread of worry winds through his inner voice, though.

I can't blame him for being uneasy. *I* don't totally trust that the Seelie had nothing to do with it. Arch-Lord Celia took Corwin prisoner unprovoked just a few weeks ago. It's not that difficult to imagine she might have had a change of heart and arranged some kind of sabotage that wouldn't violate the terms of the agreement. Or it could have been other fae who simply objected to the idea of letting the Unseelie use any of their lands.

The tensions between the realms have been building for a long time. It'd be ridiculous to think they could be smoothed over with a few days of conversation.

What will it mean for Corwin's plans of unity if it turns out someone from the Seelie side is behind this act of destruction? It could set off a whole new war.

I restrain a shiver and lean into Corwin just slightly, not wanting to make too big a show of our closeness with so many from his flock right here. He squeezes my hand with a wash of affection and reassurance.

The summer arch-lords didn't want the Unseelie settlement anywhere near their own domains, so the spot they ended up picking is about halfway out to the fringes, far enough from the Heart that no vow is required to cross the border there. But when we cruise through the thick haze, the air warming by the second, we emerge to find a small band of Seelie warriors stationed there.

They bristle at our swift arrival, a few raising swords. "Halt, there. What's your business in the Seelie realm?"

Corwin stands, and I scramble onto my feet beside him. "I'm Arch-Lord Corwin of Heart's Cadence," he says, even but firm. "One of my flock informed me of a destructive incident at our settlement here, and I've come to determine the cause of it and confirm my people's safety. Is that a problem?"

The guards murmur to each other discontentedly, but one steps ahead of the others. I recognize him from Donovan's typical retinue—I think he's one of the arch-lord's cadre-chosen. "Arch-Lord Corwin is our ally," he tells the others. "He's the one who pushed for the peace." His gaze comes back to the carriage. "You appear to have brought a fair bit of company."

I speak up, hoping they'll listen to my words with a little less suspicion than the Unseelie's. "If there's some kind of danger, we need to be ready to defend ourselves and the other villagers. We just want to go to the settlement and find out what's going on."

They hesitate for a moment longer, and then Donovan's man waves us onward. "There are people from the bordering domains keeping an eye on the area. We'd appreciate it if you stuck to the settlement territory and didn't pass farther into our lands."

Corwin nods. "Our only interest is in the situation in the settlement."

"Trying to stop an arch-lord from seeing his own people," one of Corwin's warriors mutters as we glide onward.

Corwin shoots him a sharp look. "They're being cautious, as we would in the same situation. They *did* let us pass. If we want them to assume good intentions on our part, we need to stop assuming the worst of them."

The warrior snaps his mouth shut, chagrinned. Then, as the sparse stretch of trees thins further, the settlement comes into view up ahead.

I don't need any bond to sense the horrified shock that sweeps over our entire party. It was one thing to hear the young man's story and another to see the result. We stare silently at the scene as we draw closer.

A broad swath of rubble runs the length of the village, with chunks of wood, stone, shell, and other building materials scattered all across the grass. Fae are gathered all along it, some tending to others: murmuring over wounds, examining limbs. I can already see splotches of blood on some of the injured people's clothes.

Heart help us, Corwin mutters, rage mixing with his horror. *When we find out who did this...*

Looking at the destruction, I wish I could say that I'm sure none of the Seelie would have shattered the hard-won truce like this. But I really don't know. I've seen the Seelie attack their own, attempt to frame colleagues for crimes and even to murder them... I'd just hoped that all three of the arch-lords were committed to their agreement and that all the other fae would respect their rulers' decision.

"Verik, Frain," Corwin says out loud as he stops the carriage at the edge of the settlement. "You're the strongest healers among us—see if there's anyone who needs more tending to. The rest of you, stay with me."

He helps me out and turns to face the Unseelie settlers. Several of them straighten up, still looking weary and upset but clearly relieved at the sight of one of their arch-lords. Corwin's colleagues might not have a lot of faith in his abilities, but his people recognize and respect his authority.

"Are there any casualties?" he asks, striding forward.

One of the women who's been helping the injured moves to meet him. "Not yet, but we have one who took a bad enough blow to fracture his skull. Thankfully, our main healer wasn't caught in the attack and is doing what he can to repair the damage. He thinks he'll come out all right."

Corwin inclines his head in acknowledgment. "One small mercy. Have you faced any further assaults since the initial blast?"

A man who's rubbing his bruised temple pipes up. "Nothing else, but what they did to begin with is bad enough. Convince us to trust them, to let down our guards on their territory, and then lash out at us at the first opportunity…" He lets out a disgruntled sound.

"From what I understand, we don't know who exactly is responsible," Corwin says, his gaze taking in the two fae who've spoken to him and the others assembled around him. "Has that changed, or are we still only speculating?"

The woman scowls. "It must have been the savage

curs. It's been clear enough they aren't *that* happy about us being here."

I don't see any Seelie within the town itself, but a small contingent appears to be stationed in the field a short distance away, simply keeping an eye on things. I nod toward them. "When did that group show up?"

"Not until about an hour after the attack," the woman admits. "But that doesn't mean they didn't know about it."

"Have any of the Seelie approached you to speak with you?" Corwin asks.

"No. They've been keeping their distance." The woman pauses. "Well, one came close enough to ask if we needed healers sent in, but we told them we could look after our own."

"Can't be sure they'd cure us and not kill us," the bruised man mutters.

Corwin walks along the swath of destruction, checking on each of the injured and offering whatever words he can of concern and comfort. I limp along beside him. Nothing jumps out at me as evidence of how this happened or who's caused this ruin.

We've covered most of the line of rubble when Corwin stops with a jolt of alertness. He's caught a sound my human ears can't pick up.

He glances around, and I follow his gaze. A Seelie-style carriage is just coming into view in the distance, flying toward the settlement at a fast clip. Apprehension twists in my gut.

Then a figure stands up by the bow of the vehicle, the sight of him sweeping all my newer worries away. It's August.

The Unseelie around me aren't having the same reaction. "What do the bastards want now?" one of them says in a low voice.

"Probably going to pretend to offer help while gloating over our troubles," another mutters.

I swallow hard. The peace we managed to form was shaky as it was. Whatever the hell happened here, this incident may have been enough to completely shatter it. Are we going to be starting all over from scratch?

Well, they can think whatever they want, but I'm not afraid to show how much faith I have in the Seelie—especially this particular man. "He's here to help," I say, pitching my voice to carry, and set off to meet the carriage without waiting to hear any more grumbling.

August

'm not sure what makes my heart sink farther: the ruin of several buildings stretching along the nearest edge of the Unseelie settlement or the unmistakable hostility in most of the gazes that're fixed on me as I bring the carriage to a stop. The report we'd gotten from the Unseelie settlement hadn't been *good*, but I still hadn't expected to see quite so much destruction.

Talia is already limping across the field toward me. She must have come with Corwin, who I spot speaking to a couple of the winter fae before starting after her. I hop out of the carriage, motioning for the two warriors I brought with me to follow but stay at my flanks, and hurry to meet her halfway.

"I wasn't expecting to see you here," I say, resisting the urge to ruffle her bright hair or, even better, pull her into a hug. I'm not sure how our Unseelie audience would react to a show of affection when at least some of them may know by now what she is to their arch-lord. I settle for giving her shoulder a light squeeze.

Talia offers me a tight but relieved smile in return. "We came as soon as we heard. It's awful. No one seems to have any idea how it happened."

"That's what I'm here to try to figure out. I'd imagine Donovan and Celia have their own people making inquiries."

Talia nods. "We ran into some of Donovan's pack-kin when we crossed the border…" Her voice tenses. "They seemed more focused on protecting the summer realm from the Unseelie than protecting the Unseelie from whoever attacked them here."

I'm not totally surprised, but there isn't much I can do about that fact. The only people I have authority over at the moment are the two men with me. I glance past Talia toward the settlement. "I guess I'd better take a closer look and see what I can make of it."

"You might not get the warmest welcome," Corwin says as he reaches us. "My people are convinced the assault was carried out by the summer fae."

I bristle instinctively, even though he spoke with no accusation in his tone and it's a possibility I was already considering. I will my own tone to stay even. "Has anyone found evidence of that?"

"No," Talia says, rubbing her arms. "But it's understandable that they'd assume that, isn't it? The summer and winter fae haven't exactly been friendly in a long time."

Corwin glances back toward the village, his mouth pressed into a tight line. "And unless you'd suggest that my people sabotaged their own efforts—and risked the lives of their companions—who else *could* it have been?"

I'm debating whether I can reasonably say that I wouldn't put it past some of his colleagues to orchestrate something this malicious just so they could frame us for it when Talia goes still. Her gaze jerks to me, her eyes widening. "There is another option, isn't there? You're not the only fae in the world. Wasn't there an attack on Aerik's domain by some of the Murk a little while ago?"

I never would have connected that incident to this one, but Talia wasn't there to see how different they are. She doesn't understand just how feeble the rats' power generally is with their scorning of the Heart.

"That was a petty prank," I say, "only turned murderous because one guard caught them at it. To blast down several buildings… I'm not sure many of those vermin would even have the power to crumble *one*."

Talia raises her chin. "That kind of thinking is how Sylas got his scar. At least a few of the Murk have powerful magic. And if they mostly want to make mischief and cause chaos, wouldn't disrupting our new truce be a perfect way to do that?"

It would, come to think of it. I turn to Corwin. "Have your people had any difficulties of your own with the Murk lately?"

Corwin considers for a moment. "Not that I'm aware of. But—the curse and our dwindling population have made for much more chaotic times in general. It's possible they've been stirring up trouble now and then that we haven't realized they were to blame for."

Talia grasps his arm. "What about those beasts at

Lakeshine? No one ever figured out why they'd targeted that town, did they?"

He gives her a crooked smile. "I'm not sure why the rat shifters would want to target it either. But I suppose they wouldn't need a clear reason. They do often delight in simply sowing whatever confusion they can."

"It should be easy enough to determine," I say. "The attack only happened a few hours ago. The culprits will have left at least a small trace of scent. If there were rats around, we'll smell them out." I gesture to my men. "Make a wide circuit of the area around the settlement, noses to the ground, alert for any hint of the Murk."

They leap into wolf form and lope off in opposite directions. Talia hugs herself. "What if they don't find anything? If it *was* some of the Seelie deciding to break the peace, will you be able to figure out who?"

I grimace. "That'll be harder. There are plenty of us around, and we've been coming to and from the settlement to oversee the construction for days. It's one thing to sniff out the essence of the animal and another to narrow it down to a specific individual. But there are other kinds of evidence we might turn up. I'd better join in and see what I can find."

I step back from them and let the shift wash over me, stretching my limbs and bringing my senses to even sharper alertness. As I set off with the warm breeze licking over my fur, the uncertainties that were gripping my gut fall away. Everything feels simpler as a wolf.

The one thing I am still sure of is that I need to get to the bottom of this fast. The fragile peace depends on it— our chances of keeping any kind of relationship with Talia while she's bound to the Unseelie depend on it. I will not let her down, even if it means taking my fellow summer fae to task.

Skirting the settlement, I quickly determine that the spell that blasted through that entire row of buildings must have come from the west. Whoever cast the magic would have needed to remain out of view. I head toward the nearest patch of forest in that direction, about half a mile away, taking whiffs of the grass as I go just in case. Nothing's been trampling this field except Seelie feet.

Once I reach the trees, I slow, both to inhale more deeply and thoroughly and to keep my ears pricked for movement. I'd imagine the perpetrator fled the scene to avoid detection, but that's not a guarantee.

I weave between the trees, drinking in the rich, living scents of the forest. Here and there I catch a wolfish musk, but none of that sharper ratty odor I've come across only a few times in my life. No hint of ravens in this area either.

Was it my own people then, turning against their own arch-lords? My lips curl back from my fangs at the thought.

With the motion, a thicker wave of scent trickles through my senses—and it occurs to me that the forest smells in this exact spot are a little *too* rich. I pause, taking one slow breath and then another, my nerves tingling to high alert.

The scents I'm taking in are the sorts I'd expect, but there's something unnaturally strong about them, as if they've been enhanced or saturated... to cover up a different scent someone didn't want being detected?

I shift back into my man form so that I can intone a

few words of my own magic. They resonate against the spell I suspected was lingering in the air. With a couple more syllables and a sweep of my hand, I manage to dispel the enchantment cloaking the space. Then I drop back down on my wolfish feet to take another whiff.

My fur nearly stands on end. There it is. Faint but undeniable now that the villain's efforts at covering their tracks have been dealt with—the prickling tang of the Murk.

Those mangy vermin. I cast about in increasingly wider circles, but I can't tell how many of them were involved or where they might have gone from here. It happened recently enough and they stood in this spot long enough that they couldn't erase all trace of their presence, but it is only the faintest trace.

Curse them. I'm not sure the ravens' noses will even be able to pick up the scent to accept it as proof. It's fading quickly even while I search for more.

But would the Murk really have pulled off this prank and then left the area without waiting to watch any of the chaos they wrought? They like to revel in their mischief the way Whitt revels in dancing and alcohol. Wouldn't they want to know the outcome of this particularly vicious "prank"?

But how in the lands am I supposed to find them if they didn't leave any trail? I could send out more magic to chase after that rodent essence, but unless they're right nearby, they *will* flee the second it touches them.

An idea glimmers in my head. I almost dismiss it because of what it requires, but then I push myself to spin and race back toward the settlement.

If Talia can find a mate in one of the Unseelie, then I can manage to work together with one for a few minutes. And if the arch-lord doesn't like being asked for favors, then he can say so.

Corwin is crouched at the edge of the field examining the spot where the blast must have hit the first house. He tenses a little as I charge up to him in wolf form but holds his ground. Talia hurries over at the sight of me, reaching us just as I've shifted.

"It was the Murk," I say in a low voice. "I caught a tiny bit of their scent in the forest to the west. I'd like to see if we can catch any of them that might have remained in the area to keep an eye on the results of their efforts."

Surprise flashes through the arch-lord's eyes followed by a grim setting of his jaw. "I would very much like to have a few words with the culprit myself. How do you propose we track them down?"

I motion to the landscape around us. "I can send out a searching spell that'll latch onto the presence of any Murk within a few miles. But they'll feel it when it reaches them. I'd suggest that you take to the sky while I cast the spell so that you can watch for the vermin when they make a run for it. I think I can add an element to the magic that'll light them up a bit temporarily when it touches them, to make them easier to spot."

Corwin doesn't even hesitate. "Of course," he says. "Make a sweep of it, from north to south—that way I'll have a smaller area to focus on at a time. Signal me when you're ready?"

I nod, and he springs into the air, transforming into a large blue-black raven in an instant with a flap of powerful wings. I've never thought much of the feathered form before, but I have to admit to myself now that flight is a pretty handy ability.

"I want you to wait here," I tell Talia. "The Murk become vicious when cornered."

She draws back to the shelter of the nearest unharmed building but watches from there. I wait until Corwin is circling against the sky, and then close my eyes, concentrating on the spell I want to perform.

I've never stretched my powers as far as I want to today, but the more ground I can cover, the more chance I'll actually catch the rats.

As Corwin suggested, I propel the energy out to the north first, as far as I can will it to go. With the words I murmur under my breath, I twine my memory of the rats' scent into the magic. *Find it. Make it glow.*

I have only a vague sense of the spell rippling across the terrain. When my chest starts to ache with the strain of being stretched too thin, I tug it to the left, swinging it across the land as steadily as I can. Searching, searching, extending myself even farther as I catch a second wind—

At the same instant that a jolt of success hits me, Corwin lets out a croak loud enough to reach us down below. When my eyes pop open, he's already diving— toward a spot beyond the forest where I caught the scent. I hurtle forward, releasing my wolf in mid-stride.

My paws pound the earth. In my mind's eye, I see exactly where the raven plummeted. I can't let him tackle the fiend alone. This is my lord's realm—this is my responsibility.

My muscles strain just as I strained my magical

abilities before. I throw myself forward even faster, the ground falling away beneath my feet. Another ravenish cry rises from up ahead.

I charge through the patch of forest, heedless of the twigs and pebbles scattering under my feet, and burst out the other side. At the far end of a grassy plain stands a cluster of narrow boulders. I catch the flash of dark wings amid them.

I rush across the rest of that distance in time to find Corwin in the form of a winged man, pinning a sinewy, spiky-haired woman to the ground. She hisses through her teeth at him. The stink of rat clogs my nose.

Springing to his side, I shift at the same moment and draw my sword. When I bring it to the woman's throat, she doesn't so much as flinch, but she does stop struggling against Corwin.

"Did you act alone, or do you have companions here?" I ask. "Where are they?"

The Murk woman lets out a ragged laugh. "Ooh, there are so many more of us. Just you wait."

"That's not a real answer. Tell me who was responsible for—"

I don't even get to finish my demand. Corwin must have loosened his hold just slightly seeing my sword in place, and the Murk woman doesn't value her life. She smacks her fingers against her palm—and a current of energy slams through her body, making it spasm.

Her eyes go dull, her lips parting slackly. In a matter of seconds, she's nothing but a limp shell.

Corwin stares down at her. "What—how—"

I bare my teeth. "She had a suicide spell on her. I've

heard they defy the Heart that way too—casting it on each other with a trigger they can use if they'd rather die than be trapped."

With a few vicious words snarled under my breath, I shove myself away from her. We know who attacked the Unseelie settlement, but the perpetrator has managed to flee us on her own terms after all.

Talia

Normally being back in Hearth by the Heart would comfort me. But even surrounded by all four of my men and Astrid, my frequent protector, in the familiar cozy atmosphere of Sylas's study, my nerves stay on edge.

I thought I had a pretty good idea of all the threats we were up against. Now it turns out there's a major one I never really considered.

"I don't like it," Whitt says from where he's in his typical pose propped against the built-in shelves. "The settlement had barely finished construction. We didn't put out any big announcements. How closely must the Murk have been watching to realize it even existed, let alone was a significant target?"

"It's possible it was just chance," Astrid puts in, shifting her weight near the doorway. "Good luck for them and bad luck for us that one of them stumbled on the new village and figured they could upset a lot of fae by striking at it."

I can't help worrying at my lower lip. "They don't usually pull 'pranks' that big, though, do they? It doesn't feel like a spur-of-the-moment thing."

"I agree." Sylas steeples his fingers where he's sitting behind his desk, a frown darkening his face. He glances at August, who's standing as if on guard by my chair, and then Corwin, who's sitting in the armchair next to mine. "You discerned nothing useful from the rat you caught?"

August shakes his head with an apologetic grimace. "She activated the killing spell too quickly. There was no evidence on her. I don't know if she was even responsible for the spell in any way—she had no true name marks on her. I guess it could have been a different sort of magic, though. Who knows how the Murk might twist the small blessings they scrape from the Heart?"

"The one thing she did say to us was quite ominous, if vague," Corwin says, sounding a little cautious to be giving his input when he's the lone Unseelie in the room. "Perhaps it was an empty threat meant only to unsettle us, but she implied that they had more planned that we wouldn't like."

Astrid lets out a dismissive huff. "I wouldn't trust a word that comes out of those vermin's mouths. If she saw the opportunity to confuse and distract us, she'd have taken it without a single concern to the truth."

"The Murk can lie, then?" I ask.

"Any of us *can* lie, mite," Whitt says. "It's just most of us value our connection to the Heart too much to risk damaging it by doing so. The Murk have fewer qualms on that score. Although it sounds as if the vagueness of this one's remarks might have avoided outright falsehood anyway."

Corwin nods. "She certainly wasn't remotely specific about what we should be waiting *for*."

Even after months in the faerie world—years if you count the time when Aerik held me prisoner and I never saw more of this place than his one room—I barely know anything about the rat-shifting fae. I motion to Astrid. "What was that rhyme you told me humans used to sing about all the different fae?"

Her lips twist into a slanted smile. She recites the words in a faintly wry tone.

"Wolves of summer, winter ravens

Where they dwell find no safe haven.

But most beware the rats of Murk

Sowing spite wherever they lurk."

My stomach knots. "I guess there isn't anything much more spiteful than wrecking the peace we're trying to build." Does that mean the Murk are going to keep trying to ruin our truce?

Sylas rubs his jaw. "They've generally preferred to sow that spite among humans, since the mortals make easier targets. But we've had more significant incidents with the Murk in the past few weeks than for decades before now. Perhaps they've gotten bored of their human victims and decided they needed a larger challenge."

"You don't think—" I feel abruptly ridiculous suggesting this with none of the much more experienced fae around me have, but I can't help going on. "They dislike you, and they want to unsettle you. The curses—"

Whitt snorts, and even Sylas, who's faced the hostility of the Murk directly, shakes his head. "Magic on that scale would be an incredible feat even for a host of Seelie or Unseelie dwelling close to the Heart. It's an order of magnitude thousands of times beyond the destruction in that village, which was a bigger effort than we generally see from the rat shifters in itself. But..." His forehead furrows. "The curse has struck us on both sides of the border. It's possible it has affected the Murk as well."

I see his reasoning immediately, with a chill that wraps around my gut. "It could be what's making them act out more than before, just like the Unseelie's version of the curse was driving their raids along the border."

A tremor of revulsion reaches me from Corwin at the thought of being bound in a curse connected to the rats. The thought leaves my skin crawling too. If that's what's happening, if they find out that I'm involved in curing it, will they try to call on me?

Would I even want to help them? The winter fae had only been attacking the Seelie for a few decades, with millennia of peace before then. The Murk have always been "sowing spite." With every new thing I learn about them, the less I want to have to do with them.

Whitt makes a dismissive gesture. "Somehow I doubt they'd let us in on that knowledge even if it's true. We can only work with what we know."

"Whatever their motives were, they won't disturb the Unseelie settlement again," August says, drawing himself up a little straighter. "We have sentries patrolling all through that area now, watching for any sign of the rats."

"And the repairs to the destroyed buildings?" Sylas asks.

"My people wished to see to those themselves," Corwin says. "I appreciate the help the Seelie offered, but… feelings are still somewhat raw, and even having heard the Murk were to blame, it's hard for them to shake their initial suspicions right away. I'm sure tensions will ease again when the rest of our plans proceed unhindered."

Sylas inclines his head. "I hope that's true, but I understand their wariness. Thank you for coming so quickly and for working together with August to find the perpetrator." He looks toward the window. Outside, the sky is darkening, the purple haze of the sunset fading. "You've lost the better part of the day because we failed to guard our lands well enough. I think it's only fair if I give you leave to extend Talia's visit by a day to make up for the loss, assuming that suits both of you."

I feel the leap of Corwin's spirits through our bond. My own heart skips with a bittersweet sort of happiness. It warms me that Sylas is going out of his way to be generous, that he's honoring Corwin's claim on my company, but at the same time I don't want him to think I'd rather be in the winter realm than with him and my other lovers here.

Why can't that shared castle Corwin talked about be built already? No more negotiating over where I'll be— having a space that can be a home for all of us.

"I appreciate that," Corwin says with a dip of his head in return. *Talia? There should still be time to arrange the ceremony in that case.*

Yes. I want that, I do, but sitting here with my other

lovers around me, the thought feels suddenly overwhelming. I can't just come back in a few days and announce that the confirmation of my bond is already finalized. They need to be prepared—and they need to know how generous Corwin's intentions are too.

"That does make sense," I say to Sylas. "Thank you. But I'll still look forward to coming back." Then to Corwin, silently, *And before we go, I think I should tell them I'm going to confirm the bond… Can I share your idea about the joint castle with them too, or do you want to wait until you're more sure it can be done?*

Corwin hesitates, but I sense it's mainly nervousness over whether Sylas will approve, not any reluctance to pursue the idea. *I don't think we'll know what's possible until we put our magic together on it regardless. Perhaps it would be better for you to bring up my proposal first so you can gauge their reaction. I can give you some privacy for that.*

He gets up, reaching to give my hair a brief caress. "I believe there is something my mate wishes to discuss with you before we go." He meets my eyes. "I'll be appreciating this domain's natural wonders. Let me know when you're ready to leave."

As he steps out, Astrid glances around at the rest of us. "Somehow I get the feeling this is going to be a discussion that doesn't require the full cadre."

My lips twitch with an unexpected smile. "It doesn't."

"Perhaps you could watch over our honored guest and make sure my colleagues don't act out any hostile inclinations on the spur of the moment," Sylas says dryly.

Astrid gives him a little bow and heads out, and all three of my Seelie men fix their attention on me.

"What's going on, Talia?" Whitt asks, his blue eyes intent, his tone gentle. I'm suddenly sure he's already guessed—the first part of my news, at least.

They're all too far away from me. I stand up, reaching out beckoningly, and they move to encircle me without question. I lean into August's touch on the small of my back, grasp Whitt's hand, and slip my other arm around Sylas's, tugging them even closer. The heat of their bodies and their combined, wild scents wrap around me.

I have to simply spit it out. "I'm going to confirm the soul-twined bond with Corwin."

There's no mistaking the tension that grips the men gathered around me. I hurry onward. "It doesn't mean I don't still want all of you, or to be part of the summer realm, or—or anything like that. I just don't think it's helping anyone leaving it up in the air, and I'm sure of Corwin now—I definitely don't want to put either of us through whatever *breaking* the bond would do to us... And I think having an official position among the Unseelie will make finding a compromise easier."

"How's that, my love?" Sylas asks, his voice only a little gruffer than usual. He strokes his fingers down my cheek, no sign of resentment or anger in the gesture.

"Corwin thinks we may be able to set things up so that I could be with all four of you pretty much always. It sounds like the magic side of it will be a little tricky, but he's done some research—I'm sure he can explain the details better if you agree to give it a chance." I drag in a breath and go over everything my mate told me about his plan for the shared castle—how it would be constructed and where, how they'd explain it to their respective colleagues.

My Seelie men listen quietly and thoughtfully. When I'm finished, they stay silent for several seconds. Nervous impatience itches at me. "What do you think?" I can't help prodding.

August looks at Sylas over my head. "Could it really work?" The hopeful note in his voice melts some of my anxiety.

Sylas cocks his head, but a small smile touches his lips. "I haven't looked into it myself, but Corwin seems a conscientious man. I doubt he'd have brought it up unless all the evidence he found indicated it was possible. I can't think of any reason it definitely *wouldn't* be."

A giddy bubbling sensation rises in my chest. "Then— you'd be willing to try it? I know it's a lot to ask—"

Sylas grasps my shoulder. "It isn't, Talia. Not after everything you've done for us. Not when you mean so much to us. It *would* be beneficial to both our peoples to have regular contact between the realms, so it'd hardly be selfish besides. It's hard to know how such an arrangement might work out in the long run with the tensions that have existed between us, but I'd say it's more than worth the attempt."

He glances at the other two. Whitt lowers his head to kiss my temple. "If your soul-twined mate came up with this scheme, then it only convinces me he's worthy of you —and worthy of us offering our own trust and cooperation. He didn't have to make such an offer."

"You know if there's a way to stay by your side, I'll take it, Sweetness," August murmurs. "I only—" He cuts himself off with a shake of his head. "We'll make it work. Wolves and ravens may have been at odds for a short time, and we may never have been great friends, but that can change."

He sounds as if he's trying to convince himself more than speaking from certainty, but maybe that's the best I could hope for. *They like your idea*, I tell Corwin as I tug each of my other men to me in turn, giving them a quick kiss farewell. *They're willing to give it a try. Do you want to talk to them about it now?*

His reply comes with a rush of relief and gratitude. *I think we've had enough on our minds today, and it may be best to let them think the contributing factors through some before we get down to the decision-making. But you can tell them we'll discuss it further when I return you here at the end of your stay. I'll meet you in front of the castle.*

I pass on his words to Sylas, who gives my jaw one last lingering caress before waving me off. I make my way downstairs, buoyed by more lightness than I've felt all day, and nearly bump into Harper coming out of the kitchen just beyond the stairs.

"Talia!" she says, her over-large eyes opening even wider than usual, and throws her arms around me before I can respond. "You're all right. I heard there was an attack at the Unseelie settlement, and someone said you were there with Corwin, and that the Murk were making trouble…"

With a startled laugh, I hug her back. "I didn't even see any of the Murk. We came a couple of hours after the attack happened. It was pretty awful, but I'm perfectly okay."

"Oh! I didn't really get the clearest details." Harper pulls back with a bashful smile. "Well, I'm still glad you're okay. Are you staying here now, or…?"

She looks so eager that my answer comes with a pinch of guilt. "No, actually, we just stopped by to discuss the situation with Sylas and now I'm heading back to the winter realm. Corwin's waiting for me." A spark of inspiration propels more words from my mouth. "But— I'm going to accept the bond—there'll be a confirmation ceremony in a few days. Maybe you'd like to come back to the winter realm to see it?"

I nudge Corwin through our connection as I ask, hoping I'm not breaking some rule I didn't know about, and he reacts with surprise but fond enthusiasm. *It's a moment of celebration. Any guests you'd like to have are welcome.*

Harper claps her hands together. "Really? I— Yes, of course. You should have someone from our pack there, shouldn't you? And I've never seen any confirmation ceremony before, let alone an Unseelie one."

She's so obviously excited at the prospect that I find myself beaming at her. "Great. When I know exactly where and when it's happening, I'll send a message back." Maybe I should invite my Seelie men as well—or would that be awkward? Would they even be able to leave the summer realm on a trip like that when Sylas has so many responsibilities?

I guess it can't hurt to ask them once I know what'll be involved. I say my good-byes to Harper and hurry out to meet Corwin so he can get on with making those arrangements.

As we walk to the border, the Unseelie arch-lord takes my hand to twine his fingers with mine. *I'm glad that this incident hasn't dampened your eagerness for our union.*

Not at all, I say. *If anything, seeing you and August taking on the Murk together made me think of how much I'm looking forward to seeing you all collaborate more often once we've worked out all the official stuff.*

He chuckles out loud and teases his thumb over my knuckles in a way that lights up the skin all up my arm.

I don't get to enjoy it for very long, though. When we pass through the border into the chilly air on the winter side, a sentry is waiting for us beneath the glinting starlight.

"Arch-Lord Corwin," he says without even looking at me. "Your fellow arch-lords request your presence in the Hall of the Heart for an urgent meeting about the Seelie catastrophe."

Corwin peers at him. "There was no 'Seelie' catastrophe. My people should have made it back here hours ago. Didn't they explain that the Murk were behind the attack on our settlement?"

The sentry keeps his posture rigid. "It may be so, but we can't be sure the Seelie didn't put them up to it to get around their oaths, my lord. At least, that's the sort of speculation I've heard among the flocks, if you don't mind me saying."

Corwin's mouth tightens, and my heart plummets. *I know none of the wolves would ever associate with the fae they consider vermin. Are the Unseelie, even the other arch-lords, really going to blame the summer fae for a crime they had nothing to do with?*

Talia

"No one's outright insisting the Seelie were behind it," Corwin tells me over breakfast the next morning, looking weary. "They're just unwilling to assume they definitely *weren't* involved. I've gone over everything we saw and discovered, and explained that I have every indication that the summer fae would never associate with the Murk, but... you've seen how stubborn my colleagues can be."

I nudge the scrambled eggs on my plate half-heartedly, not able to summon much appetite despite the creamy smell of them filling my nose. "Do you think it'd do any good for me to talk to them? I know just how unfriendly the Seelie are to the Murk. They've had their issues with the winter realm, but they still recognize you as equals. The Murk they barely see as fae at all." And considering the way the Murk behave, it's easy to understand why.

Corwin shakes his head with an apologetic pursing of

his lips. "I already suggested they speak with you, but they've banned you from the Hall on the basis of your connections to the summer realm. I even told them we're going to be confirming the bond so that you'll officially be lady of Heart's Cadence… Maybe once the ceremony has happened, they'll recognize your loyalty."

Or if I could finally figure out a way to consistently stop the curse. No wonder the other Unseelie arch-lords are skeptical of me when I cure all the Seelie once a month but can't seem to bring more than one of the winter fae out from their icy illness.

I rub my forehead. "Has the curse struck anyone while we've been dealing with this? If I could manage to heal someone else…"

"Not that I've heard," Corwin says. "And I'm sure I'd be notified immediately if there had been." He sighs. "I'm meant to consult with my colleagues again this morning. I think I can at least talk them down from demanding a full contingent of our warriors be stationed at the settlement. I'd imagine the Seelie will allow at least a few guards given the circumstances."

His gaze goes distant in thought. He pokes at the last few bits of food on his own plate and glances up at me with a flow of warmth through our bond like an inward embrace. "I'll let you know as soon as their tempers are more settled. We have more to discuss about the ceremony, after all—and I would like to spend a *little* more of your time here on matters that have nothing to do with politics."

I offer him a small smile. "Keeping the peace and looking after your people have to come first. If we can solidify the truce between the realms, then we'll have a lot more time just for enjoying ourselves in the future, right? I just wish there was more *I* could do."

Corwin makes a humming sound. "You push yourself too hard. There are a *few* things that aren't your responsibility. You should take some time while I'm gone to think about happier things—perhaps come up with some ideas of what you'd like to see in our joint castle, which I'm still determined we'll build whether the rest of the fae like it or not."

The defiance in his voice makes my smile widen a little, but after he's left, I find I can't concentrate on anything that far in the future. How can I get excited about sharing a home with my men of both realms when I'm not even sure their peoples won't be inciting war against each other in the next few days?

Corwin has closed off our connection while he meets with the other arch-lords, so I have no idea how their discussion is going. I wander through the palace, searching for inspiration in the halls and rooms that are becoming increasingly familiar. After a while, I end up in the alcove where the locked door leads up to Corwin's mother's room.

I stop there, eyeing it, considering grabbing the key that'll take me to the entrance to her rooms. I don't know how to do the calming spell Corwin cast over her so that he could talk to her without her becoming violent, but I could try to speak to her through the door up there. She should be able to hear me.

I'm just not sure what I'd say to her. Is she aware enough to care what happens to her son anymore? To take any joy in the knowledge that he's found his own soul-twined mate? Maybe hearing that would only make her more upset over her loss.

As if answering my unspoken questions, a scratching sound and a low moan reach me from up the stairs. Knowing who's making them doesn't make them sound any less unnerving. I hug myself, rubbing my arms, and turn at the tapping of soft footsteps.

Zelpha comes around the bend. She cocks her head when she sees me. "What are you doing over here?" she asks mildly.

I don't know how to explain it in a way that'll make sense to her. It doesn't even make sense to me. I look back toward the door. "I guess I was just thinking about all the people the curse has hurt… Wondering if there's anything I can do to make *any* of it better." I pause. "Maybe it goes against the Heart to say this, but it kind of seems wrong to me that she has to keep living if she's in so much pain and doesn't want to. The Murk…"

The Murk offer each other a way out if they feel it's better to end their life than continue it. August told me that's how the woman they caught was able to avoid questioning. Maybe working a spell like that means they have less magic to draw on in general because of the Heart's disapproval… but I can't help feeling like your own life *should* be something you have control over.

Zelpha shudders. "You don't want to be taking any cues from how the Murk handle their problems. If we offered her a way out, then there'd be no chance of helping her if we got the opportunity later. Once we have a handle on the curse, maybe it'll be easier to cure her grief too."

"I know that's possible. It makes sense. I just—" I think back to a moment months ago when I stood in front of the former Arch-Lord Ambrose holding a knife at my own throat. "There was once a time when I'd rather have died than let our enemies get their hands on me. I used that fact to save myself. I wouldn't want anyone taking *that* opportunity away from me either. I've already been through enough to know there are things worse than dying."

If I was ever wrenched away from my men and my friends, if I knew they were lost to me and there was nothing but pain up ahead—or that my captor would use me to cause all kinds of pain for others— While I hope to the Heart I never find myself in that position, I wouldn't want to go on living if I did.

But the Unseelie are too rigid to consider that point of view—as rigid in their opinions as their bodies become in the grips of the curse. The answer must have something to do with that strictness, but I still don't see how I fit in. With the Seelie's curse, I don't stand up to their savagery or prevent it, I let them indulge it, and *that's* when they snap out of their rage.

My head hurts just trying to think the problem through.

Zelpha gives my back a light pat. "The way we see it, it's true that some things can't be fixed. But when that's the case, we must make the best of them in their broken state. There can be beauty even in what's damaged."

Is that how they'll think about relations between the summer and winter realms if they can't resolve all their conflicts and suspicions?

My chin comes up at the thought. "Well, I think there are a lot of things we can still fix." The arch-lords don't want to hear from me, but what about all the other Unseelie? What are *they* saying about the attack on the settlement now? From what the sentry who summoned Corwin yesterday said, everyone's been speculating about the Seelie's involvement.

I turn to Zelpha. "I want to go down to the village common again and speak with the flock."

Zelpha raises her eyebrows. "Did Corwin give that plan the okay?"

"I hadn't come up with it the last time I talked with him, and he's busy with his meeting now. He didn't mind you taking me down there before, did he?"

She looks uncertain, maybe because last time she was bringing me to see the flock for her own purposes and now she's unsure of mine. "They know you have ties to the summer realm. They might not be as friendly today."

"Well, that's exactly why I should see them. So they can realize that the summer fae had nothing to do with what happened and there's no reason to be unfriendly about it." I study her. "I know where the path is now. I can go on my own."

"Now hold on—"

I hold her gaze steadily. "Would you be telling me whether I should take a walk down to the village if I were fae? I might limp, but I'm not an invalid. In a few days, I'm going to be standing by Corwin as his confirmed mate. I hope you wouldn't think of treating me like I'm a servant who can be ordered around then."

Zelpha winces. "All right, all right, you know how to

drive a point home." She gives me a considering glance up and down. "Are you sure you don't have a sizeable portion of fae blood in you after all?"

I have the ridiculous urge to stick out my tongue at her. "Humans have minds of their own too."

"Clearly." A laugh sputters out of her. "I still think you'd be better off with a coterie member along for backup. Just in case."

"Come on then."

I head through the palace and out to the cliff overlooking the village. It isn't hard to find the path again now that I know what I'm looking for. I march down it without waiting to confirm Zelpha is following, hearing the rasp of her boots trailing behind me. My heart is thumping faster both at the thought of what I might face in the village and from the argument with her, but all of Corwin's coterie need to see me as more than some frail human girl who somehow stumbled into their lives and might have a cure to the curse accidentally up her sleeve.

When I reach the village common, it's busier than last time. Many of the winter fae are standing around in clusters, talking with each other in terse voices. Those tending to the garden are frowning, barely seeming to notice what they're doing with their hands.

Several of the fae's gazes turn my way as I walk out under the reflected light that streams from the diamond fixtures overhead. I stop in the middle of the space, steadying myself against the smooth stone of the floor, and look around me.

"If anyone has any questions about the Seelie or what happened in the summer realm yesterday, you can ask me," I say, raising my voice slightly. "I visited the settlement with Arch-Lord Corwin. And I've lived among the Seelie for a long time. I know them."

The conversations fall off. Most of the Unseelie drift toward me, their expressions hesitant. The wariness in their stances unsettles me. Has the attack made them so suspicious that they see even me as a potential threat?

"We don't need anyone to tell us that most of the wolves would like to tear us to bits," one of them says.

"No one should tell you that, because it isn't true. They never attacked you even when you were launching raids on their territory, did they? All they wanted was for *your* attacks to stop."

"Or maybe they were just scared to step into our lands," another Unseelie pipes up. "As soon as we set foot in the summer realm in an attempt at peace, our people are getting blasted and battered. That doesn't seem like a coincidence."

"Your own arch-lord caught one of the Murk who was responsible," I remind them. "You don't think *he* would lie about that, do you?"

They murmur discontentedly. "The Seelie could have hidden an alliance with the Murk," the first man says. "From Arch-Lord Corwin and from you. Who knows how much they might be hiding?"

As far as I've seen, the Seelie aren't anywhere near as in the habit of hiding things as the winter fae are, but I don't think it'll help relations for me to point that out. "I've been around a lot of different Seelie during my time there, and I've never heard any of them show anything but hostility toward the Murk," I say. "I promise you, they think of the rat shifters as the enemy and are just as eager to catch them and stop them from hurting you again as you are."

A woman near the back of the bunch steps forward, her eyes narrowed. "Maybe *you're* in on it with them. You're a human—you could lie for them if they wanted you to."

Zelpha moves closer to my side. "I hope you're not making accusations of our lord's honored guest."

The other fae stiffen a little at her intervention. I raise my hand to Zelpha, motioning her back. I have to show I can handle this confrontation myself.

I turn back to the gathered fae. "I don't want to see you hurt either. That's why I'm here—why I've been trying everything I can to cure your curse."

"How can we be sure of that?" another fae man demands. "All these offers of help could be just a way to set us up for some greater trick. Have you really cured anyone?"

A voice rises from off to one side. "I heard you pushed for the arch-lords to agree to the settlement in the first place."

"You came from the summer realm," a woman says. "You've been part of one of their packs. You don't even really belong here."

I swallow hard, groping for the right words, and it hits me. *I've* been hiding too, and maybe it's time I stop. Not in every way—I remember Corwin's warnings about revealing my magic too well—but it can't hurt for me to admit the main reason I've come here, can it? In a couple of days, we'll be announcing it to everyone anyway.

I suspect Corwin would have preferred to be here to tell his flock himself, but he's not. And this is my truth as much as his. I've accepted it—his people will have to too.

My heart pounds even harder, but I pull my spine straight and speak as steadily as I can. "I do belong here. I belong here in this domain alongside Corwin, because I'm his soul-twined mate. That's why I came in the first place —that's why I've kept coming back."

The fae around me gape at me. Someone sputters a laugh. Zelpha's face has tensed, but she sets a hand on my shoulder and glowers at the crowd. "I can verify it. I've heard it from our lord myself."

"Then why hasn't the bond been confirmed?" a woman demands.

I can be honest about that too. "Because I wasn't totally sure I wanted to confirm it. I *do* have loyalties to the Seelie as well—to summer fae who've supported me and looked out for me. Being bound to Arch-Lord Corwin doesn't change that. But that's why it means so much to me that you and the Seelie can make peace with each other. I belong to *both* realms, and I want to see them united, not fighting each other. Especially when it looks like you're both facing another enemy you could tackle more easily together."

Restless talk echoes through the cavern, blending together in a mishmash of voices I have trouble picking apart. Zelpha's stance remains on guard. No one is speaking to me now, only their fellow fae.

My stomach sinks. Did they not believe me? Or they believe but don't approve?

But even if that's the case, I don't regret having the truth out in the open.

Maybe I should let them stew on the situation for a while rather than expecting them to embrace me as their ruler's partner right away. I ease back, lifting my voice to make one more promise. "When I'm the lady of Heart's Cadence, I'm going to do everything I can for this flock, just like Corwin does. But part of that will be making sure you can see the Seelie for who they really are, just as I know them. I promise you, they aren't villains any more than you are."

"I suppose that depends on which specific fae we're talking about," Zelpha mutters as we hustle back up the path.

I can't summon a smile at her attempt at humor. If the Heart wants me to bring the realms together, I can't help thinking we've still got an awfully long way to go.

We cross the plain in silence. As we reach the terrace wall, a servant comes darting out of the palace to meet us, his eyes wide.

"Zelpha," he says with a bob of his head and a flick of his eyes my way that suggests he's not sure whether he needs to address me or how. "I didn't know what to do— Arch-Lord Corwin hasn't returned from the Hall of the Heart yet—"

"What's the matter?" Zelpha says evenly, drawing to a halt.

"Well…" The man wrings his hand. "We have a visitor. From the summer realm. It's one of their arch-lords —he says his name is Sylas."

Talia

For all the times I've wished that the men I love weren't so separate from each other, I've never actually imagined what it'd be like to have Sylas sitting here in one of the armchairs in Corwin's study. It's weirdly thrilling and unsettling at the same time.

Corwin doesn't appear to know exactly how to handle the unexpected visit either. At first, he sat behind his desk as if it were a professional meeting, but now he's gotten up again, standing beside it instead. He eyes the Seelie arch-lord, opening his mouth and closing it again before he finally speaks beyond initially ushering us in here.

"I could ask my kitchen staff to bring refreshments, if there's anything you'd like. I wouldn't want you thinking ill of me as a host."

"I'm fine as I am," Sylas says, although the massive fae man looks a little awkward too surrounded by the diamond walls and pale furniture. Like he's a little worried he might break something if he moves too quickly. "I simply hoped that we could talk, and I believed it was only fair that I come to you this time after you've made the journey to the summer realm on multiple occasions. But if this is a bad time for you, you certainly don't need to drop everything for us to have this conversation now. I wasn't sure how to arrange it in advance."

"No, it's all right." Corwin's hand flexes, and I can feel he's suppressed the urge to rub it over his face. He's doing his best to keep a cool composure despite his agitation underneath.

I reach out through our bond with the equivalent of a squeeze of his hand. *I'm sure he isn't going to make any problems for the confirmation ceremony. It's a pretty big show of trust, him coming into Unseelie territory on his own like this.*

It is, Corwin agrees, and his stance relaxes enough that he lets himself sink against the front of his desk, using it as a temporary seat. "I'd just finished speaking with my colleagues when you arrived. They're still quite disturbed by the attack on our settlement. If you wanted to check in about our response, I expect we'll be putting forward a couple of new requests within the next day, but I've managed to keep those within reason. They still want the experiment to continue in case it proves to be our best hope of avoiding the curse."

"I'm glad the Murk haven't managed to disrupt our truce completely despite their efforts," Sylas says, matching Corwin's even tone. "But I actually came to address a more personal matter."

He pauses, his mismatched eyes focusing on me for a

second where I've settled into one of the other armchairs, a hint of a fond smile touching his lips. Then he returns his attention to Corwin. "I'd imagine you know that Talia conveyed your idea of a joint castle straddling the border to me and my cadre."

Corwin draws his posture a little straighter. "Yes. She said you were open to the possibility. I've been looking forward to discussing it with you directly. First I'd like to say just how much I truly do hope we can work together to continue the peace between our realms."

Sylas nods. "As do we. And also to see that our lady receives all the adoration the four of us can offer in combination—that's your intention as well, unless I'm mistaken?"

A muscle ticks in Corwin's jaw hearing Sylas state it so openly, but he inclines his head. "Yes. I—I do understand how important you are to her and she to you, and this is the best way I could think of to honor your connection. Regardless of the bond the Heart has blessed us with, I can't see how it could be its will that I shatter the happiness she's already found. The more love she has in her life, the better."

I can sense the traces of discomfort that statement still provokes in him, even though I know he means it. Sylas must catch some of it with his own senses as well, or maybe it's easy enough to guess. He knows what the attachment of a soul-twined bond is like.

"I agree," he says. "But I'm also aware of how difficult it can be to go against one's instincts to claim and possess, especially with so strong a connection of your own... I wasn't sure I could accept sharing her affections when she first made it clear she wasn't willing to pick me over my cadre-chosen, and I didn't have the same depth of bond stirring up my emotions."

"I've given it plenty of thought," Corwin says a bit stiffly. "I wouldn't suggest it if I wasn't committed to seeing it through."

Sylas holds up his hands. "I don't mean to question your commitment. I'm only being... practical, as I understand you ravens appreciate. Thinking about a thing and actually seeing it through are very different propositions. Before we go forward and provoke all the chaos we're likely to create by asking to build this castle between the realms, I thought we should make sure you really can tolerate that kind of sharing of affections in practice."

A giddy tingle washes over my skin as I guess what he's getting at. Corwin studies him, his stance tensing even more. "What do you mean?"

"Consider this a sort of experiment in itself," Sylas says. "It's perfectly all right if you find you can't accept it after all. Say the word, and I'll withdraw. I won't blame you either. We've been prepared that compromising might not actually be possible since the soul-twined bond first took hold. I simply think it's best that we determine that up front... It'll be much more complicated to discover it's unbearable for you once we've already proceeded with your plan."

The Seelie arch-lord extends his arm toward me beckoningly. My heart skips a beat.

Corwin has frozen against his desk, a conflicted tangle of emotion reaching me through our connection. He's seen glimpses of my intimate moments with my other men through my memories, fragmentary impressions that I couldn't totally shield him from when I've been with them, but he's never had to watch anything happen right in front of him.

Sylas is right, though. We should know exactly how far we can take this compromise before we try to put it in motion. I'm not sure it'd change anything about what I do in the next few days, but *I'd* like to know just where my mate really stands when it comes to my relationships with my other lovers before I make the ultimate commitment to him.

I have to at least go forward with my eyes fully open.

I get up and walk to Sylas. When I'm close enough, he reaches to trail his fingers down my arm from the elbow-length sleeve of my dress to my bare wrist. Heat sparks in the wake of his touch. I gaze into his mismatched eyes, sharply aware of both how much desire this man can stir in me with a simple touch and how much turmoil is rippling through my mate witnessing it.

Corwin? I say tentatively. If he asks me to stop this, I will. I don't want to hurt him. But then I'll know where we really stand.

He grapples with his answer for a moment before he voices it. *Go ahead. I swore I'd let you have this. If he can bear to see you in other men's arms, then I have to manage to tolerate it too.*

I'd like us to get to some point beyond mere tolerance, but that'd probably be asking too much right now.

I step closer to Sylas, touching his cheek. He loops his arm around my waist and tugs me right into his lap. One of his hands comes to rest on my thigh, tracing delicate circles there. The other tips my head to the side so he can press a quick kiss to the side of my neck.

The brief heat of his mouth sends a heady jolt through my body, one that travels into Corwin as well. A flicker of his own desire rises up in response. He may not be overly enthusiastic about watching another man bring me pleasure, but that pleasure still affects him.

His voice comes out a bit ragged. "You want me to simply watch, while you and she…"

Sylas looks at him over my shoulder, pausing to nuzzle my hair. "That's up to you. You can stick to watching if that's all you're comfortable with. But I'd hoped we could make this our first collaboration, if you're willing."

A collaboration. The image flits through my mind of both my arch-lords skimming their hands over my body, grazing their mouths against my skin, and a deeper heat swells inside me. I meet Corwin's eyes, wanting to encourage him without pushing him beyond what he's ready for.

Holding my gaze, he wets his lips. My excitement has stirred more of his own, and an ache is running through his chest to please me any way he can, to show he can handle everything he proposed. But the sight of Sylas caressing me has set off a flare of possessiveness he hasn't quite mastered.

He clenches his hands against the edge of the desk. Sylas dips his head to nibble at the crook of my shoulder, and I can't help tipping my head back to welcome the teasing kisses. *It feels good, but it'd feel even better if you were with me too.*

Corwin lets out a rough sound, and then he's moving, crossing the space between us in a few quick strides and tangling his fingers in my hair. He claims my mouth with a determined kiss. Sylas nips my shoulder, and hungry flames surge all through my body.

I'm caught between two of the most powerful men in the fae realms, and I can't imagine wanting to be anywhere else.

Corwin deepens his kiss, his tongue delving between my lips. I whimper encouragingly. When I arch toward him, my body quivering with the need for more contact, he drops his hand down my side. He strokes his fingers from collarbone to hip over my dress and then cups my breast.

Sylas lets out a low growl, tasting my eager reaction. His hand slides over my leg to caress the even more sensitive flesh of my inner thigh, close but not quite reaching the spot where I'm already burning hottest.

Corwin sucks in a breath, and another pang of hesitation reverberates through him. Feeling my arousal has already made him hard, but it unsettles him how much of our shared desire is being conjured by another man.

Don't think of him as an outsider, I suggest, with as much coherence as I can summon in the moment. *He's adding to the experience, not taking anything away from you. We* both *get to feel more.*

Corwin kisses me again, even harder than before. He swivels the heel of his hand against my breast, sending blissful shivers through the stiffening peak. Then a sudden sense of resolve comes over him. He pulls back, brushing his lips to my cheek and my temple, and looks at Sylas behind me.

"Touch her sex," he says with a husky note I've never heard from him before. "She's aching for it."

An approving rumble emanates from Sylas's chest. He dips his fingers right between my legs, tucking the fabric of my dress with them, and a gasp slips from my throat. I press into his hand, seeking more of the pleasure that floods me with the contact, and satisfaction echoes through me from my mate.

I grasp Corwin's shirt, tugging his mouth back to mine. Sylas brands the side of my neck again, his fingers working against me through my dress as Corwin massages my other breast, and it's hard to imagine we could ever have thought this was anything but a fantastic idea.

I love you, I think at Corwin, running my hand down his lean chest, gripping Sylas's arm with my other hand. *I love you.*

I love you too, he replies, his inner voice full of tenderness and hunger. *You deserve all the love this world can offer.*

"Her dress," he rasps out loud. "It needs to be off."

Sylas gives no objection to the command, dragging the fabric up over my hips as Corwin opens the fastenings that tighten the bodice. As I adjust my position on Sylas's lap, the rigid length of his erection rubs my bottom. Corwin senses it and the flare of lust it provokes through me. As soon as they've tossed my dress aside, he grips my thighs and settles me right against that hardness.

I can't help squirming, and Sylas's breath catches. He delves his fingers between my legs again, humming happily at the feel of my soaked panties. I tip back against him, and Corwin leans over me, his hand braced against the arm of the chair, his head dropping so he can suck the nub of my breast into his mouth.

The swipe of his tongue and the rocking of Sylas's hand take me from burning to scorching. I grasp Corwin's hair, bowing my back to offer myself up to him, swaying with Sylas's touch. It's all so good I don't know how to ask for anything else and yet I want more, everything, the rush of release I can already taste the edges of.

Corwin teases my nipple between his teeth, my urgency egging on his own. He rises to rest his forehead against mine, both our skin damp with sweat. Desire resonates through me, through our bond.

"She needs to be filled," he says, the invitation clear in his tone. "Let's take her as high as she deserves."

Sylas loosens his slacks and frees himself from his drawers while I shimmy out of my panties. As I sink down over Sylas's length, Corwin keeps his hand against my face, his thumb stroking over my cheekbone, drinking in the giddying stretch and the heated fullness that brings a moan to my lips.

Sylas adjusts his position under me to drive in even deeper and holds me there, pressing a kiss to my shoulder blade. "Have you ever taken your soul-twined mate into your mouth?" he murmurs.

The suggestiveness of the question sends an eager quiver through me. I push back against him, reveling in the fullness where he's entered me, and gaze up at Corwin. My mate's eyes gleam darkly with a longing he can't suppress.

He shouldn't need to suppress it. "No," I say, nudging him to straighten up. "But I'd like to."

I slip my fingers over the front of Corwin's trousers and the bulge straining beneath them, and he can't hold back a groan. He helps me open the ties, caressing my hair with a gentleness that sends tingles over my scalp. I dip forward, still taking Sylas in as I angle myself to flick my tongue over the head of Corwin's stiff erection.

There's something so intoxicating about the effect of that simple gesture. Awed bliss washes through Corwin's body. His fingers tighten in my hair, not so much pulling me to him as holding on for the ride. *So good, my soul—it feels so good.*

I know, because I'm feeling every bit of that delight flooding into me as well. I take him right into my mouth, absorbing the woodsy flavor of him, reveling in every twitch and stuttered breath brought by the pleasure I'm giving him. Even more giddy heat flows through me from where I'm locked in Sylas's embrace as well.

The Seelie arch-lord grips my thigh and rocks into me with increasing force. I let his rhythm carry me up and down over Corwin's shaft. Sylas reaches his other hand to fondle my breast, and Corwin gives my hair just the slightest tug that toes the line between pain and pleasure. Dear God, if every collaboration between summer and winter worked out this spectacularly, I can't imagine anyone would be complaining.

Talia, Corwin says with a tremor of concern, the force of his release ready to burst inside him.

I only suck him down harder. *I want you. I want all of you.*

He comes with a salty spurt in my mouth and a thrill that sings through his veins and mind, so ecstatic it throws me over my own peak. Sylas thrusts inside me, and I clench around him with a cry. The Seelie arch-lord mutters a curse as he pumps into me a few more times before spilling over inside me.

I lift my head, seeking out Corwin's lips. He bends to meet me, no hesitation over his flavor on my mouth, only a fresh wave of fervent appreciation. I turn, slipping off Sylas's shaft, to kiss the other man as well. The Seelie arch-lord hugs me to him with affection I don't need any magical connection to feel. "My love."

"My love," I whisper back.

I turn in his arms and hold my hand out to Corwin. A momentary awkwardness settles over us as the impact of what we've just done sinks in. My mate wavers, and then steps in to squeeze my fingers and brush his lips to my temple, sharing the embrace.

"Have I proven myself acceptably adept at compromise, Arch-Lord Sylas?" he asks with a trace of wryness.

Sylas offers him one of the rare wide grins that turns his fearsome face absolutely stunning. "I think our lady will be well taken care of. It will be an honor to stand with you by her side."

Corwin bends to offer me my dress, and we all get our clothes back into proper order. Then the Unseelie arch-lord draws in a careful breath. "I'm not sure if you would want to witness it or be able to attend, but it would please me—both of us—if you and your cadre could attend the confirmation ceremony. It'll be the start of a step forward for all of us, I hope, and you should be a part of it."

I grasp Sylas's arm. "Yes—I'd like for you and August and Whitt to be there, if you can. And maybe, if the joint castle works out and we can keep the peace, we could have a ceremony of our own, even if it's not quite the same."

Sylas watches Corwin's reaction, but my mate only nods at the suggestion. A softer smile touches the brawnier man's lips. He sets his hand over mine. "I'll speak with the others, but I expect their answer will be the same— nothing would make us happier than to be a part of your life in every way we can."

I beam back at him and then at Corwin, able to tune out the tension in my gut for just a few more minutes in their presence.

Now if only the rest of the fae world would accept the cooperation between our peoples just as willingly.

27

Sylas

I purposefully called the meeting at the Bastion for a time a little later than I intended to arrive myself so that I could have several minutes to wander that glowing space and reflect in the presence of the Heart. The veins of gold pulse with the thrum of energy, their warmth washing over me. I take in the flow of magic, searching it for any sign that my decision is misguided.

But the images that stir in my mind are of my interlude with Talia and Corwin yesterday. The passionate heat generated between our bodies. The way the Unseelie arch-lord's defenses dropped and he gave himself over to the sharing of pleasures.

I hadn't been sure when I'd arrived how he'd react to my proposal. I'd been prepared for him to delay seeing it through or outright reject the suggestion, as would have been his right. He means well and he wants Talia to be happy, but putting a plan into action is a very different thing from merely imagining it. It was too easy to picture catastrophe if he didn't have to face the reality of not just a joint castle but a joint relationship until we'd already invested in bringing it into being.

But he didn't just face it—he was an active participant. I think we even started to find our footing with each other, a give and take of power and commands with Talia as our focus, without balking too much at giving one another due room. How that might play out once all four of us are in the mix, I can't predict, but I feel certain now that we can navigate those waters without veering into disaster.

And how wonderful was it seeing the glow in Talia's face as *she* discovered just how well we could cooperate given the chance?

I know what she wants, I know what my cadre-chosen and I want, and now I know that Corwin will meet us halfway as promised. I wish those were the only concerns I needed to consider. But I don't believe I can explain our dedication to a castle within the borderlands without finally acknowledging our dedication to *Talia* to my colleagues—not without skirting closer to outright lying than I'm comfortable with.

I meant to claim her as my own in their eyes weeks ago. The only difference now is that there's one more mate who owns a piece of her heart. The rest of the Seelie would consider our relationship odd regardless. I was prepared for this.

I don't need them to celebrate our romantic commitments, only to agree not to get in the way. Whether that's too much to ask remains to be seen. Celia has already expressed some reservations about my interest in Talia.

The Heart doesn't give any indication that it disagrees with my purpose here. If anything, the rhythm of its pulsing soothes my nerves. My connection to Talia is born out of love, as is that of my cadre-chosen. When she welcomes that love, it can't be wrong. It certainly doesn't hurt anyone. I haven't let it interfere with my duties to my people. And if we were still living on the fringes in banishment, it wouldn't be anyone's business at all.

As if roused by that thought, an image forms before my deadened eye. I see a filmy figure of myself standing in the middle of the Bastion's main room, surrounded by three arch-lords sitting on their thrones: Celia, Donovan, and Ambrose.

A snarl twists Ambrose's mouth as he says something with a swipe of his hand cutting through the air. My past self's jaw is clenched, but the turmoil of emotions that was roiling inside me echoes into me now while I watch.

The vision fades away as quickly as it appeared. I shake the lingering uneasiness it brought off as well as I can. It was showing the day my pack's banishment to the fringes was proclaimed.

Is it an ill omen that my eye focused on that moment in my history? Or perhaps I should take it as an attempt at reassurance. Who would have thought I'd have come so far from that moment to now own one of these thrones myself?

No matter what troubles we face, we'll find a way to rise above them.

Celia's arrival prevents me from dwelling on the matter

any further. I recognize her elegant, poised stride from the soft tapping of her shoes across the stone floor before she comes into view.

As I requested, she's come alone. Before long, word of our relationship with Talia will spread through the entire summer realm, but I'd like a little privacy for the initial announcement.

"Sylas," she says with an acknowledging tip of her head, and crosses the room to her throne, though she doesn't sit in it, only positions herself in front of it. That's fine. If she'll feel more secure standing by the symbol of her authority, perhaps she'll find less to argue about in my news.

"I trust your pack-kin have picked up no further activity from the Murk?" I say. She should have passed on the word if they had, but if there's a particularly recent development, it might not have reached me yet.

Celia shakes her head, her pale hair hissing over her ebony shoulders. "Other than the one you caught with Arch-Lord Corwin, there's been no sign of them. They do have a knack for vanishing into the shadows." Her lip curls with distaste. "I don't like how quickly they're increasing in boldness. They take too much delight out of startling us."

"I agree. Perhaps, once we're sure of relations with the Unseelie, we could pull many of the troops who've been stationed along the border to seek out whatever communities the Murk have been forming within the realm or along the edges of it."

Celia frowns, but she doesn't reject the idea. "I suppose that will depend on the ravens."

Donovan approaches with a brisker rapping of footsteps. He strides across the central room to meet the two of us, a faint furrow in his brow but his tone upbeat. "It's good to see you both looking well. I hope that will continue after we hear what you have to say, Sylas."

I give him a mild smile at his gentle teasing. Between my two colleagues, I have less idea how he'll react. Celia, at least, has had the experience of taking mates of her own, both soul-twined and not, even if she might hesitate over my specific choice. As far as I know, Donovan has yet to commit himself to anyone. He's been on my side more than once in recent months, but I have no sense of his views on more intimate relationships.

"I don't think what I wanted to speak to you about *should* cause any distress, if you take it in the spirit I mean it," I say. "It shouldn't take very long for me to explain either. This matter has simply been a long time brewing, and it appears that I'll be taking some action in regards to it soon, so I felt you should know."

Celia cocks her head. "And what exactly is this matter?"

I inhale slowly, girding myself. "It involves Talia. You know that she's confirming her soul-twined bond with Arch-Lord Corwin tomorrow."

Both of my colleagues nod. "But the oath she swore to return here regularly is still in place, is it not?" Donovan asks. "We have no need to worry when it comes to the curse."

"We don't. Corwin has expressed the intention of letting her offer her aid as she always has before for as long as she wishes to—and I know Talia is determined to continue helping us in every way she can."

Celia is studying me with a knowing gaze. "I suppose that will be difficult for your cadre-chosen August. He became quite attached to her."

Well, she's given me the perfect opening. "That's a factor in what I need to tell you. There are actually two aspects you should be aware of. The first is that it isn't only August who's formed a more personal attachment to Talia. I don't expect you to understand because you don't know her as we do, but she is quite a remarkable woman regardless of her heritage, and both Whitt of my cadre and I myself are quite devoted to her as well."

Donovan's eyebrows leap up. "What are you saying, Sylas?"

I keep my tone as even as possible. "I'm saying that before the unexpected soul-twined bond appeared, the three of us had intended to bond with her in our own way in a shared mating of the sort that isn't unheard of among cadres."

Celia lets out a startled cough. "It's highly unusual for a lord to join in such an arrangement, let alone an *arch-lord*."

"Perhaps, but she's a highly unusual lady. It is both her preference and our own not to force any limitations on her affections. We have managed to balance our fondness for her without issue for months now; I don't think it should affect anything beyond the walls of our home."

"Other than she's about to be bound to another man —an Unseelie, of all things," Donovan points out, still staring at me.

"Yes, well, that is the second part." I meet his gaze and then Celia's with all the calm authority I can summon, even though my wolf stretches inside me with the urge to roar out that we will have her as we wish regardless of their hesitation. "Talia hasn't hidden her pre-existing ties from her soul-twined mate. To do so would have been quite difficult. And he has come to accept the role we play in her life even if it isn't quite as close a bond as theirs."

Celia's lips part with a slackening of her jaw. "You're not really saying— How could he possibly agree to give up his own soul-twined mate, and to his enemies, no less?"

I give her a sharp look. "We aren't enemies anymore. I should hope we all expect the truce to last if we stay faithful to it. And he wouldn't be giving her up. In the interests of both cherishing this very special woman who's sacrificed so much to stem the tide of our own curse and allowing an ongoing dialogue between the summer and winter realms, we are going to attempt to create a single home for her that we and Corwin would share, if the Heart will allow it."

"You're going to construct a dwelling *within* the border," Celia says, catching on quickly. She rubs her temple. "Sylas, this is all without precedent. Are you sure you've considered the full implications—she may have done a lot for us, but she is still a mere human woman—"

"*Can* they even do it?" Donovan breaks in. "With the spell on the border—unless you mean to build it farther from the Heart—but you have your responsibilities here—"

I hold up my hands to halt both sets of questions and protests. "My domain by the Heart and Corwin's in the winter realm lie across the border from each other. We would attempt to work with the required vows to create this new castle there. And neither of us would treat it as a permanent residence. It would primarily be Talia's home— a place where she could be safe, as no one could enter without the proper vows taken, and where either side could call on her if we would request further help with our curse or any other concern."

Celia gives only a sputter of a laugh, still looking bowled over by the entire situation.

"Nothing is finalized yet," I go on. "Corwin needs to put the matter to his own colleagues, and we'll have to see what flexibility the Heart's magic will offer us. But the Heart has blessed Talia with both the means to subdue our curse and a soul-twined mate, so I believe we have reason to expect it to accommodate our attempt at collaboration. And it will be good for both of the realms to have two arch-lords in regular contact with one another—with all necessary discretion, of course."

"Discretion," Celia mutters. "When you're sharing a lover."

"I'm certain we can manage not to spill political secrets while enjoying our mate's company," I say dryly.

"You sound like you've made up your mind," Donovan says. "There isn't any way we could persuade you not to attempt it?"

I turn to him. "Would you try to persuade me? If you have worries about the end result, I'll do my best to address them."

He opens his mouth and hesitates. "I don't actually

know. I'm just so surprised—it seems as if there must be a dozen ways it *could* go wrong."

"You've trusted my judgment in the past," I say quietly. "*Both* of you have, if not always at the same time. The very fact that neither of you realized the depth of my connection to Talia shows that I'm capable of staying discreet. But you are my colleagues, and together we have the highest responsibility in the realm to our people. My association with Corwin will affect that responsibility, I believe for the better. I felt you deserved to know my intentions before I began carrying them out."

"I appreciate that," Donovan says, but his expression is still tense. Celia looks no less uneasy. I don't know what else I can say to ease their fears when I suspect neither of them can fully justify those fears to begin with.

"We still need to be careful of the ravens," Celia says finally. "You must stay wary of this Corwin—and watch what you say around Talia, regardless of your feelings for her, since he can glean whatever he wants from her mind."

I inclined my head. "I will not jeopardize the safety of my people for anything. You have my word on that. If you can point to a moment when she's distracted me from fulfilling my duties in any way thus far, please do."

She lets out a huff. "Your point is taken. I can't say I approve, but I can't say I have grounds to fight you on this either, Sylas. In the end, it is your personal decision. But I will be keeping a close eye on your associations with the Unseelie and this proposed building on the border. If I see any hint that your judgment or our security is being compromised…"

My stomach twists, but I can't argue against her need

for caution. "I understand. You *should* be monitoring these developments, as we all monitor each other to ensure our realm is ruled with the highest standards of accountability and loyalty. Heart willing, we can usher in a new era that benefits all the fae who deserve it."

Celia gives me a skeptical look as if she assumes my intentions are mainly to do with keeping Talia in my bed. I suppose I can't blame her for such speculations.

We'll simply have to prove to my colleagues just what a good thing this step can be for all of us—and before they stumble on any reason to cut our efforts short.

28

Talia

It seems strange that an hour before I officially swear myself to Corwin for the rest of my life, I'm only just meeting his entire coterie for the first time. Zelpha, Olander, and Verik have been around all week, of course, and Domhnall joined us at Heart's Cadence last night for the largest dinner I've had in the winter realm. But it was only this morning that the fifth member turned up to help with the final preparations.

Meriol reminds me of a hummingbird flitting around the temporary cabin constructed at the base of the cliff. The bright green and mauve streaks in her fluttering hair must be magically dyed like my pink and purple shade, because her ears are nearly as smoothly round as mine are, so she's definitely not true-blooded. She looks me over with small but bright eyes, like dark pebbles in her pale face.

"Well," she says in her high, sweet voice. "They

definitely won't be able to say you're not fine enough to be our lord's lady."

She and Zelpha have been overseeing the two folk of the flock who've been fiddling with my hair and my dress for the past hour. I guess the male members of the coterie are fussing over Corwin in the cabin's other room. I'm just trying not to think about the large stage that's been formed out of diamond just beyond the thin walls around us, where I'm going to confirm him as my mate for a large crowd of his people to see.

Not just his own flock, either. Corwin felt that making as large a spectacle of the ceremony as possible would help the rest of the Unseelie recognize me as one of their own, as much as I am by association with him. Give them lots of positive associations to go with the sight of me attaching myself to one of their arch-lords.

Musicians are playing on the stage right now to entertain the hundreds of fae who've already shown up to watch, many from the other arch-lords' domains but quite a few from farther abroad as well. I caught a glimpse of rows of carriages lined up across the icy plain when Corwin flew me down to the cabin. The swelling melody carries to my ears, cajoling me to sway with it, but my nerves are jumping too much for me to get totally wrapped up in it.

My Seelie lovers and my closest friend have arrived too. A buzz ran through the crowd when Sylas and the others arrived. Corwin assigned several of his warriors to "accompany" them, by which I suspect he means to provide a barrier between them and the winter fae in case anyone's hostile feelings toward the summer realm spill over.

I hope he's not second-guessing his decision to invite my other men to begin with. The last thing we need is a skirmish in the middle of the ceremony. But I know that even if the Unseelie try to provoke my men, they'll do whatever they can to keep the situation peaceful. They'd leave before they let blood be shed during this special moment.

I'd just rather it didn't come to that. Having them here is helping keep my uncertainties at bay, reminding me that I'm not losing them by accepting Corwin.

Zelpha nudges me toward the full-length mirror at one end of the room. The woman who's been working on my hair trails after us, her hands twisted together in front of her, looking oddly nervous about a mere human's opinion. But then, as soon as I'm officially Corwin's lady, I *won't* be just a human anymore. I'll be an Unseelie arch-lord's closest companion, with a certain amount of authority granted just by my connection to him.

Not that I want to go lording it over the fae in any significant way.

And my attendant has nothing to worry about when it comes to my opinion anyway. At my first sight of myself, my jaw drops. I stare at myself for several seconds before I can form words. "Wow. I—this is wonderful. Thank you."

I touch the tendrils of hair streaming over my shoulders tentatively, afraid of breaking the spell. Because it does feel like some kind of magic has been draped over me, elevating me from my regular human self into a much more ethereal figure.

The dress is one that Harper brought especially for this occasion, following the same theme as the first gown she made me for the winter realm. The spider-weave fabric overlaid with the most delicate of glittering lace hugs my slim frame from shoulders to hips and then flares out to drift like a gust of snow around my legs down to my ankles. Swirls of pale, iridescent blue, gray, and ivory mingle together, seeming to flow across the silky cloth with every move I make.

And my attendants must have added some kind of literal spell to the dress as well, because the lace no longer just glitters faintly but twinkles as if embedded with tiny stars.

My hair has undergone an unearthly transformation too. Swept back from my face, the top section has been braided into an elaborate crown atop my head, woven with diamonds and delicate ice-blue flowers. The rest streams down to the bodice of my dress in perfect waves that mimic the waterfall outside. I swear I can see them rippling as if with a current even when I'm standing still.

I notice with a grateful pang that for all the work they've done, the folk of the flock haven't hidden the tips of my ears with their human curves or attempted to disguise my boots with the brace for my warped foot. I still am who I am—just a more fantastical version of that woman.

Zelpha grins. "Corwin's going to trip over his feet the second he sees you. Maybe we should make sure he gets a good look before you go out on that stage so he doesn't melt down out of admiration in front of the audience."

Meriol snorts and swats her colleague. "I'm sure he can

hold himself together in front of a beautiful lady, soul-twined mate or not. The hard part is getting him to loosen up, not keep himself in check."

"True, true."

I sense the rest of my coterie is gossiping about me, Corwin says through our bond in a dry tone, but I pick up on his own jitters of nerves and eagerness underneath. *Are you faring all right?*

Better than all right, I reply, and focus on my reflection in the mirror again, encouraging him to see me through my own eyes.

The waft of awe that rushes through me tells me Zelpha wasn't totally off base about his reaction. His voice wraps around me like he wishes his arms could in this moment. *I already knew it, but I'm undoubtedly the luckiest man in the realms.*

I suspect most people watching will think it's the other way around.

They don't know you as I do. But they'll come to see just how honored we should be to have you among us, starting today.

Meriol sets her hands on her hips. "Ask him if he's ready to get started, because you definitely are."

My cheeks flush, realizing she must have been able to tell I was communicating with Corwin, but she only looks amused. *Did you hear that?* I ask him.

I think we can begin now. Verik says the other arch-lords have arrived. They'd have been annoyed if we started without them.

"He says yes," I tell Meriol for simplicity's sake.

She grins and then snaps her fingers with a brief

darkening of her expression. "I almost forgot. Something to be prepared for—the curse struck in one of the more distant domains last night. I heard that the lord and the victim's mate have brought him here in the hopes that you might try to heal him, but they won't want to interrupt the ceremony. Just keep an eye out for them when it's complete."

My pulse hitches, but I nod. I may be proving myself Corwin's partner today, but I'm still a long way from showing I can help the Unseelie in all the ways I'd like to. What if I fail again? We still don't know why all our efforts last time went nowhere.

Don't dwell on that right now, Corwin says. *We'll give it our best attempt when it's time. The moment ahead is about celebrating the bond the Heart blessed us with.*

I nod, knowing he can feel my agreement through our connection. Maybe solidifying that bond will make all the difference anyway. I can tell I'm so close to breaking through the curse's grip…

After. I'll focus on that after the ceremony is over. I have plenty of other things to be nervous about already.

The attendants from the flock hustle over to the door to hold it open for me. Zelpha and Meriol escort me out into the cool wintry air and then up the shining steps to the diamond stage. Corwin is just mounting the platform at the other end, his other three coterie members at his flanks.

He hasn't gotten quite the same beautification treatment I have, but he's stunning all the same. The brilliant sunlight beaming down on us brings out the blue highlights in his glossy black hair, and tiny diamonds gleam all through the silver thread that embroiders his formal padded jacket over the dusky violet fabric. He's wearing his silver crown for the first time I've seen it since he and his fellow arch-lords appeared before the Seelie months ago, nestled amid his curls.

But as we walk toward each other, the coterie hanging back at the sides of the stage, it's his eyes my gaze is drawn to. They're the same deep burgundy as ever, intent and thoughtful, but with a pleased glint dancing in them that matches the happiness thrumming through our bond.

We meet in the center of the stage. Corwin holds out his hand, and I take it. Then we turn to face our audience, the fae faces forming a sea so expansive I lose my breath. There must be thousands of people here to witness us confirming our bond.

I've heard that there hasn't been a confirmation ceremony for an arch-lord in over a century. And after everything these people have been through in the past few decades, I'm not surprised they'd jump at an excuse to celebrate such an occasion.

My attention leaps to my Seelie guests in their little cluster by the left side of the stage. Zelpha and Meriol have already stepped a little closer to them, scanning the crowd warily. I shoot a quick smile at my lovers and Harper. The warmth in the eyes of those men gazing back at me steadies me on my feet.

I have so much love to offer and so much given back to me. This ceremony is just one more way of recognizing that love.

Corwin draws in a breath, readying to speak—and another figure steps onto the stage.

Staggers is more like it. It takes me a moment to recognize Terisse, she's so hunched over, her normally copper-brown face grayed to a sickly tan. Laoni hurries after her, grasping her arm to help her balance. She looks out over the crowd and pitches her voice to carry.

"We hate to interrupt this honored ceremony, but it appears that the curse has taken one of our own arch-lords. With time of the essence, we're sure Arch-Lord Corwin's new mate wouldn't want to delay in helping her with her supposed skills."

A murmur carries through the audience, and my back stiffens. They're staring at me even more avidly now. News and rumors about my attempts to cure fae of the curse will have spread all over the realm by now. I thought I was going to make my next attempt in private, afterward…

My gaze darts to Meriol. Her mouth has slanted into a tight frown, her brow knit with confusion. No, this isn't the curse victim she mentioned would be here. She said it was someone from a distant domain—someone who traveled with their lord, not an arch-lord themselves. Has the curse hit *two* fae in less than a day's time?

Corwin and I step back to make room for the two approaching arch-lords. My gut twists into a tighter knot. *Did you have any idea she was sick?*

No, Corwin replies with a mental shake of his head. *It must have just struck her. I'm sorry—if I'd known, I would have prepared you.*

It's not your fault. I'll just—I'll have to do whatever I can. I glance in the direction of the Heart for just a second, sending out a plea to it to show me what to do.

If I fail to cure one of the arch-lords in front of all

these people who count on them, they won't see any cause for celebration here today.

And Laoni doesn't expect me to be able to help. I can tell that the moment she reaches us, her cold eyes fixing on me for just a second before she turns back to the crowd. The way she spoke about me: "her supposed skills."

She *wants* me to disappoint everyone. So she can use my failure as proof that Corwin's judgment is shaky? Would she be able to prevent us from confirming the bond?

I can't let any of that happen. I *have* to make this work. Too much depends on it.

Terisse comes to a stop in front of me by the edge of the stage. She sits down on the diamond surface, her head drooping, even her dark, green-tinted hair looking wilted. The sickness is taking her so quickly.

If I *can't* heal her, who will take her place among the arch-lords? What will it mean for the truce?

There's a lot more at stake than just my bond with Corwin.

I swallow thickly and walk up to her. My anxiety has already brought tears prickling to the back of my eyes, so at least I don't need to fight to force them out. I think back to the pregnant woman I healed, to the warmth that seemed to flow from my touch right through her skin. I wanted so badly to cure her, and something in me or in her responded.

I need Terisse to be well. I need her to stand with Corwin and the others at the table in their Hall of the Heart, to make decisions for the good of all her people. I need the Unseelie to stay strong and united so that they can stand up to whatever enemies threaten both them and the summer fae.

A few tears trickle from my eyes. A hush falls over the audience as they watch. I kneel next to Terisse and bring my hand to her cheek.

She simply shivers. A chill seeps from her face into my fingers. I dab at the tears streaking cool over my skin and touch her again with damp fingertips. I reach my other hand to squeeze hers.

Please. Please, let me send this curse away. Let me fend it off. If I'm not doing it right, show me how.

No bolt of inspiration comes to me. Terisse's pallor doesn't budge. Should I try singing to her or hugging her or— But none of those things worked before, and I have the weight of thousands of stares pinning me in place. What if it looks as if I've made her *worse?*

Corwin moves to join me, maybe to offer to create one of his draughts in case that will help, but Laoni draws herself up to her full height in front of him, her chin raised.

"It is as I thought. This human woman our colleague means to join himself to is proving to be a traitor who only pretended to hold some sort of cure to our curse. She's cured all the Seelie with her blood dozens of times over—why can't she do the same for even one of us when asked? Clearly all her loyalty is with the vicious wolves."

A chill rushes through me that has nothing to do with the curse. "No," I say, but I can already see the victorious edge to her smile. She doesn't want to be proven wrong. She set this up to make me look feeble or unwilling, either because she honestly believes that I'm too dedicated to the Seelie or that I've been lying, or she simply—

She set this up.

That one fragment of thought sticks in my head. The crowd shifts restlessly, a few voices calling out harsh words, but my attention narrows in on the woman beside me. On Terisse with her faded skin and crumpled pose.

What are the chances that the curse *would* strike two fae so close together, and that one of them would just happen to be an arch-lord? Right at the perfect time to interrupt our ceremony too?

The certainty tingles over me that what I'm seeing isn't a curse but some kind of illusion. There's magic on Terisse, but it came from herself or one of her colleagues, making her *look* sick when she isn't really. Laoni even phrased it that way, saying she "appeared" to be cursed, not that she was. To avoid a lie?

If that's the case, there's no way I could have cured her when she isn't suffering from the curse to begin with. It's all part of their plan to discredit me.

Even as the understanding rises up inside me, I realize what I need to do. I need to shine a light through this deception and prove that I'm more than an ineffectual human.

Talia, Corwin says, but I can tell he doesn't have a solid argument to stop what he can read of my intentions. If I don't do something, in a matter of moments the crowd before us will turn on me.

I'm tired of hiding so much. Let them see everything that I am, just as the men I love have.

I can dispel whatever magic is on her, Corwin offers.

No. Laoni could just claim that your magic was the illusion, trying to hide that she's still sick. That you're protecting me. They need to know what I can do. They need to see what I stand for.

I glance at him, feeling him braced to leap to my defense and awash with adoration even though I'm being used as a tool against him. Then I look toward my Seelie men, who are watching with taut expressions. Sylas, who would whisk me away from here the second I seemed to be in clear danger. August, who'd fight off the entire crowd to save me if he had to. Whitt, who looks ready to spring onto the stage and proclaim my goodness to the realm.

How could I possibly cherish them more? No matter what challenges we've faced, I've never been happier than when I'm with them.

Love swells inside me and fills me like a glow. I open my mouth and let that glow spill out of me. "*Sole-un-straw!*"

Light flares from my hands and washes over the woman I'm kneeling by. With a shudder that ripples over my skin, it burns through the illusion that dulled her skin and weakened her stance.

Terisse jerks away from me, startled, as the copper tones of her true skin shine through. The appearance of stiffness melts from her limbs. She stares at me and then down at herself. "You—"

I raise my voice. "The Heart has given me some of its magic as well as a soul-twined bond, and the light I call on shows what is real. There is no curse here."

Talia

The audience stares at the cluster of figures on the stage in stunned silence. Laoni recovers first, jabbing a finger at me. "It's impossible —unnatural—"

My hands clench at my sides. "What's unnatural is pretending someone's sick who isn't to try to hurt me and my soul-twined mate. Whatever magic I have must have come from the Heart, mustn't it? It's let me push back the curse, find a bond with one of your own arch-lords, and understand some of the true names, so it must want all of that from me."

She strides toward me. "You still haven't proven you can cure *any* of us. If this power comes from the Heart, if you're as devoted to us as you are to the curs across the border, why haven't you given us the same benefit you offer them?"

She holds herself tall and defiant, her muscles flexing

all through her body, but up close, I catch a tiny tremor that runs through her body. Is she *scared*? Of *me*?

Maybe that isn't so hard to believe. I came from the summer realm, and she doesn't trust the Seelie at all. She doesn't understand what I am or how I can be so entwined with the fae—even more so now that I've shown just how much magic I can wield. She doesn't understand, and so I'm a threat to her.

But she'd never admit that. No, that's the real curse the Unseelie suffer from: this insistence on hiding so much away, of pretending they have no emotions about anything...

The idea hits me so hard a gasp slips from my lips. Laoni stares at me, but I spin toward the crowd, ignoring her.

"I've tried," I say. "I did heal one woman, but I didn't know what I'd done right. There's still a lot about the powers I have that's unclear to me. But I think—I think I know what made the difference now. I heard there really is someone here who's in the grip of the curse, who wanted to ask for my help after the ceremony. If that person is here, I'll try to help them now. You can all watch. And if I fail, then maybe I don't deserve to stay among you after all."

Talia, don't say that, Corwin protests, coming up behind me. He rests his hands on my shoulders, and I reach to set my hand over his.

It'll be okay. I see how it is now. I hadn't worked it all out before—but the cure has to come from the same place as the curse, I think. Whenever I give blood to the Seelie, it's through violence, even if I accept that violence. They cut me with a knife or magic or their teeth… we've never tried magicking blood straight out of me without any wound.

But we don't need violence. That isn't our curse.

No, your curse is locking you up inside your own body. Freezing out all your emotions so you feel nothing but cold. I was trying to skip straight to warming people up again without recognizing what's gone wrong first.

At least, I hope that makes sense when I act it out. It *feels* right, deep inside me, with a headier pulse of energy that seems to hum straight from the Heart.

The crowd is parting, three fae moving through the gathered bodies toward the stage: a man partly supported by an older man and a young woman gripping his elbows. His skin has an icy pallor that hasn't been faked.

Laoni's jaw works, but the voices carrying through the crowd are eager with anticipation. Her people won't want her stopping the demonstration I offered. She can at least tell when she's lost, even if she doesn't intend to stay defeated.

She motions to Terisse, who backs away with her. They both stay on the stage to watch, their cold gazes watching for any hint that I've faltered and given them another opening to dismiss me.

If I do, maybe I deserve to be dismissed. Because if this last try doesn't work, then I really might be useless to the Unseelie.

I can't believe that's true, though. I must be here—I must have the powers I've been given—for a reason. I won't stop believing that until it's proven otherwise.

Rather than make him come around to the steps leading onto the stage, several of the other fae lift the man up right in front of me. The woman who I guess is his mate scrambles up to help him catch his balance on the diamond surface.

The cursed man gazes up at me, his eyes hazed with growing frost. His voice comes out in a croak. "You think you can take away the cold? There's still—there's still so much left I want to do. I don't want to leave this world yet."

Of course he doesn't. I choke up, emotion burning behind my eyes. So many fae have had centuries of their lives cut short because of this awful curse. There are so many that I wasn't here in time to save—or didn't see the answer in time to. But now, now I can make a difference.

Not tears offered freely. Tears hidden away just as the Unseelie would try to disguise their own grief.

In some ways, that answer is harder to get at than what I give the Seelie. The bodily pain the summer fae's curse demands is immediate and innate. With this emotional pain, my impulse is to show it for all the fae before me to see—to prove how much I care. It never even occurred to me to hide it once I thought my distress could heal them.

That's what's so tricky about the curse. It twists the Unseelie to mimic the strictest part of their nature and requires a cure from me that goes against my own instincts.

I force myself to turn away from the cursed man even though his anguish tears at my heart, even though I can feel the entire audience watching and thinking I'm rejecting him. I blink back the tears until I'm facing the back of the stage and the cliff beyond it, where they can't see them. But that isn't enough. I turned away from the man from Uzziah's flock too.

Then, I was only repeating that one motion. I let my tears fall freely, let him see them as soon as I'd summoned them. This time, I have to scrub them away. Pretend I'm not experiencing this sorrow.

Drawing in a shaky breath, I wipe the tears from my cheeks and rub my eyes like I did when I tried to stop my sadness from upsetting the pregnant woman all those days ago.

My grief *is* weakness, in a way. And I don't really want the fae to see me weak any more than they want to show their own weaknesses to each other. But that weakness can become a strength when I pass it from me to them.

"Please," the man rasps.

Surely I've held back for long enough? I allow myself to swivel toward him, still blinking hard. In time with the thudding of my heart, I walk up to him and crouch down. The faintest tingle of dampness remains on my fingers when I bring them to his face.

"I don't want you to leave either," I tell him. I might not know anything about him other than what he's said in the last five minutes, but I mean it all the same.

The man stares back at me, and my chest starts to constrict. Was I wrong? Has it still not worked?

But then, with a flare of joy right through the middle of me, I catch a whisper of warmth spreading over his skin.

The man's eyes widen. A blush of color blooms across his cheek, and the woman with him gasps. She touches the other side of his face and then spins toward the crowd.

"She's done it! The chill is leaving him. He feels—he looks—he's turning back to normal, as he was before."

More gasps and startled murmurs rise up from the crowd. Many of the figures push in for a closer look.

I step back, and the man sways to his feet. He looks down at himself, testing his increasingly limber joints, running his hand over his face, and letting out a startled but delighted laugh.

He turns toward me with a smile that's almost nervous. Even after all that, it doesn't come easily to him to show any emotion to me, to make himself vulnerable.

That's all right. That's how the Unseelie are—how my mate is too. I can't expect them to change completely.

"Thank you," the cursed man says, his voice emphatic even if his expression isn't. "You—I don't know how to thank you enough."

"I'm just glad you're okay." Relief rushes through my limbs as I realize that's true. I've done it again—I've repeated my cure. We know what the curse needs now.

Corwin steps up next to me on the stage like he did when we first arrived and clasps my hand. He raises it with his into the air. "You've seen how much my soul-twined mate cares for our people and the gift she can offer us against our curse. Will you all support us in confirming our bond and making her a full part of the winter realm?"

His voice rings out across the plain, and a chorus of responses rises up like a cheer, all of them eager and approving. Next to us, Laoni's expression tightens. Terisse has ducked her head, her mouth twisted with what looks like shame, but the self-named leader of the arch-lords strides to the front of the stage.

I stiffen, but she's clearly recognized that there's no turning the tide against us after what I've just done. She brushes her fingers across my shoulder, ruffling my hair with the faintest pinch of my scalp that vanishes an instant later. Before I can react, she's rested her hand on the cursed man's head.

"It gives me great happiness to see you well again," she says to him. "Any ruler can only claim to be an authority if they're willing to admit when they're wrong. I apologize for misjudging my colleague's mate and hope we can all celebrate the boon her presence brings to our people."

She says all that looking out at the audience without so much as glancing at me, which provokes a jab of consternation in Corwin, but I find that I don't care. Let her save face with her people, as long as she's giving me credit at the same time. Today, thousands of fae saw that I can cast away the curse. There's no way she can deny it ever again.

Terisse speaks up too, her voice more strained. "I only wished to ensure none of us were misled. Our test has brought out the best in this woman, and for that I am grateful."

Sure she is, Corwin mutters silently, and I squeeze his hand. Somehow I suspect he's going to have significantly less patience for his colleagues' dismissiveness going forward.

He shifts his attention to me with a flicker of affection like a caress down the middle of me. *Shall we continue with our confirmation as intended?*

I smile up at him. *Yes, I think it's about time.*

Corwin lifts his other hand, and the crowd quiets. "I

am pleased to acknowledge and welcome my soul-twined mate before all of you, and to ask you all to welcome her too. I know she will be a shining light of truth in all things, not just today. Before my people and the Heart, I confirm my commitment to my soul-twined mate, Talia of Hearth by the Heart. May our souls be ever twined."

Magic resonates through his last two sentences, the official vows of the ceremony. I drag in a breath, nearly overwhelmed with a giddy sort of nervousness, as if something more might go wrong. But nothing stops me from following his voice with my own.

"I'm so happy to have found a home here with my soul-twined mate and all of you, and I look forward to doing all I can to serve you alongside him. Before the Unseelie gathered here and the Heart, I confirm my commitment to my soul-twined mate, Corwin of Heart's Cadence. May our souls be ever twined."

With the final syllable, a shock of magic hits me, the connection between Corwin and me flaring brighter with a deeper sense of each other's presence and consciousness than I've ever experienced before.

A flash of surprise lights in Corwin's eyes and through our bond. Then, all thought of the watching crowd melting away, he leans in to kiss me, propriety be damned.

Another cheer goes up, even louder than the first. Joy flows between us like a whirling star. I have my mate, and the bond between us couldn't be firmer.

As Corwin eases back and signals for the musicians to return, I look toward my Seelie men in the crowd, half-afraid I'll see consternation on their faces now that the ceremony is complete. But August is beaming at me,

Sylas's expression is full of pleased relief, and Whitt's eyes are alight with sly affection. I extend my hand to them just for a moment, like a promise. Someday, before much longer, we'll confirm our own bonds in our own way.

Then the music washes over us. Corwin tugs me into his arms for the first dance, and there's nothing left to do but rejoice.

Talia

Harper ambles over and plops down next to me on the soft grass where I'm watching the early stages of construction at the border. She cocks her head, following my gaze. "It'll be an interesting building, that's for sure. No one will ever be able to see the whole thing at once, will they, with all that fog in the way?"

My mouth twitches with a smile. Of course the dressmaker would be most concerned about the visual impact of the building. "I guess that's true. I'm interested to see whether the fog insists on sticking around inside the castle or if it'll be content to flow over it."

So far no one's gone inside the fledgling castle at all. I can only just make out Sylas and his cadre's forms and the trunks of the trees they're slowly urging out of the earth within the border haze. The summer side of our shared home will look a lot like the main castle of Hearth by the

Heart, just as I expect the diamond side Corwin is erecting will look a lot like Heart's Cadence.

My mate's excitement tingles through to me from where he's working alongside a few of his coterie members across the border. This is the first time he's created a castle that's all his own. The main palace of Heart's Cadence was constructed centuries ago by his ancestors, and he's only needed to do minor repairs and adjustments in his decades as arch-lord.

I'm glad that the first home you're bringing into being yourself is something we can enjoy together, I say through our bond.

He sends the impression of a smile in response. *As am I.*

Harper wiggles her bare feet in the grass and leans back on her hands with a happy sigh. "So, you're going to be living in that place most of the time after it's fully built? You won't really belong to either realm."

"I'd like to think of it as belonging to both," I say. "And you'll be able to come by and visit whenever you want, no matter which side I'm paying the most attention to right then. All you'll have to do is make your border vow at the summer-side door and you'll be able to enter."

"Hmm. I don't think I should drop by unexpectedly *too* often, considering you'll have plenty of things—and people—to keep you busy." She raises her eyebrows mischievously at me.

My cheeks flush. When Sylas announced to the Seelie around the Heart that he and Corwin were collaborating on this joint castle so that they could act as ambassadors to each other's realms, he also expressed his intention to formally recognize me as his mate—in a ceremony that'll recognize August and Whitt as well. After all the chaos of the past few months, most of his pack-kin seem to have taken it in stride, although at larger gatherings, I've gotten some odd looks from the fae of the other nearby packs.

The memory sends a prickle of discomfort over my skin despite the summer warmth. "I'm not sure everyone is totally happy about that part."

Harper lets out a dismissive huff. "They're just frustrated to have three very prominent bachelors taken off the market, I'd bet. But they've got a whole new arch-lord's pack to get to know." A dreamy smile crosses her lips. "Maybe I'll find a mate of my own in one of the other domains by the Heart. Besides, with you being human—"

She cuts herself off with a pained expression. I glance at her, and understanding clicks. With me being human, I shouldn't be competition for my lovers' attention for very long by fae lifespans.

I grimace. "It's okay. We all know I'm not going to live centuries upon centuries like you do. I'm just... glad to have what I do while I can have it."

"Yes. Exactly. Maybe it makes sense that you should get to have extra loving while you're here since you don't get as much time to enjoy it."

A laugh tumbles out of me. "You'll have to put it that way to the other fae and see if they buy that explanation."

I think it's a perfectly good one, Corwin remarks, and a broader smile crosses my lips.

Harper glances up, her fae ears picking up some sound mine couldn't. A shadow crosses her previously peaceful face. "I think that's one of Arch-Lord Celia's sentries lurking around again."

I follow her gaze just as the woman she noticed ducks out of view between the trees at the other side of the field. I didn't get a chance to recognize her, but I wouldn't be surprised if Harper's right. The other arch-lords on both sides of the border have remained uncertain about the continuing alliance between the realms—and about my role in that alliance.

I turn back to Harper. "I guess it can't hurt for them to be keeping an eye on things. Then they can see for themselves that nothing so horrible is going to come out of us working together."

The Unseelie have decided to keep their summer-side settlement for the time being, just to see if it has any more permanent effect on who the curse strikes. I've managed to lift the cursed chill off two more winter fae in the past week, but we're still not sure how long my "cure" will last. I can't believe it'll be permanent when my blood doesn't offer that kind of benefit to the Seelie.

A quaver of uneasiness and confusion passes to me from Corwin. I sit up a little straighter, my senses going on the alert.

A few moments later, his voice reaches me through our connection. *Talia, can you come across the border? Have Sylas or one of his cadre escort you if you'd like. Laoni and Uzziah have come to speak to me—they say there's something you should hear.*

That sounds ominous. I shake off my own unsettled nerves and get to my feet.

Corwin must have communicated the situation to my

Seelie men, because as I step toward the border, August emerges from the fog to meet me. "Do you have any idea what this could be about?" he asks, offering his hand.

I slip my fingers around his, my pulse thumping faster. "No. Considering how they've treated me so far, I'm guessing it isn't going to be a house-warming party."

"Well, let's see what they're up to now. Sylas, Whitt, and Astrid are at the ready if we need them."

I'd like to say I'm sure Corwin's colleagues would never attack me outright, but then, I'd never have thought they'd fake the curse to try to prove me a liar and a traitor during our confirmation ceremony.

Holding my head high, I walk with August into the cooler atmosphere of the winter realm. We pass the looming diamond walls of Corwin's side of the castle and come out to find him, Verik, and Meriol facing the two other arch-lords.

"Here's my mate," Corwin says, beckoning both me and August over. He takes my other hand without a hint of rancor that I'm still holding onto one of my other lovers as well. "What is it you have to say about her?"

Laoni looks at me, her cool eyes hardening even as she puts on a thin smile. Uzziah stirs on his feet next to her, placing his hand on his stout belly as if he's got indigestion.

"We took a small sample of Talia's flesh some days ago," Laoni says evenly. "It seemed only reasonable to investigate her exact origins."

A small sample of my flesh? My mind darts to the moment she touched my shoulder during the confirmation ceremony, the momentary pinching I felt. She must have pulled out a hair by the root and smoothed over the pain with magic.

My back stiffens, and anger trickles through my bond with Corwin. Before my mate can speak up, August shakes his head. "My lord has already tested her essence in every way we can think of. You already knew as much as we do about her connection to the Heart."

Laoni aims her icy gaze at him. "You'll forgive us if we'd want to make our own tests, but that isn't what I meant. We wanted to discover more about her history in the human world."

Despite my uneasiness, a tremor of excitement runs through me. Have they found out something about the trace of fae ancestry in my family? "And you did discover something?" I ask.

Laoni motions to Uzziah, who clears his throat. "A few of my people did their best to trace your bloodline—and one of them uncovered a direct, living connection we can't help suspecting may have his own ties to the Heart if your own were born through your family line."

My stomach sinks. "Like a distant cousin or something?"

Ambrose already tried to push for the Seelie to gather any relatives of mine they could find, however distant, to use in whatever ways they could. Sylas managed to dismiss that idea, but if the Unseelie have taken it up too…

Uzziah's next words knock those suddenly minor concerns out of my mind in an instant.

"No," he says, gazing at me with what might even be a

tiny bit of sympathy. "It seems the wolves didn't slaughter all of your immediate family after all. We believe we found your brother, alive and well."

ABOUT THE AUTHOR

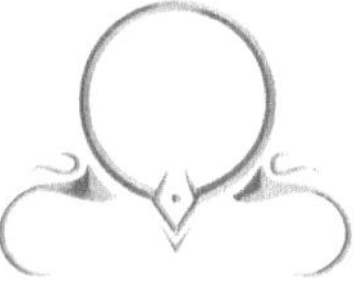

Eva Chase lives in Canada with her family. She loves stories both swoony and supernatural, and strong women and the men who appreciate them. Along with the Bound to the Fae series, she is the author of the Flirting with Monsters series, the Cursed Studies trilogy, the Royals of Villain Academy series, the Moriarty's Men series, the Looking Glass Curse trilogy, the Their Dark Valkyrie series, the Witch's Consorts series, the Dragon Shifter's Mates series, the Demons of Fame Romance series, the Legends Reborn trilogy, and the Alpha Project Psychic Romance series.

Connect with Eva online:
www.evachase.com
eva@evachase.com